KISSING HER COWBOY BOSS

TEXAS LONGHORN RANCH, BOOK 2

EMMY EUGENE

CHAPTER
ONE

Laura Woodcross bent her head into the wind, her spirits as low as the temperatures had been falling this December. It wasn't exactly what she'd classify as cold, but it wasn't warm either.

That was about how everything in Laura's life had become. Neutral. Stale. Boring.

Her father had had hip replacement surgery several months ago, and he was doing okay. Just okay. Not great, but not in as much pain as he'd been in before.

She lived with another cowgirl, and they hadn't become best friends, despite Laura's attempts to talk to Josie and get to know her. They existed together, and Josie basically left Laura alone to live her life.

After her bust of a first date with Todd Stewart, which Laura had actually enjoyed, things between the two of them had been good. Fine. Okay. She saw him every day.

They spoke in person and on the phone, through texts, all of it.

He'd asked her out again, and they'd gone to dinner a few times. She'd celebrated his birthday with him, but she'd gone back to Hidden Hollow for Thanksgiving.

Laura's relationship with Todd had cooled as the work around a cattle ranch never really slowed or stopped. Deep down, she knew it wasn't work keeping them apart.

It was her.

Every time she thought about kissing Todd, her cells lit up and her brain told her to get the job done. She'd kissed him once, but it had been a very emotional moment triggered by an event in her past she still hadn't told him about.

He hadn't tried to kiss her again, and Laura wasn't sure she'd even let him. The single time she'd lost her mind and touched her lips to his had caused so much guilt to fill her. She'd been tripping over it since, and he seemed to know it.

The only saving grace was her job here at the Texas Longhorn Ranch. That presented her with a new challenge every single day. Or at least some variety.

They'd moved into birthing season, and that meant Laura had to check her pregnant cows every single day, multiple times throughout the day. Morning, noon, evening, midnight. They didn't seem to care about her sleep schedule when it came to giving birth.

She took a deep breath and looked up into the shrouded sky. She didn't talk to Hans anymore, and she wasn't going to start today. He deserved to Rest In Peace, without her constant chatter to him about how she missed him and wished they'd gotten more time together.

The people she had time with right here on earth she'd started to shut out again. She didn't like this version of herself, but she didn't know how to change it.

She'd thought the Longhorn Ranch would be the answer to all of her prayers. For the first few months there, it had been. The people were nice, the job nothing she couldn't handle, and that handsome Todd Stewart…

Laura pushed him out of her thoughts as she swung into the saddle, but he simply galloped right back in. "All right, Miss Dolly," she said to the horse. "None of the momma cows are gonna have their babies in the next little bit. Let's go check the tree line."

Dolly didn't move too fast or too slow, just another medium in Laura's life. To be honest, she could use a runaway bull or a lightning strike only ten yards from her. Something to jolt her out of this funk and back to the land of the living.

The growl of a truck approached, but she wouldn't know if it was Todd or someone else until they rounded the bend. By the throatiness of the engine, it wasn't Todd. His truck purred like a kitten, and this one sounded like it could cough, sputter, and die on the next turn of the tires.

Sure enough, Little Nick came around the corner in a beige ranch truck. When he saw her, he gunned the engine and flashed his lights.

"Whoa," Laura said to Dolly, because Little Nick clearly needed to talk to her.

"Laura," he called out the open window. "There's been an accident at the demo. We need you."

Her brow crinkled. "The demo?" She didn't memorize all of the activities that went on at the ranch, especially the commercial side of it. She enjoyed the free breakfast and dinner every day of the week, and she'd signed up for the monthly grab-and-go lunches too. She definitely didn't want for food.

"Yeah," he said. "It turned into a pig stampede, and we've got someone who's bleeding."

"Okay," she said, still not getting it.

"Switch me," he said, coming to a stop. "I'll take Dolly in. You take the truck." The sandy blonde cowboy got out of the truck, but Laura's mind couldn't quite keep up.

"I'm a veterinarian," she said. "I don't patch up people. Isn't there a first aid kit at the lodge or something?"

"It's a little girl," Little Nick said. "She's here with his mom and gran, and they're deathly afraid of hospitals. Won't go." He took the reins from her, and Laura saw no way out of this.

She also knew exactly how that girl and her family felt. She'd spent so much time in hospitals, she wouldn't feel bad if she never had to step foot in one again.

"All right," she said, sliding from the saddle. "I still need to check the pasture out at the tree line."

Little Nick frowned, but he nodded, swung into the saddle, and said, "Yah, Dolly. Let's pick up the pace."

Above them, the sky grumbled with thunder, and Laura realized what a blessing she'd been given. If she'd stayed out here, she'd have been caught in the coming rain for sure.

As it was, she got behind the wheel of the truck, rolled up the window, and enjoyed a drama-free return to the ranch.

The outdoor demo area sat to the east of the main lodge, in the barn next to the one where Todd kept his office. Quite the crowd lingered there, as it sure seemed like people possessed a morbid streak and accidents and pain attracted their attention like nothing else.

If that were really true, everyone would be staring at her all the time, not just right now as she pulled up in the rickety ranch truck.

"There you are," Adam Stewart said, pulling open her door before she'd even put the vehicle in park. "She's freaking out, and none of us can calm her down."

Laura gave him a calm smile. "Species?" He blinked at her, his eyes widening, and Laura shook her head. "Sorry," she said. "Bad joke." She joined him on the ground. "How old is she?"

"Four, maybe," Adam said. "I don't know. She's little."

"What happened?"

"Our huge six-hundred-pound sow stepped on her foot," another man said, and Laura came face-to-face with Todd Stewart. The man took her breath away, though he frowned with everything inside him. At least she'd never seen his face this unhappy before.

Face-to-face was a stretch too, as Laura usually had to look up to see everyone. The downfalls of only being five-foot-two.

"Hey," he said, sliding his hand along her hip. "Thanks for comin' in."

"Did you text?" she asked.

"Several times," he said, glancing up as the first drops of rain splattered the windshield with fat, splashy sounds. "I figured you were out too far, and this storm isn't helping anything."

Todd slid his hand away, and Laura's whole body went cold. How he did that so casually, she didn't understand. Because of his touch, she also couldn't quite figure out where their relationship stood.

She followed him as he turned and strode back the way he'd come. "We're under the demo roof, so we should stay dry."

Laura jogged to catch up to him, his longer legs covering so much more distance than hers. "So it's her foot? Her calf? Her whole leg? What?"

"I don't really know," he said, sliding her a look. Something burned hotly in his eyes. "She's hysterical, and her mother's not much better."

"Someone should get all these people inside," Laura said, and Todd lifted his hand. Two of his brothers came straight to him as if he was their king and they his servants.

"Get everyone inside the lodge," he said. "They don't need to be out here in the rain."

Adam nodded, immediately calling for everyone to follow him into the lodge to wait out the rain. Laura once again bent her head against the weather, this time to keep her face dry as the rain increased.

She and Todd went under the roof a moment later, the sound of the droplets on the metal above soothing to her. Beyond soothing. It meant she was outside, on a ranch, and she'd wanted this life for as long as she could remember.

A flicker of new light and extra life entered her heart and mind, and Todd got his brother Blake to move aside, revealing the little girl down on the ground.

Laura sucked in a breath at her dark, richly-colored hair. She looked like she'd been dipped in tar, her hair was so dark. She sat on the ground, her shoulders shaking violently as she cried.

"Honey," Todd said in a careful, gentle voice. "She's here." He looked up at Laura, who got herself moving again.

Her heart had lodged itself in the back of her throat, where it bobbed with every beat. *Keep it together,* she told herself as she dropped to her knees beside the girl.

Her eyes swept her from head to toe, catching the blood and the injury on her lower leg, just above her ankle. Maybe below it too.

"Hello, baby," she said in a calm quiet voice. She smiled at the little girl, who looked at her with wide, teary eyes the color of earth that had just been plowed under in preparation for planting.

"Her name is Ally," Todd said as a woman sobbed nearby. "Blake."

His brother moved over to the mother, and Laura shifted her body to shield the little girl from her mother's hysterics. A first aid kit sat on the ground beside her, and Laura reached into it to pull out a pair of gloves.

"My name is Laura," she said. "Do you like animals, Ally?"

The girl couldn't be more than four, and Laura guessed she was more like three. A pang of sadness hit her hard, the reverberations in her ribcage like that of a gong.

She didn't answer Laura, but Laura didn't need her to. "Once," she said as she finished putting on her gloves and reaching for the wet washcloth laying on top of the kit. "I knew a girl just like you."

She offered Ally a smile, never taking her eyes from the girl's. "Her name was Letty, though. She could speak another language. Can you do that?"

She stroked the cloth down the girl's leg softly, glancing there to see what wounds she was dealing with. Some of the blood had started to dry, and she quickly saw the enormous scrape that extended a good three or four inches along the front of Ally's leg.

The shin bone could be so sensitive, on all kinds of mammals.

"Do you have any pets?" Laura asked.

Ally looked around as if just now realizing her mom wasn't there. When she didn't see her, her teary eyes came back to Laura. "A cat," she said.

"My momma loves cats," Laura said. "Is it your cat or your momma's?"

"My gran's," Ally said, sniffling. "She named it Moonbaby."

Laura gave a light laugh. "Moonbaby. I like that." She

KISSING HER COWBOY BOSS 9

nodded to Todd, who took the cloth from her and handed it to someone she couldn't see.

Laura put her hands on her thighs and kept smiling at Ally. "Miss Ally, you've got a scrape here. Scrapes aren't that big of a deal." She took a fresh cloth from Todd and started on the back of Ally's leg this time, the heat from the cloth seeping into her fingers.

Ally's chin shook, and she turned to look at Todd. "She needs a blanket."

"Shock," he said, getting to his feet with a groan.

"Hold her," she said to him as he called for a blanket. He got back on the ground, and he pulled the little girl into his lap. He hummed to her in a quiet, low voice, and Laura blinked, seeing Hans and the life she'd once had right there in front of her.

Her anxiety tripled, and she swallowed against it. Nash arrived with a blanket, and Laura used the movement as Todd shifted Ally to get the last of the blood cleaned off her leg. She pressed the cloth right over the wound and Ally didn't even make a noise.

She curled into Todd's chest so much the way Hans's little sister had only a few days before he'd died. Laura couldn't look away from the sexy cowboy holding that little girl, and every nerve in her body screamed at her to get out of there.

Finish, she commanded herself. *Focus. Flee.*

She quickly dabbed some anti-bacterial ointment over the open wound, then bandaged it all up, saying, "All done, Miss Ally." She grinned at the girl, and Ally smiled back.

Laura got to her feet too and turned to go talk to the girl's mother. Todd joined her, and she gave the directions as quickly as she could. Todd transferred Ally to her mother, both of them calmer now.

Laura stepped away and peeled her gloves from her hands, her chest vibrating in a horrible, violent way. She had to get out of here. Now.

She spun and strode away, not caring that the rain hadn't let up, not even a little bit. Her hair and skin got soaked within a few seconds, and behind her, Todd called, "Laura, wait up."

She didn't. She couldn't.

She'd come here to get a fresh start after the ordeal of losing someone she loved so very much. Why did she have to see reminders of him literally everywhere?

A sob wrenched its way from her stomach, and it was going to come out of her throat.

"Laura," Todd said again, his voice closer.

She couldn't face him. Not right now. She broke into a run, praying the Lord could give her winged feet just this one time. She'd never ask Him for anything again, if she could just get away from everyone and find somewhere to cry her soul empty again.

CHAPTER
TWO

Todd Stewart slowed his step as Laura broke into a run. Confusion struck his mind the way a snake did. Quick and without warning.

Every time he watched her work, she amazed him. She was always calm in the face of the stormiest of seas, and he'd seen her calm hysterical horses with a simple touch of her palm along their spines, deliver breech lambs, sew up a gash on a goat's side, and deal with all manner of diseases with their chickens and turkeys.

Now he'd witnessed her calm, beautiful spirit comfort a child, and she had never been more attractive to him than she was now.

He looked behind him, surprised how far from the demo arena he'd gotten in just a few seconds. Facing forward again, something told him to go after Laura.

He could barely see her through the rain anymore, and he didn't move as wild indecision raged through him.

"Where'd Laura go?" Blake asked as he came to stand beside Todd. "They've gone inside." He sighed and wiped his brow. "I told them I'd have Doc Hanson come out and look at her leg in a couple of days."

"Okay," Todd said, still not sure what to do. Laura had run off in the direction of her cabin, and he'd often seen her walking the road between the cowboy cabins and the barn where he divvied up the ranch responsibilities each day.

She owned a car, but she only drove it to town or home to Hidden Hollow. So many things about her intrigued him, and he disliked that he'd let her talk about simple things and not what really mattered.

He'd seen the pain on her face just now, even when she'd been smiling, and that got him moving across the gravel in the direction Laura had gone.

He took shelter under the eaves of the ice cream shop they opened and ran in the summer months and pulled out his phone. Laura didn't answer, and his frustration now was as sharp as it had been when he hadn't been able to get in touch with her when that little girl was screaming.

His phone tucked safely back in his pocket, Todd headed out into the rain again. He didn't care about being wet. Like he'd told Blake once, if he wasn't dry, he was wet, and whether that was a lot or a little didn't matter.

Laura lived in a cabin close to the front of the row of them, and he spotted her car parked out front. That didn't mean anything, and he climbed the steps and knocked on the front door.

He realized that he should've called all his men and women in off the ranch the moment the first drops of rain fell, and he got his phone out again to do that.

If you're still out on the ranch, come in, he tapped out. *The rain's not supposed to stop for a while.*

Only a moment after he'd sent his text, one came in from Starla. *Hot chocolate bar in the dining hall. Come one, come all.* She'd included an emoticon of a steaming cup of cocoa, and that screamed Starla.

Todd could see why both Jesse and Nash liked her, as she had the strong personality Jesse liked, with the brains and the beauty. Nash had a crush on Starla, and had for some time, but to Todd's knowledge, he hadn't asked her out in the five months since Jesse had ended his fleeting relationship with their kitchen manager and head chef at the lodge.

Todd's mouth watered for chocolate and mint, whipped cream and marshmallows, but his heart yearned for Laura Woodcross.

No one had come to the door, and he raised his fist to knock again. She still didn't come, and neither did Josie, the other cowgirl who lived here.

Frustration filled him, and Todd tried his phone again. He turned away from the door, his phone pressed to his ear, and went to the edge of the porch. The rain fell only a couple of inches in front of his face, and he saw something light up in Laura's car.

His pulse jumped and skipped through his veins, and while he feared he might be overstepping his bounds and drive her further from him, he jogged down the steps and toward her sedan.

Sure enough, he saw her sitting in the front seat now, and he bent down and peered in her window. She cracked it a few inches, and he asked, "Can I join you?"

"The doors are unlocked," she said. The window went up a moment later, and the thunder crashed through the sky with a noise great and terrific.

That prompted Todd to move, and move fast, around the car and into the passenger seat. He had to slide the seat back to make room for his longer legs, and he took off his cowboy hat, which held about as much water as the ground outside.

"It's really coming down," he said, hating himself for talking about the weather.

Laura had gathered her hair into a very low ponytail at the nape of her neck, as it wasn't long enough to do much more than that. She raked her fingers through it, pushing it back off her forehead. She usually clipped it on the sides, but Todd saw no evidence of barrettes this afternoon.

"They're doing hot chocolate at the lodge," he said in a lame attempt to make conversation.

"I got the text." She didn't look at him but leaned her head back against the rest, her eyes drifting closed.

Todd's frustration moved up a rung, and he considered what to say. He prayed for the right words, in the right order, but nothing came to mind.

"Laura," he started, his mind whirring. When he didn't continue, she turned toward him and opened her eyes. "You look tired," he said.

"Just what every woman wants to hear." She offered him a small smile that sent a teaspoon of joy into his heart.

"What can I do to help you?" he asked gently.

"Who says I need help?"

"I do," he said, adding some oomph to his voice. "I can see you're in distress, Laura. Even when you're smiling and working miracles with little girls, I can see the absolute…pain in your eyes."

Those lovely eyes filled with tears, and the last thing Todd wanted was to make her cry. "I'm sorry," he said quietly. "I—I wish you'd talk to me though."

He swallowed, now committed down this path. "I've enjoyed our dates, but I can feel the distance you keep between us." He gripped the brim of his cowboy hat, kneading it with his fingers until it was bent all out of shape. "And blast me, I let you, because I don't know how to make you talk to me. I can barely say what I want to say—and usually I can't at all. That's why I let you."

His lungs felt like someone had wrapped them in rubber bands, and they couldn't expand enough to get him the air he needed. He really didn't do well in talking to women. He could say hard things to any of his siblings. Anyone who worked for him—except Laura.

She reached over and took one of his hands away from the misshapen brim. "You're ruining your hat."

"It's just a hat," he said. "I have others."

Sunshine filled her face on this very rainy day in December, and Todd found himself returning the smile.

Her fingers wound around his and then slipped in

between them. She curled them and squeezed, and Todd liked this soft, quiet connection between them.

He dropped his hat completely and reached over with his other hand to tuck her hair behind her ear. "I've missed you, Laura."

"I know," she said, her eyes drifting closed with his touch. "I miss myself right now."

"Where does she go?" he asked.

"To things in the past," she said.

"I wish you'd tell me about it."

Her eyes opened, and she searched his face. "You can trust me," he said, remembering that she'd said it was ridiculous to think everyone could be trusted.

"I do trust you, Todd."

He let his hand come back to his lap and waited. Laura maybe needed a few moments to find her words and her voice, and he'd been pushing her too soon, or jumping in with his own thoughts when she needed the silence.

"I had a girl like that one once," she said, her smile made only of sadness now. "She wasn't mine, but she belonged to my fiancé." She gave a light laugh that carried no joy. "We were to be a family."

Todd's neck throbbed with his rapid pulse, and he had no idea what to say. Something—maybe the Good Lord Himself—told him not to say anything at all.

He just needed to be here with her, so Laura knew she didn't have to weather everything alone.

Laura's smile dissolved into a sob, and Todd wished they weren't seated in a car so he could take her into his arms and hold her tight. "Come on," he said, not caring about the rain. They both wore soaking wet clothes already.

He got out of the car and rounded the hood to get her out. She let him, and Todd swept the waif of a woman into his arms easily. He couldn't help the way his hormones fired, but he told himself now wasn't the time to be attracted to her.

Laura obviously had some serious things she was dealing with, and Todd wanted to be her safe place should she need one. In his opinion, she definitely needed one.

"Is the door unlocked?" he asked.

"Yes," she said, her voice hardly her own. "Who locks their doors out here?"

"Fair point." He opened the door and took her inside. As wet as they both were, he didn't dare sit on the couch, so he used his foot to kick a dining room chair out from under the table and he sank into that, cradling her on his lap.

She curled into his chest, sniffling. Todd once again felt prompted to give her time, and he stroked her hair back with one hand and kept her securely on his lap with the other.

His phone rang, but he ignored it. His jeans started to itch, but he didn't move a muscle. His throat turned dry, but he didn't ask for a drink.

Finally, Laura sat up and got to her feet. "I'm okay now."

"You're always okay," he said, watching her walk into

the kitchen and get a towel. She wiped it over her hair and faced him. "You're strong, Laura. You've always been a ray of sunshine on this ranch, and I want to help you get that back."

She smiled, and this time, it did hold some remnant of its old luster. "So I was obviously engaged," she said.

"I know what a fiancé is," he teased.

Thankfully, she didn't take offense to that, and she nodded to show her appreciation of his barb.

Her face crumbled, and she turned away from him. "His name was Hans, and he took care of his four-year-old half-sister after his dad passed away."

Todd got to his feet as Laura wiped her eyes. He approached her slowly, not wanting to overwhelm her or scare her back into silence.

"Ah, so that little girl reminded you of her."

"Yes." She looked at him, tears clinging to her eyelashes. "Hans was very ill, and he died before we could be married. I was supposed to still have Letty, but his aunt —who'd said she wouldn't take her from me—did exactly that."

She shook her head, smiling and half-scoffing as she tried not to burst into a sob. "It's okay. I went back to my veterinary program, because Hans hadn't wanted me to quit in the first place. I couldn't have done that with Letty."

"Doesn't mean you don't miss her." Todd ducked his head and watched her, her pain so raw and so real, he could almost feel it as if it belonged to him.

He opened his arms, a clear invitation for her to seek

refuge with him. She did, practically flying into his embrace. "I'm sorry," she said.

"You don't need to apologize to me." He pressed his lips to the top of her head. "Like I said before, you belong here, and I want to help you if I can."

"I love this ranch," she said. "I love my job here. Everyone has been so nice. Maybe not Josie, but it's okay. We get along okay."

The news that Josie wasn't nice surprised him, but he said, "I'm glad you like it here."

She ran her hands through his hair, her fingernails drawing shivers from him. His cold clothes probably helped with that, but he didn't try to still them.

They breathed in together, and Laura touched her nose to his cheek, and his mouth sought her jaw, then her earlobe. She pressed into his touch, the passion between them suddenly heating everything in his body.

Their lips caught for a moment, and then she ducked away. Todd wasn't sure if he should stop, step back, or stay. Laura looked up again, and he witnessed the conflict in her expression.

She'd kissed him last time, after he'd sung to her for her birthday and presented her with brownies and ice cream. This was different. This was attraction and desire—and pain.

This time, he lowered his head and kissed her, the fireworks just as loud in his ears, and the fire just as smoking hot as last time.

He could kiss her all day and never tire of it, but she

pulled away far too soon. Last time they'd kissed, she'd wanted something lighter and easier after that.

This time, Todd asked, "Okay?"

She looked up at him, her eyes full of a sexy softness, edged with fear. She didn't tell him the kiss was okay, and the longer the silence stretched, the more doubt filled him, until he was practically choking with it.

CHAPTER
THREE

Laura wanted to kiss Todd Stewart, but she didn't want it to be under these circumstances. The first time had been done out of an extremely emotional situation too, and that wasn't what she wanted.

He waited for an answer, and Laura didn't want to lose him over this. "It's okay," she finally got herself to say. "I just…" She exhaled heavily. "I don't want to kiss you when I'm super emotional."

"Oh."

"I want it to be…this happy thing. Something amazing and not because I'm crying or whatever."

"I'm sorry," he said.

"You don't need to be sorry." Laura paced away from him, her clothes wet and annoying. "I should get back to work."

"I called everyone in off the ranch," he said. When Laura turned back to him, Todd had stuck both hands in his front pockets. He offered her a small smile, and Laura found it easy to return it. His handsomeness struck her right against her heart, as did his kindness. He'd always been extraordinarily kind to her, and he'd always made her feel like she belonged here at the Texas Longhorn Ranch.

She wanted that again. She just didn't know how to get it. It lingered just out of her grasp, but she could see the happiness here on this ranch. She could reach out and wrap her fingers around it, but it wisped into smoke the moment she closed her fist.

"Laura," he said, really drawing out her name. "Would you like to go to dinner with me?"

She considered him. They'd gone out a few times, but nothing recently. "Like a do-over?"

The corners of his mouth curled up, but only for a moment. "Yeah," he said. "Like a do-over." He took a step toward her. "I'd like to go out with you again, and this time, see if we can try to put each other ahead of the ranch."

Laura wasn't sure if that was possible. Todd ran everything here at Longhorn, and though he had help, everyone looked to him for final decisions. He knew every detail, every single thing that happened, every need someone—or some animal—had.

"Okay," she said slowly.

"But?"

"But." She drew in a deep breath, so deep it hurt her chest. She imagined her chest falling, then her ribs closing as the air left her lungs, then she let her belly soften as the last of the oxygen fled her body. "Can we go out in the new year?"

"The new year?"

"Yeah." She smiled at him. "Like, you know, in a couple of weeks?" She took a step closer to him. "I'm going home for Christmas, and I…need to get in a better mental space before we go out."

Todd nodded. "All right. Dinner after the new year."

Laura nodded with him, unable to verbally agree. She wanted to go out with him. She did. It wasn't right for her to say yes, then back off, then go out with him again, then freak out about it. She wasn't going to do that. Not this time. Not again.

She'd work through some things before she went out with him again, that was all. She could start with her counseling app, talk to her mom over Christmas, and then come back to Chestnut Springs and…see.

"All right," Todd said. "I'll see you later. Are you going to come over to the lodge for the hot chocolate bar?"

"I'm going to shower first," she said. "Then, maybe."

He gave her a smile and headed for the door. "'Bye, Laura."

He had the door open and had stepped outside before she said, "'Bye, Todd." As the door swung closed, Laura pressed her eyes shut too. "Lord," she prayed. "Help me to do the right thing."

That was all she wanted to do. The right thing. With the right person. At the right time. Every time she pictured her future, it was blank. Except for right now, as she thought about it again, a handsome, tall cowboy walked toward her.

It was Todd Stewart, and Laura gasped as she opened her eyes. Could Todd be her cowboy in shining armor? The prince she'd been dreaming of? The man who would be good for her even if she still had one foot still stuck in the past?

She'd bought herself a bit of time to figure that out, and Laura went down the hall to get changed out of these wet clothes. She thought about Todd in a crown the whole time, and it was a very, very enticing picture.

––––––––

"I DON'T KNOW, MOM," SHE SAID A COUPLE OF WEEKS LATER. Laura had barely set her purse on the built-in buffet in her childhood home. She still had her bag and presents in the car. "I have to run to the bathroom. Can you wait a minute to fire questions at me?" She gave her mom a smile, glad when they both could laugh. She then escaped down the hall to the bathroom, where she drew in a deep breath, exhaled, and looked at herself in the mirror.

"You want to talk about this," she reminded herself. She'd called her mother a couple of weeks ago, after the rainstorm and the injury in the demo barn. After she'd kissed Todd again under the wrong circumstances.

The cowboy clearly liked her, and Laura liked him too. There just seemed to be so many hurdles she needed to clear before she could go out with him. He hadn't asked her again, and everything had gone back to their new normal after their earlier dating last summer and early fall.

He texted her. They laughed and talked when they were together, but they didn't leave the ranch, and neither of them made any special attempt to see one another outside of getting assignments, doing meetings, checking in on the animals at Longhorn Ranch, and anything else work-related that brought them together.

Laura used the restroom, washed her hands, and headed back into the kitchen. Her bag and laundry basket of gifts sat on the couch, and she smiled at her daddy. "Thanks, Daddy." She moved into him and hugged him hard. "I could've gotten them."

"I know." He held her tightly too, and Laura had always felt loved by her parents. They didn't understand some of her struggles, but they'd done the best they could to help her and support her through them.

She sighed as she sat at the bar and accepted a cup of coffee from her mother. Mom's eyebrows went up, and Laura reached for the spoon and the bowl of sugar. "What was your question again?"

"I asked when you were going to go out with Todd," she said.

"Right." Laura hadn't really forgotten, but she also didn't want her mom to know she'd been carefully planning her answers for days now. "I don't know, Mom. I asked him to wait until after the new year."

"That's next week," she said. "Maybe you could talk to him, and—"

"Becca," Daddy said, and she looked at her husband.

Mom fell silent, and Laura wondered what they'd talked about before she'd arrived. Daddy had clearly just reminded Mom of it, and something itched beneath her skin. "I talk to him," she said.

"Of course you do," Mom said, turning back to the fridge. "I've got a cheese ball in here. Daniel, get out the crackers, would you?"

"When's Eddie coming?" Laura asked, though she wouldn't wait for her brother and his family to start in on the cheese and crackers. She wasn't surprised Mom had it ready—it was one of Laura's favorite foods. Her mother was a very, very good cook, and while Laura could get by, she wasn't instinctual in her cooking the way her mom was.

"Should be here soon," Daddy said. "If you don't want to talk about Todd in front of him, you maybe better start talkin' now." He plunked two boxes of crackers on the counter too, and together, he and Mom pushed the food toward Laura.

She definitely took after her mom, who'd passed on the short genes and the reddish highlights in Laura's hair. The dark eyes and hair and the longer nose came from Daddy. Laura looked between them, finding all the pieces of herself in them. Except for the bravery and courage she needed. Maybe the mental strength and toughness.

"I want to go out with him," Laura said. "I'm feeling a little…disloyal is all. It's creating this mental block I'm having a hard time moving past."

"You're talking to Gene, aren't you?" Mom asked.

Her counselor. Laura nodded. "Yes, and you guys will be thrilled to know what he said to do."

"Do tell." Her dad took off the lid to reveal the cheese ball. It was creamy white, with green and orange specks, and Laura's mouth watered.

She smiled and reached to open a box of wheat crackers. As she did, she said, "He said to talk to you two. Get your opinion."

Her parents looked at one another, having a whole conversation without saying a word. Laura knew what that felt like, and it lifted her heart to be in a relationship so trusting and close as that. She'd had that once, with Hans, and her mind whispered at her that perhaps she could have it again with Todd.

If only she could get out of her own way.

"Well," Mom said slowly. "I understand how you feel. You loved Hans so much. You—" She took a long breath in. "You know what? I found a couple of journals in the barn while I was out there these past couple of months helping your daddy. I think you should have those, and they might help you."

Laura's throat went dry. "Journals?" In the barn?

"Yes," Mom said. "Let me get them." She bustled off to do that, and Daddy scooped up a thick layer of cheese ball with a saltine.

Laura shook her head at him. "Those are the wrong kind of crackers to eat that with."

"You have 'em your way; I'll have 'em mine." He grinned at her and tucked the whole thing in his mouth.

"What do you think, Daddy?"

He chewed and swallowed, and Mom still wasn't back yet. Laura wasn't sure what that meant, but she did value her father's opinion. When she called home, it was to talk to Mom, but she knew all the conversations got repeated for him.

"Laura, men and women are different, you know? I'd have moved on by now, but I'm not you." He cleared his throat. "I think it's great you're talkin' to someone who can be objective. I do. I think it's amazing that you're at this new ranch you love so much. I think the Lord probably guided you there, even if you didn't like the path you had to trod to get there." He picked up another saltine, looked at it, and then back to Laura.

"I think you're holdin' so tightly to the past that you're afraid to take a step forward, when that single step is all you need to do. Then you'll be free, and you'll be able to see if you and this Todd cowboy could be happy together."

Laura nodded, instant tears welling in her eyes. *Holding so tightly to the past* sounded about right. Hadn't she said almost those exact words to Gene yesterday? A version of them at least.

"All right," Mom said, hurrying back into the kitchen. "Here they are." She carried a lot more than a couple of volumes, and Laura stared at the books as she set them on the countertop.

"Mom," she said. "What are all of these?" She moved her gaze from them to her mother. "And there's no way you found all of these in the barn."

Mom wound her hands around themselves nervously. "No, all right, I didn't. Some of them I did. Yours."

"Mine?"

"Nellie brought me the rest," she said, her voice tight. "She said she and Miller had read them a bunch of times each, and they were ready to let them go. Ready to give them to you, but they didn't know where you were, and I said you were coming home for the holidays, and I'd pass them on." She threw a nervous look to Daddy, then back to Laura.

Laura reached for the top volume. "These are Hans's." His parents had journals of his, and she didn't know it? Apparently.

She flipped open the dark blue book, and her fiancé's handwriting stared her in the face. She expected to start sobbing, for her memories to flow thick and fast in her mind, to render her a blubbering mess of a woman.

That was how she'd been when Hans had finally passed away. Now, though, she read the first page with unwatered vision, smiling fondly at the story he told about taking Letty to see a fallen bird's nest out by their calving shed.

She finished the entry, noting the date had been a year before his diagnosis. He hadn't known how cruel life would be to him yet. She hadn't met him yet.

Laura looked up and smiled at her parents. "Thank you," she whispered. "I can't wait to read these."

"If it's too hard for you," Daddy said, but Laura shook her head.

"It's not going to be too hard." She gathered the books into her arms, noticing the two or three she'd written in after she'd learned of Hans's terminal condition. She'd needed an outlet that wasn't crying, running, or turning into a mime, and writing had provided that. She'd laid in the barn at night, up in the hay loft with the cats, and written out everything in her mind and heart. Often, Daddy would find her there in the morning, as she'd fallen asleep pouring out her emotions onto paper.

She took the books to the couch, where she swapped them out with the wrapped presents, which she put under her parents' Christmas tree. She'd barely finished that job when the front door opened, and in ran a pair of footsteps that belonged to a little boy.

"Gramma! Grampa!" Nelson shouted. "Come see what we got for Christmas!" The five-year-old streaked into the kitchen, his high-pitched voice more excited than Laura had ever heard it.

"My goodness," Mom said. "You got something already? Christmas isn't even until tomorrow." She laughed as Nelson grabbed her hand and started towing her toward the door.

Laura watched them with fondness, a smile filling her face and her soul. Coming home was exactly what she needed, and she hoped she could find the answers she needed here—and perhaps in Hans's journals—so she could close this chapter of her life and move into another one.

Outside, a dog barked, and Laura startled, her gaze flying to Daddy's. "They did not get a dog."

Daddy simply started laughing, and Laura hurried around the couch and out onto the front porch too. Eddie held a leash in his hand while his wife, Margery, carried their toddler on her hip. Lacey grinned and giggled at the black, brown, and white puppy, who kept jumping up and licking her brother's face.

"My goodness," Laura said, sounding very much like Mom. "They got a dog for Christmas." Happiness poured through her, and she wanted to tell Todd. The man adored canines—and Laura did too—and instead of fighting that instinct, she pulled out her phone, snapped a picture, and sent it to him with a message.

Look what my brother got his kids for Christmas.

Todd's response came lightning quick, as if he'd been waiting for her to text so he could strike back. *I love Australian shepherds. That'll be a good farm dog.*

He's adorable, Laura said as Daddy moved past her and down the steps to meet Eddie's puppy. *Can I have a dog at Longhorn Ranch?* That was about as close to flirting as she got, and she wished she could see Todd's face, giggle at him, and assure him she'd take good care of the animal.

Sure, Todd said. *I seem to take care of them for anyone who doesn't want to. What's one more?*

Laura laughed, because he did have his brother's dog more than Blake did. *By the way, I made it here safely.*

I see that. I'm glad.

She sobered, because she didn't doubt Todd's authenticity at all. If he said he was glad, he was. The cowboy didn't seem to have a disingenuous bone in his body, and that only made him more attractive to Laura.

She'd be here on her family farm in Hidden Hollow for the next three days. Then she'd return to the Texas Longhorn Ranch and all the Stewarts. Animals needed care three-hundred and sixty-five days a year, and she was blessed to have time off around the holidays at all.

She wanted to read through all of Hans's journals before she returned, but standing on the porch with all the family excitement happening a few steps down, Laura found she didn't want to wait to get a date on the calendar with Todd.

So, she typed out. *When I get back, can we go to dinner? Or lunch. Maybe you could meet me in town on my way through or something.*

Without second guessing herself, she sent the text, feeling braver and more like herself than she had in months.

CHAPTER
FOUR

Todd choked on the mouthful of orange juice he'd just swallowed. Or tried to swallow. His throat suddenly forgot how to push things down it, and he fumbled for his phone. That didn't work, and the juice burned as it came out his nose and went down the wrong pipe in his chest.

"Hey," Kyle said. He reached behind Todd and pounded him on the back. "No choking today."

"Starla is already worried about the menu," Jesse hissed. "Why are you making it worse?"

Todd coughed a few more times, took the napkin Blake handed to him, and glared at Jesse. "I choked on some orange juice." He shook his head. "It's not like I yelled about how salty the freaking chicken sausage is." It *was* salty, too, but he'd gotten the text from Nash—yet another brother—about the breakfast menu that day.

They were serving meals later this week due to the

holidays, and Todd didn't mind that at all. He usually faded into the background at a table filled with his family, even during a choking incident. To his left, Gina came out from the kitchen carrying another tray of cinnamon rolls, and at least three guests got up to go get one. There was nothing wrong with that morning's breakfast service.

"What caused the choking?" Blake asked, his eyebrows high as he looked pointedly from Todd's face to his phone.

Todd flipped it over quickly, but Blake had probably already seen it. Kyle too, as he knew all about Laura and Todd's insane crush on the woman. They lived together, and Todd saw no reason to hide anything from the brothers he trusted most.

At the table this morning, just the four of them ate together, and Todd flicked a look toward Jesse. His eyebrows had already straightened out of their frown, and he watched the kitchen door like a hawk. He had a mad crush on Starla Masters, the head chef and kitchen manager here at the lodge, even if he had broken up with her because Nash also had a crush on her. Neither of them were dating her right now, and Todd knew the three of them weren't happy with one another.

Or Jesse wasn't happy with Nash. Starla wasn't either. Nash wasn't happy with anyone, it seemed. Todd got lost about that point, which was why he preferred to work with animals and fields than people.

"Todd," Kyle barked, and he blinked.

"Yeah, uh." He cleared his throat and didn't reach for his orange juice again. "Laura just suggested we get together for lunch or dinner 'or something' when she returns in a few days."

"That's good," Kyle said. "Right?" He took another bite of a yogurt and fruit parfait, his eyes full of hope.

"Yeah," Todd said.

"But?" Blake asked.

"But I don't know," Todd said.

"I thought she said she didn't want to go out until the new year," Jesse said, his eyes finally getting torn from the kitchen door.

"She did." Todd flipped over his phone. "I think she wanted to talk to her parents about us." That wasn't speculation. Laura had all but told him her parents had helped her reason through a lot of hard life decisions in the past. He hated thinking that going to dinner with him was a "hard life decision," but now that he knew a little bit more about where she'd been and what she'd gone through, he understood that dating was difficult for her.

She seemed so happy on the outside, but Todd had started to see deeper. Not only that, but their first date had gone wrong at every turn. Laura had laughed and said she'd just liked the time with him, and now he knew why. Time was important to her. *Time* was what she hadn't had with Hans.

"So I should say yes, right?" he asked.

"Of course you should say yes," Blake said. "For how fast you were answering her before, she probably thinks she blew it."

"Answer her," Kyle said.

Jesse nodded, then exploded to his feet in the next moment, dislodging the table.

"Hey," Blake practically yelled, but Jesse was already gone. Todd joined his brothers in watching him nearly run over to Starla.

"He has *got* to calm down," Kyle muttered.

"Too obvious," Blake said.

Todd said nothing, because if Jesse wanted to date Starla, and Nash wasn't going to make a move, then Jesse should. Or else Nash should. The stalemate between the three of them made zero sense to him, but he reminded himself he wasn't the one living inside it. He also didn't want to get called to the lodge to break up a fistfight between his brothers again either. So perhaps they should all simply exist inside their misery.

He could put Laura out of hers.

Yeah, sure, of course. He tilted the phone toward Blake. "Too obvious?"

"Mm, tone it down. Just say yes."

Todd deleted the whole message and started again. *Yeah, I'd like that. You tell me when you're leaving, and I can pick a place? You're coming back on Tuesday, right?*

It took a few seconds for her to respond, but Todd's heart tap-danced with the message. *Yes, Tuesday. I won't stay long that morning. It'll probably be halfway between break-fast and lunch. It's only an hour from here to there.*

Hmm, halfway between breakfast and lunch, he typed, his soul expanding and smiling in every direction. *Gonna make it hard to pick somewhere.*

You like breakfast for every meal, she sent back, and Todd read it in her teasing voice. He hadn't heard it for a while, not directed at him, but this texting session definitely felt more flirty than their others in recent months. *So pick somewhere that we can get breakfast all day, and we'll be good.* "Bacon Barn," Kyle said, and Todd looked up at him. "Sorry." Kyle averted his eyes. "I'd like to take someone to the Bacon Barn." He sighed, because the only people in the dining room were guests.

"Then do it," Blake said, plenty of conviction in his voice. "You date, Kyle. You know how to meet women."

Kyle shook his head, his gaze still somewhere in the distance. "Yeah, maybe. I don't know."

Todd exchanged a glance with Blake, who nodded toward their younger brother. Blake, Todd, and Kyle were all two years apart, almost exactly. They'd palled around a lot as kids and teens, and they'd been friends on the ranch their whole lives.

"Not everyone is going to be Maggie," Todd said.

Kyle whipped his attention to him. "I know that."

"You haven't dated since her, that's all." Todd shrugged. "I don't care if you do or not. But if you want to, it's...you know a lot of women. You have a lot of contacts out there."

"I don't want someone in country music," he said, and he might as well have tacked on the word *again*.

"Plenty of women not in country music," Blake said. They fell silent again, and Todd went back to his breakfast. Kyle worked a lot around the ranch, especially in the summertime, when all of their concerts happened. He also put in long hours arranging those concerts in the off months, and he brought in seasonal guests too. He worked year-round, though he definitely had a slower season and a high-stress season.

Todd felt like his life was high-stress season, and he took his time over the rest of breakfast. No one needed him, and no one texted. At least for a few minutes. Then Little Nick needed to know where he should put all the extra feed they'd ordered that week, and Todd pushed away from the table.

"See you later, boys," he said, and he picked up his empty plate and Jesse's and took them both to the dish return before heading out to their storage barn to assist with the work on the actual ranch side of the Texas Longhorn Ranch.

"WE BEST BE GETTIN' OVER TO MAMA'S," TODD SAID THE next afternoon.

Sierra, his youngest sister and the youngest Stewart sibling, looked up from her tablet. "Is it time?" She yawned, because she'd gone out overnight to assist with the birth of one of their cows. She'd been on the midnight patrol, and they'd actually delivered two calves overnight.

Birthing season reminded Todd of low-battery smoke detectors. Those always went off in the middle of the night, the annoying beeping something a man couldn't just ignore until the sun came up. Cows giving birth were the same way. They had to be watched and attended to, in case something happened that jeopardized the life of them or their baby.

Since the ranch made about half of its income from the sale of their cattle, as well as some dollars that came in from the extra hay they grew, which other local farmers and ranchers would buy from them if they couldn't produce enough, Todd didn't want to lose any cattle. Not if it could be helped by having a human out there at two in the morning.

Sometimes that human was him, and sometimes it was Sierra. Four other cowboys assisted around the clock too, and they all took shifts in the winter months.

"Yeah." He sighed as he stood up. "It's time. No sense in bein' late if we don't have to be."

"Except she's going to make us carol around to the guests." Sierra wore a sour look on her face, and Todd couldn't blame her.

"It's good for business," he said. Most unsavory things around the ranch could eventually come back to that. The commercial side of the dude ranch was all about entertaining and educating the guests who paid good money— and a lot of it—to come stay in the lodge or one of their cabins.

The family all had private residences here on the ranch, and Todd was grateful for that. He needed an escape sometimes, and the wide open field across the dirt lane offered him a good view of the sunset in the evening. The woods behind the cabin he and Kyle shared—that bordered all the backyards of all the family cabins—gave them privacy from anyone who might go out that way.

No one ever did, or at least very rarely. Today, he tossed his keys to Sierra, and they both stepped into their jackets before going outside. The wind had driven in some storm-clouds, but it hadn't started to rain yet. The past couple of days had been gray and dreary in the morning, with the sun finally showing its face about four o'clock in the afternoon.

Todd didn't think they'd be that lucky today.

"You've got your gift?" she asked, and Todd patted his coat pocket.

"You?"

"In my truck." She detoured over to it to grab her red-wrapped gift, and they trundled over to their parents' in silence. Sierra could get going and once she did, stopping her mouth became almost impossible. She could remain silent too, and Todd liked sharing an office with her. She worked hard; she cared about animals; she loved being outdoors; she never complained about the long days, oddball hours, and how dirty ranching could be.

It seemed like everyone else had arrived ahead of them, and Todd and Sierra weren't even late yet. They got out and went up the sidewalk to the house where they'd all grown up. This house was by far the biggest one here, as there were eight kids in the family. Still, rooms had been shared and quarters close for all of Todd's life. He didn't normally mind it—and he didn't today either.

Sierra went in first, with Todd following her to shut out the wind. Chatter and laughter filled the house, as did the scent of roasted meat, bacon, a bit of wood smoke, and pine trees. Totally Christmas.

Todd smiled as he walked toward Jesse, Adam, and Holly. The three of them stood in a triangle that they expanded for Todd while Sierra went to get a cup of the strawberry punch their mother made every Christmas.

"Merry Christmas, Todd." Holly, his oldest sister, hugged him.

"Merry Christmas," he said back. He didn't work with Holly a whole lot, and that made them great friends. She managed the lodge in the evenings, so she'd probably be over there tonight to lead everyone in the carol-singing, make sure they got their Christmas dinner on time, and that everyone was happy with everything this holiday.

Jesse and Adam worked together quite a lot, as Jesse was the controller at the lodge. Basically anything Blake couldn't handle in terms of admin, Jesse did. He focused a lot on customer service and relations, and he could go from hot to calm in less time than it took to blink. Todd admired his people skills, and deep down, it turned to jealousy. Jesse could handle almost any situation with grace and ease, even if he did complain about it later.

Adam…wasn't so much like that. He took care of their stable of horses, and Longhorn Ranch had about thirty of them. They all required constant care, play times, exercise, training, and more food and water than one might think possible. He was a saint in Todd's book, because dealing with the varied horse personalities on the ranch was no picnic. Not to mention their health needs…hoof rot, pills for this, an injury during horseback riding with that one, an attitude on Lady. The list of equine problems was long, and Adam happily dealt with it seven days a week.

He had to, because he got along better with nonverbal creatures than those who could talk back, and with him out on Todd's side of the operation, everyone was happy.

"Did you see that text from Sammy Boy?" Adam asked. "He's figured out where those huge chunks of hay have been going." He wore a glint of amusement in his dark eyes, and Todd smiled.

"I didn't get it. He must've just sent it to you." He peered over at Adam's phone as he started a video.

Sammy Boy narrated as Todd watched. "Look at 'im. He's puttin' his front hooves up on that blasted bar." Sure enough, one of their more rascally horses—King Louis—did a balancing act to get to the hay he wasn't supposed to have.

He twisted his long neck, and because horses had the biggest heads on the planet, he reached the hay easily. He took a big bite of it, pulled hard, and fell back into his stall, his treat getting chewed.

"I can't believe him," Sammy Boy said, his voice loud on the video. He started to laugh, and Adam, Jesse, and Todd did too.

"He's a piece of work," Todd said. "Are you gonna move him?"

"Sammy Boy already did." Adam tucked his phone in his back pocket. "He put Winchester in that stall, because he's a short little thing, and we need the room to store the hay."

That they did, and Todd nodded his approval. "What are the chances we can get out of singing before we eat?"

Jesse cocked one eyebrow. "Null." He chuckled. "You should do what Adam does."

Todd switched his attention back to Adam. "What does Adam do?"

"Nothing," he said at the same time Jesse said, "He lip syncs."

"We can't all lip sync," Holly said, shaking her head. "It's not that bad."

"It's like fifteen minutes of *Silent Night*," Adam rolled his eyes. "When we're all starving."

"You ate at the lodge this morning." She swatted his arm. "Be nice to Mama."

"I *am* nice to Mama."

"Everyone," Mama called in that moment, and Todd turned to face her. She held up both hands, one of which still had an oven mitt on it. "Let's gather 'round for our devotional."

Todd exchanged a glance with Adam, but they did as instructed. Everyone bunched up in the kitchen, and Mama stood at Daddy's shoulder. Todd didn't mind the family time, because it felt precious to him. Everyone here had a role to play on the ranch, and each of them was important. He didn't like it when he wasn't getting along with one of his siblings, or some of them weren't getting along—like Nash and Jesse.

He noted that they didn't stand next to one another. In fact, Nash stood way on the other side of the kitchen island, next to Daddy and no one else. He'd always been a bit of a loner, even inside the family. Todd tried to catch his eye, but he seemed fixated on Mama.

"Everyone put in your vote for the songs we'll sing," she said, pushing out the pens and slips of paper. "We'll just do three, as usual."

"Please, no *Silent Night*," Adam murmured from beside him, but he stepped forward and got slips of paper for himself, Todd, and Holly. Jesse got his own, and Todd wrote down three songs that couldn't really be counted as hymns. He didn't mind those either; they usually just went on too long.

"The food is ready," Mama continued as slips of paper started to rain down on the counter. "So Holly will play for us, and we'll sing. Then Daddy—who did you ask to pray, dear?"

Daddy looked like he'd been caught in the headlights. "Uh." He scanned the lot of them, which was only his children, plus Blake's new fiancée, Gina Barlow. Sometimes they had more people with them for the holidays, and this felt like a rare thing that they didn't have someone from the lodge or ranch dining with them.

"Todd, would you?"

"Yes, sir," he said dutifully, though he didn't like the spotlight all that much. He'd prayed plenty in his life, though, and it was Christmas Day. He wasn't going to say no.

"Okay," Mama said. "Then Todd will pray, and then we'll eat. Gina and Starla set the table, so we'll eat over there." She picked up the first slip of paper while Todd looked around for Starla.

He finally saw her standing back in the mouth of the hallway, out of the way. She simply observed, and Todd got the feeling she felt out of place here with them. He didn't like that, and he nudged Jesse.

"What?" he asked, making an exaggerated move away from Todd as Mama said the first song would be *Jingle Bells*.

"One verse," Blake said.

"Fine," Mama agreed, though she obviously didn't like it. "One verse."

When she went back to reading papers and tallying song votes, Todd leaned toward Jesse. "Starla looks a little lost." He nodded across the group to where she stood, her arms now folded.

Jesse swallowed, everything about him changing and softening as he followed Todd's gaze. "I'll be right back," he whispered.

"Up on the Housetop," Mama said, nodding to Holly at the piano in the living room behind them. She wore a pursed look, and Todd knew it was because everyone had put in secular songs. She was probably the only one wanting to sing *Away in a Manger* or *O Little Town of Bethlehem*.

"And *Silent Night*," she said, not even looking at the rest of the papers.

"Mama," at least three people said, but Todd kept his voice quiet.

"What? I'm sure that'll be the third highest one." She held her head high and started sweeping all the papers into her arms, lest anyone grab them and check. "Let's go, Holly."

"You can't just pick the songs," Adam said.

"Yeah, you had us vote." Blake shook his head, but he was teasing. Adam wasn't.

"It's fine," Daddy said, adding his voice to the fray. He and Mama had had their fair share of problems, but in the end, they always backed one another. "It's three Christmas songs."

"We hate *Silent Night*," Kyle said. "It's so long."

"And slow," Sierra said.

"Holly will speed it up," Mama said. "Come on. It's our tradition, and it's my favorite Christmas song."

More grumbling happened, but most of it stayed under people's breath. Todd said nothing, because he'd come knowing he'd have to sing *Silent Night*. He didn't mind it the way Adam and Sierra apparently did, but as his stomach gave a painful growl, he hoped Holly would speed it up a whole lot.

Holly started with a rousing rendition of *Jingle Bells*, and Todd didn't do any lip syncing during that. He enjoyed the vibrancy and energy in the cabin, and he felt a keen sense of belonging to his family. It was beautiful and kind, and while they had problems like any other family, today, while they sang, everything was okay.

He couldn't help letting his mind wander during *Silent Night*, especially the third verse. It went straight to Laura and what her family traditions surrounding Christmas looked like. Did she have to sing? Go around the table and talk about something good that had happened that year? Exchange gifts with her siblings?

The Stewarts did all of that, and Todd wished she was there with him to experience it. Especially when, after dinner and pie, he presented Nash with a bolo tie, and everyone started to laugh. At least Nash did too, and he even put on the tie to model it for the family.

"I'm so wearing this to church," he said. "Then I can be in the Cattleman's Club too." He sat with it on while the rest of the gifts got exchanged, beaming like he'd just won tickets to his favorite country music band.

Todd got a new blanket for his bed, something he sorely needed, from Adam, and he thanked his brother for the thoughtful gift. He watched Blake and Gina hold hands and share smiles, and he noted that Jesse never got too far from Starla. Nash didn't look their way, and only when Sierra caught his eye did he realize how tired he was.

She nodded toward the door, her eyebrows up, and Todd nodded. If they were lucky, they could make their escape without Mama's protest, but as they stood from the circle, they weren't so lucky.

Todd didn't mind as much as Sierra, who looked a couple of breaths away from passing out from exhaustion. That got them out of there with only three days' worth of food and more hugs than Todd needed to get through the next week.

Unless he could get one from Laura. He'd take that hug anytime. Anytime at all, and he couldn't wait to see her again…because when he did, they'd be on their second first date.

Please help it go better than the first one, he prayed as he drove Sierra home.

CHAPTER
FIVE

Laura sang along to the radio, her heart lighter than it had been in a while. She'd read all of the journals, but nothing had stuck to her so strongly that she needed to keep them close to her. She hadn't wanted to upset her mother, so she'd stowed them in the back of the closet in the room she'd grown up in.

They had helped clear her head, as had the visit itself. She'd spent the first half of the drive back to Chestnut Springs scolding herself for not going to visit her family more often. She could easily get there and back in a single day.

"An hour," she'd scoffed at herself. It was an hour there, and an hour back, and she didn't have to pack anything.

Once she'd decided she wouldn't let herself fall into such a funk again—she'd just ask for a day off and drive to see her parents—she'd turned the radio on loud and started singing. She drove down a lonely highway west of town, the two-lane road with trees lining it so comforting to her.

Her cousins from Nevada hadn't known what to do with all the trees. They'd commented on them endlessly, talking about how they couldn't see driveways and turn-offs until they were right on top of them.

Laura loved the Hill Country, and the morning sun had burned off almost all of the mist now. The winter days usually dawned gray and dark blue, lightened to white, and then provided a spectacular sunset. As long as it wasn't raining, that was.

She belted out the chorus to one of her favorite songs, then yelped as the car bumped violently. The wheel went slack in her hands, and the car started to turn sideways.

She gripped the steering wheel and braked, easing her sedan off the road and onto the shoulder. It *thu-bumped* to a stop, and her heart sank to her shoes. The radio blasted far too loudly now, and she reached to turn it down.

With things a little quieter, she could think, and she unbuckled to check the tires. Sure enough, the rear right one was flat as a pancake, the rim of the wheel sitting right on the asphalt. Laura heaved a sigh and ran her hands through her hair.

She hadn't stayed long at her mama's, just like she'd told Todd she wouldn't. Long enough to curl her hair, though. Long enough to put on makeup too. She was meeting him for a date, and she wanted to look presentable.

Her hair, makeup, and clothes were far past

presentable, and she knew it. Mama and Daddy had known it too. Had Eddie been there, he'd have catcalled and teased her about who she was going out with.

She looked up into the sky. "Really, Lord?"

No answer came, not that Laura truly expected one. Mama had said God had placed her at the Texas Longhorn Ranch, and maybe He had. Laura didn't like arguing with Mama about faith and religion. She sometimes wondered how big of a role God played in her life, that was all.

It sure had seemed cruel to give her Hans and Letty, only to take them away. She shook the thoughts from her head and looked at the tire again. She wasn't even sure she had a spare.

Moving to the back of the car, she released the trunk. It popped open, and Laura stared down at the contents of it. "My goodness."

Mama had clearly been busy while Laura had been showering and primping. The entire trunk was filled. The laundry basket Laura had brought her gifts in now held what she'd been given for Christmas. Clothes, boots, and a new saddle. Daddy had been working on that for months, and Laura teared up a little again just looking at the leather.

Not only that, but Mama had put a box of food in the trunk too, and it was as big as the laundry basket and full to the top. Laura didn't want to gripe about it. She could cook, but she didn't enjoy the activity, and this would be enough for a couple of weeks if she froze some things.

Mama had also been going through the farmhouse and cleaning it out, and at least three more smaller boxes sat behind the two bigger items, and Laura saw things like an old puzzle, her yearbooks, and other things she felt certain she wouldn't want. Mama didn't want them either, and Laura had told her to throw things away. Mama couldn't do that, and Laura would end up putting them in the bin herself.

Right now, though, she couldn't get all of this out to see if there was a spare underneath. Even if there was, it had been a long time since she'd changed a tire.

Sighing, she straightened and closed the trunk. She looked left, then right, and didn't hear or see another vehicle coming. She went to the passenger door and sank into the seat there before picking up her phone.

Something Todd said after their first date rang in her ears. *I'm cursed. You should run now.*

Or something close to that. Laura had laughed and said she didn't want to get out now. And she hadn't.

She didn't want to cancel on him, and she was only fifteen or twenty minutes outside of town. Maybe he could tow her to the tire shop in Chestnut Springs, and they could go eat as planned, and then she could wait for her car to get back out to the ranch.

She hesitated, because something stuck in her head. Maybe their relationship was a bit cursed. Nothing seemed to go right with them, and Laura gazed out the windshield as she took a moment to analyze things.

"No." She shook her head only a couple of moments later. "When I talk to him, and when we're together, that's easy. It's everything outside of that which is hard."

She tapped to dial his number, only to have a notification come up that said she couldn't complete the call. No service.

Back outside of the car, Laura checked her phone again. Nothing.

"Of course," she said, rolling her shoulders and then her eyes. She decided to begin the walk toward town, as that seemed like her best bet to find a farm or house with WiFi she could borrow, or to find a pocket of service so she could make a call.

She kept her eyes on the phone or the road as she walked, the silence around her a bit unnerving. She'd gone for a couple of minutes before realizing she hadn't turned off her car, and she spun back to the vehicle. It seemed impossibly far away, but Laura broke into a jog to get back to it.

Once she had it turned off, locked, with the keys in her purse, and her purse slung across her shoulders, she started off again. She didn't want Todd to think she'd stood him up. She'd texted him when she was leaving, and he'd told her he'd meet her at Bacon Barn in roughly an hour.

She looked at his texts, and they'd been almost an hour ago now. Her pace increased, as if she'd walk the remaining distance to Chestnut Springs in only a few minutes. She'd probably have been a bit late had her car kept running. She hadn't shared her pin with him, something she'd done with Hans. They both worked out on farms and ranches, without much contact sometimes. They wanted to be able to know where the other was if something went wrong.

Walking alongside the road in that moment, Laura no longer loved that all she could see was asphalt and trees forever. She felt totally and utterly alone, and if something happened, no one would know where she was or when it had happened.

There were several roads into Chestnut Springs; Todd would have no way of knowing which one she'd taken. No one would.

Anxiety beat behind her tongue, and Laura swallowed it away. Down, and away. A road sat up ahead, and she'd simply go down it and see if there was a house where she could make a phone call. Simple.

She did, and by the time a man answered the door at the huge mansion Laura had stumbled upon, she wondered if days and days had passed. "Howdy," he said as whoever played the piano behind him stalled the music. "What can I do for you?"

He stood over six feet tall if he was an inch, and Laura swallowed at his commanding presence. He wore the clothes of a cowboy—a working one—and she calmed when a couple of dogs came to his side. He looked down at them and said, "Sit down," and they both did.

"My car got a flat tire back down the road there," Laura said. "There's no service, and I need to call a friend who's waiting for me in town. Could I use your WiFi or a phone here?"

"Sure," he said, stepping back. "C'mon in. This here's Winner, and that's Thunder, but they're sweet as pie." He looked toward the woman standing in a doorway and added, "This is my wife, Jenna."

"He's Seth," Jenna said with a smile. "He always introduces everyone but himself."

Laura smiled at them too, wondering what they did that both of them could be home with their dogs in the middle of the day. "Thanks," she said, entering the house.

"The service is pretty bad on the road," Seth said. "But it's not bad out here." He pulled his phone from his pocket. "I've got bars."

Laura checked her phone. She didn't. Looking up, she asked, "Can I use your phone? Mine seems to have forgotten how to work."

He chuckled, handed Laura the phone, and turned to go with the dogs back into the further recesses of the house. Laura stayed in the foyer, with the room holding the grand piano on her left, and tapped in Todd's number.

It came up as a contact in the man's phone, and Laura stared at it. *Todd Stewart.*

Of course. Todd ran a huge ranch, and Seth-Whoever obviously did too. Of course they'd know each other. She wasn't sure why her heart did the strange flippity-flop it did, only that she didn't want Seth and Jenna gossiping about her and Todd.

He'd be able to see who she called on her phone now, and another dose of hesitation ran through her. The clock at the top of the device spurred her to making the call. She was ten minutes late, and she had no idea if Todd had tried to text or call.

She tapped, and the line started to ring. Hallelujah.

After only two rings, Todd said, "Seth," good-naturedly. "Howdy. What's up?"

"Todd," Laura said. "It's not Seth. It's Laura."

"Laura?" He sounded so confused, and she could only imagine the feelings she'd have if someone's name came up on her screen, but she got someone completely different. It would be like taking a sip of water and getting milk instead.

"Yes," she said. "I got a flat tire, and there's no service out on this road. I had to walk somewhere to get help, and I guess I'm at Seth's place."

"Oh, no. That's too bad."

"I was thinking maybe you could come tow me into town?"

"Sure," he said. "I can do that. You're out on the western highway? The one that runs past Chestnut Ranch?"

"I guess? I don't know."

"You didn't make any turns before showing up at Seth's, right?"

"I mean, I had to turn to walk down his lane, and then I walked for a while, and then there was this huge brick house before a bridge. I'm not even sure I made it to the ranch."

"You didn't." Todd sounded like he was walking fast now. "But I know where you are. You're at Jenna's place. I'll be there in a few minutes."

"I should wait here?"

"Yeah," he said. "Wait there. Then you can get me back to where your car is, and you won't have to walk."

"Okay," she said, but she didn't want to wait with Seth and Jenna. Laura wasn't particularly gifted with small talk, and it was nice weather outside. She could walk back to the main highway and wait there for Todd.

"I'll be there in fifteen or twenty minutes, Laura," he said.

"Todd," she said, and then paused. "Do you—? Do you still have time to eat afterward?" Twenty minutes for him to get out here. They'd have to hook up her car. Twenty minutes—or more—back to town. Drop off her car at a shop. Then go to lunch? This flat tire had added over an hour to his time away from the ranch. Hers too.

"Sure," he said. "I'll be fine."

"I just—I know you're busy right now." She wasn't sure what she was saying. Todd obviously didn't either, because he remained silent. "If you have to get back to the ranch, I understand."

"I don't," he said. "Do you not want to go out?"

"I do," she said, almost whispering the words. "I just— it feels cursed, you know? Remember you said that when we tried to go to the Sunflower Café?"

He chuckled, and the sound plucked against Laura's heartstrings. Funny, when Seth had made the same sound, she'd felt nothing for him. But with Todd's unique timbre in her ears, she heard whole symphonies.

She couldn't ignore that, and she quickly said, "I don't care if it's cursed. I'm hungry, and I want to see you."

"Great," he said. "I'll be there in fifteen or twenty minutes, and I—we—have plenty of time to eat afterward."

"Okay," she said, strengthened by the conviction in his tone. "Thanks, Todd." She didn't want to hang up with him, but she didn't have anything else to say. So she awkwardly said, "Bye," and hung up.

Neither Seth nor Jenna loitered within earshot, which she appreciated, but she didn't want to encroach further into their personal space. "Thanks," she called, and a chair scraped from somewhere down the hall that led deeper into the house.

Seth appeared there, and she moved toward him, his phone extended in his direction. "He's on his way. I'm just going to wait down at the highway for him."

Seth took the phone, looked at it though it sat with a dark screen, and looked back at her. "Are you sure? Jenna just made coffee."

His wife appeared down at the end of the hall, and Laura didn't know how to say no. "All right," she said.

Seth turned, and as he walked into the kitchen with Laura behind him, he asked, "Oh, you called Todd?" His eyes met hers, and they weren't judging her or casting anything negative at all. Just curiosity.

"Yeah," she said. "We were meeting for a late breakfast or early lunch." She bobbled her head this way and that. "He chose Bacon Barn, so my guess is he'd be eating breakfast." She grinned at Seth and Jenna.

Seth smiled on back and nodded. "He likes breakfast all day long."

"Friends of ours live out at the Texas Longhorn Ranch," Jenna said, pouring a cup of coffee and handing it to Laura. "Luke Miller and Rebecca Stewart."

"Oh, sure," Laura said, looking around for sugar.

"Becks works in the office, so I don't see her a lot, but Luke's on the ranching side. I know him."

"What do you do out there?" Seth asked.

"I'm the vet," Laura said, a bit of pride swelling in her chest.

Interest filled Seth's gaze now. "A vet, huh?" His phone chimed, and he let it distract him. A moment later, his big, booming laugh filled the room.

"What?" Jenna asked, moving to his side to peer over his forearm at his phone too. She grinned and giggled, and she took the phone and showed it to Laura while Seth continued to laugh.

Laura's eyes scrambled to read the text on Seth's phone. It was from Todd, and it said, *She's my full-time vet, Seth. Don't you dare offer her a job.*

Laura looked up at Seth, surprise in her expression. "Do you need a vet?"

"He runs a huge dog rescue," Jenna said. "He always needs a vet."

Seth took his phone back from his wife. "I value my life more than having a vet." He tucked the device away. "So I won't offer you a job."

Laura smiled at him and stirred in a few spoonfuls of sugar. Maybe hanging out here for a few minutes wouldn't be so bad.

Then Jenna asked, "Are you dating Todd, or do you just work for him?"

CHAPTER
SIX

Todd made the turn to head out to Jenna Wright's house—where she now lived with her new husband Seth. They'd only been married for a couple of weeks, and Todd thanked the heavens that they were home from their honeymoon. If they hadn't been, Laura would've been able to find someone a little further down the road. Over the bridge from Jenna's place sat Chestnut Ranch, and Todd had been there countless times in the past.

He also knew Seth's brothers had been working on the dog rescue enclosures, and that Seth always needed a good veterinarian to look at the dogs he had. Todd didn't know how many he was dealing with, but some of them came from some pretty poor conditions around the area.

His phone sat silently in the console, without a return message from Seth about not offering Laura a job. Not only did Todd and Longhorn Ranch need her, but he didn't want to have to drive forty-five minutes to see her. He liked having her closeby, and in some of his meetings, the lingering scent of her skin or perfume staying even after she'd left.

The drive down the lane to the big brick house seemed to take forever, and he didn't see anything amiss there when he arrived. Seth's huge truck sat in the driveway, and Todd glanced to the detached garage to his left. With the holidays, Jenna probably wasn't at the elementary school and wouldn't have her piano students today.

He swung down from the truck, then walked up the sidewalk toward the front door. This house stood two stories tall and looked like a great golden cube out here in the Texas wilderness. The Wrights had lived here for generations, and Todd had attended both of the Jenna's parents' funerals, as well as her and Seth's wedding a few weeks ago.

The doorbell rang inside the house, the higher tones reaching his ears out on the porch. Todd fell back a step, his heartbeat hopping up into his throat. He hadn't seen Laura for several days, and he hadn't anticipated having to welcome her back to Chestnut Springs in front of Seth and Jenna.

Seth, however, answered the door at his own house, with Jenna only a foot behind him. Laura wasn't to be seen. "Howdy," Seth said, thrusting out his hand for Todd to shake. His grin suggested he'd been having a grand old time while Todd had been driving, and Todd pumped his hand even as he narrowed his eyes at his friend.

"Howdy." He leaned in and hugged Jenna too. "Is Laura still here? I didn't see her walking down the lane."

"She's here," Jenna and Seth said together, and Laura said, "I'm right here."

Her voice came from the left, but Seth refused to move. Laura crossed behind them and smiled at Todd from around Jenna. "Hey, Todd." She reached up and tucked her hair behind her ear, drawing his attention there.

She wore earrings, something he'd only seen her do when he'd spied her sitting alone at church. Josie, her cabinmate, went to the same services, and she sat with a couple of other cowboys and cowgirls from the ranch. Why Laura hadn't been invited to sit with them, Todd didn't know, but it had bothered him.

"Hey, Laura." He tucked his hands in his pockets and denied himself the opportunity to reach for her. "You ready to go?"

"Yep." She stepped into Jenna and hugged her too. "Thanks for the coffee and banana bread."

"You ate?" he asked.

"Thanks for your phone, Seth." Laura gave him a light hug too, like the tall, broad-shouldered cowboy was made of glass and she didn't want to break him.

She joined Todd, who gave her plenty of room, on the porch. "I ate a few bites. I'm still plenty hungry." She nodded toward the driveway. "Are you ready?"

"So ready."

Laura left, but Todd stayed on the porch, the width of Seth's and Jenna's smiles somewhat alarming. "Thank you," he said to them, trying to find something else to say.

Why did he feel like he had to explain who Laura was to him?

He gave himself a mental shake. "Hope the honeymoon was amazing."

Jenna linked her arm through Seth's. "It was. Thanks."

"Dogs doing well?" he asked Seth, because his Texas manners wouldn't allow him to simply leave after two sentences.

"Great," he said. "My brothers got everything finished while I was gone as a Christmas present."

"I heard that," Todd said. "I was going to come down to help, but I had four calves born that morning."

Seth chuckled and said, "Cows ruin the best-laid plans."

"That they do." Todd grinned back at Seth. "Thanks for helping Laura."

"You two have fun," Jenna said, and Todd backed up a step and turned around. He'd taken a few steps down to the sidewalk when the door clicked closed behind him. Laura waited at the end of the sidewalk for him, and he felt like skipping toward her.

His smile, which had been real enough for Seth, turned into something soft and purely genuine as he met Laura's eyes. "Look at you," he said, letting himself do exactly that. His gaze slid down to her feet, where she wore a cute pair of cowgirl boots he'd never seen before. "New boots?"

"My sister-in-law gave them to me for Christmas." She tipped up onto her toe on her left foot, letting the heel dangle in the air. "I love them."

"I do too," he said, arriving in front of her. He

supposed Seth and Jenna could be spying on him out the window, but he didn't care. He slid his fingers between hers and added, "I missed you. Did you have a good Christmas?"

"Yes," she said, her voice low and barely loud enough for him to hear. "Did you?"

"Oh, it was about the same as usual," he said lightly. "Too much food at my mama's. She gets her way about singing *Silent Night* every year. Adam bickers with everyone, and watching Blake and Gina was almost sickening." He chuckled, glad when Laura joined her laughter to his.

"Sounds fun," she said.

"You'll have to come to our New Year's Eve party," he said, holding his breath for a moment. "Starla and Gina have been planning a menu for months, I've heard."

"Wow, months." Laura's dark eyes almost looked violet for a moment. She gave him half a smile that felt flirty and fun. "I better not miss it."

"You better not." Todd squeezed her hand and continued toward his truck. The moment he opened his door, a rush of embarrassment hit him. "Uh, let me move my bags." He'd been shopping that morning before this date, picking up a few things he needed, and he'd forgotten about the bags.

"What did you get?" Laura asked as he tried to fist them all at the same time. That didn't really work, and he dropped a couple of bags with new jeans in them.

"Clothes," he said. "Some new jeans, socks, a jacket. That kind of thing."

Laura moved back to allow him to put the bags in the

back of the truck, and then she boosted herself onto the seat. Todd's blood boiled at the sight of her in his vehicle, and he closed his door without acting like a fool.

"You're in too deep already," he muttered to himself as he circled the front of the truck. "Calm down. Tone it down." He heard his brothers' voices from breakfast the other day, then saw Jesse jump to attention the moment Starla made an appearance. He didn't want to be the overeager beaver, but one look at Laura through the window, and he almost couldn't help himself.

In the truck, he buckled his seatbelt and looked at her. "Right to your car?"

"Yes, sir," she said, checking her phone. "I still have no service. I might need to update my plan or something."

"You have service out at Longhorn, don't you?"

"Yeah, I've never had a problem there," she said.

Satisfaction drove through Todd for a reason he couldn't name. "That's good, at least."

Her car sat down the highway about a mile, and they discovered that he didn't have the required ropes to tow it back to town. "We'll stop by the tire place and talk to Rafael, okay?" He looked to her car and back to her. She'd gotten out of the truck with him, always ready to dig in and get the job done.

"All right," she said, a clear streak of worry on her face.

Todd wondered what that was about, but he didn't have to guess too much. Laura was a fiercely independent woman, and she wouldn't like being out on the ranch without her car. She'd have to ask for a ride when she wanted to get to town, to church, anywhere.

Back in the driver's seat, he looked over to her. "You can have my truck for anything you need to do until your car's fixed."

She looked at him, and he noticed the makeup on her face. She wore mascara and blush and lip gloss, and his hormones fired hard at him. "Thank you," she said.

"Or I'll drive you." He cleared his throat. "I can do that when you have to come back and get the car." He eased the truck back onto the road and accelerated.

"You don't think they'll be able to do it during lunch?"

Todd glanced over to her and back to the road in front of him. "I doubt it." She sighed, and Todd reached over to take her hand in his. "I'm sorry."

"It's fine," she said. "It's a flat tire. They happen."

"Doesn't mean it's fun or something you want to deal with."

"No," she said. "But I can afford it, and it's just an inconvenience." She flashed him a smile and looked out her window.

Todd shifted in his seat. "It's not a curse."

Laura turned back to him, a flirty smile on her face. "Isn't it?"

Todd smiled back at her, knowing what it felt like to kiss her and wanting to do it again. He wasn't going to do that until she initiated it, and he didn't think she'd do that until they were on solid footing, without high emotions between them.

"Even if it is," he said. "It's kind of exciting, isn't it? This cursed, forbidden relationship." He dropped his voice like he was telling a ghost story at scout camp.

She trilled out a laugh, and that made Todd's heart happy. His phone rang, and he tapped the screen in the truck to answer the call from Adam. He tried not to ignore his brothers on work days, especially if they actually worked out on the ranch with him.

"Go for Todd," he said, still chuckling a little.

"Todd," Adam barked. A moment of silence followed. "Oh, you're out with Laura. I forgot."

"I just picked her up," he said, cutting her a glance out of the corner of his eye. She didn't seem surprised that his brother knew about their date. "She got a flat on the way into town."

"Oh, that stinks," Adam said. "I was going to see if you could stop by the hardware store on the way back. Winchester apparently can't resist the siren's call of that hay, and Sammy Boy and I are going to put up a wall there."

Todd sighed, because he didn't like extraneous building if it could be avoided. "A wall?"

"I only need a few things," Adam said, but Todd didn't believe that for a second.

"Fine," he said with disdain in his voice. "Text the list to me, and I'll get it all while I'm here."

"Thanks, brother," Adam said. "Have fun on your date."

"Thanks," Todd said, but the call had already ended. He shook his head and waited for the truck to switch back over to the radio. He and Laura continued down the road for a minute or two in silence, and Todd didn't mind it.

"Do they all know about this date?" Laura asked, cracking everything peaceful between them.

Todd whipped his attention toward her. "Uh, probably? I don't know."

"He *knew*-knew," she said.

"Uh, Jesse was at breakfast when we were texting on Christmas Eve," Todd admitted. "Him, Blake, and Kyle. And Adam lives with Jesse, so." He took a breath, running through the rest of his family. "I had to tell Sierra, because she's in charge of the ranch when I'm gone. But I didn't specifically tell Nash or Holly."

"They know anyway," she said, looking away again. "Because nothing in your family stays a secret for long."

"Do you want us to be a secret?" he asked. "I can make that happen."

"You can? How?" Her voice carried a teasing lilt, and Todd smiled at her as she grinned at him. He loved these soft moments between them, because she felt like herself during them, and he could simply be himself too.

"Oh, I'll just act the way I have been for the past few months. Grump around, speaking in one or two-word sentences. When Blake and Kyle finally ask me what's wrong, I'll tell them you didn't like today's date, and I struck out again. It won't be that hard, honestly."

Laura laughed, and Todd marveled at how easily she did that now. She'd changed once again, right before his eyes, and he hoped he'd be able to keep her during the highs and the lows of her life—and his.

"The idea is kind of appealing," she said, still teasing

him. "Sneaking around, kissing around corners or in your office…"

It did sound enticing, but Todd didn't necessarily want to keep things hidden between them. Then he wouldn't be able to bring her to family functions or eat with her at the lodge. He remained silent, and Laura finally said, "I can't imagine not liking today's date."

"No?"

"You've already rescued me. What's not to like?" She covered his hand with her other one, and Todd sure did like having his sandwiched between both of hers.

They drove through town, and after running into the tire shop to get her car towed into town, Todd returned to Bacon Barn, where he'd been when Laura had called. "They do serve breakfast all day here," he said. "So I'll probably be fine. I seem to recall you liking bacon cheese-burgers, and they have one of the best here, so perhaps this date won't be as cursed as our first."

Laura grinned at him, something sparkling around her. "Let's go see, shall we?"

CHAPTER
SEVEN

L aura looked up at the waiter as she sat down, as he listed off their Tuesday specials. She had no idea there could be so many things on the menu at a place with "barn" in its name in the middle of the week.

Her mind got instantly overloaded, and she took the menu he offered her and focused on it instead of his voice. When he stopped talking, she looked at Todd.

"We definitely want some of that apple bacon jam," he said. "And the bacon-wrapped chestnuts." He pressed one palm against his chest. "I want a Diet Coke." He looked at her expectantly, and Laura didn't bother with the menu.

"Sweet tea," she said. "Lots of ice, please." Every restaurant in Texas had sweet tea, and while she'd never been here, she'd also never had a glass of sweet tea she didn't like.

The waiter said, "I'll be right back with the drinks," and walked away.

Laura grinned at Todd. "Apple bacon jam?"

"And they bring it with biscuits." His eyes rolled back in his head. "It's amazing. You'll love it."

"I don't think I've ever eaten a chestnut."

"They're also fantastic," he said. "They cook them really well here too. It's why the town is named Chestnut Springs."

"I thought that was from some waterfalls," she said, still not looking at the menu.

"That too," he said. "But there's a huge chestnut tree grove on the east side of town, and you can go there in the fall to gather them. They're *huge*, like *massively* huge trees." He spoke like a child obsessed with dinosaurs and she'd just asked about the rare chestnuosaurus.

She grinned at his boyish enthusiasm. "We should do that sometime."

"It won't be for months now." His eyes sparked something in her direction, and Laura dated enough to recognize attraction. Her own fired through her too, and while a teensy bit of disloyalty came with it, she managed to push past that and enjoy this conversation with Todd.

"Well, when they're ready again," she said. "I'd love to see some really huge, like *massively huge trees*." She laughed, glad when Todd did too. They both quieted, and she looked at the menu then. "You said there was a bacon cheeseburger here?"

"It's the Springing with Bacon," he said. "Another nod to the town name."

"We should go up to the falls." She kept her eyes on the menu. "I like being outside and stuff." Their eyes met, and patriotic music should've started playing for how many fireworks erupted across the table.

The water returned with cola and tea, and Laura took a moment to open her straw. She suddenly felt sweaty and like she needed a fan, and it had everything to do with the man across the table from her. He'd not only rescued her in his shiny...blue truck, but he'd handled everything at the tire shop too.

He knew everyone in Chestnut Springs—at least that was how it felt. He claimed he didn't, but she felt certain that if she'd gone inside to arrange things for her car, she'd still be there, trying to get it all done. Rafael had Todd's number, and he'd call him. Simple as that.

"Do you know what you want to order?" the waiter asked, and Laura looked up at him.

"Springing with Bacon," she said.

He went through the options for sides, the temperature of her meat, and if she wanted double the bacon. At the Bacon Barn, how could she refuse? Todd put in his bacon and eggs order, which felt so tame, and once the waiter left, she folded her arms on the table and leaned into them.

"Bacon and eggs?" She cocked her eyebrows, because she couldn't lift only one at a time. It was a skill many others had, but not her.

"What?" Todd asked, unwrapping his silverware and actually putting the paper napkin in his lap. "I like bacon and eggs."

"It's so simple."

He looked at her, reached up, and removed his cowboy hat. He tossed it into the windowsill, and as he ran his fingers through his hair, he said, "I like simple."

Laura picked up her tea and took a long drink just to alleviate the dryness suddenly in her throat. Todd's hair looked perfectly touchable, and a bit of surprise threaded through her that she wanted to run her fingers through it.

It looked the color of freshly turned earth, and it matched his eyebrows and beard perfectly. He had a strong jaw, and plenty of character in his eyes, and everything about him told her to get closer. The scent of his cologne, which held notes of blue, cool water, and red, spicy musk. The way his hands moved with grace and beauty as he picked up his own drink and took a sip. The way he smiled at her and said, "You're staring at me."

She ducked her head, but her hair wasn't long enough to hide behind. "Sorry."

"What are you thinking?"

"Oh, I can't tell you that." She put plenty of flirty vibes into her voice. "We're in public."

To her great surprise, Todd's whole face turned bright red in less time than it took for her to inhale. His neck, his ears, probably his whole scalp.

She giggled, some of his embarrassment leaking across the space between them and filling her. "What? You don't think I think about you?"

"I don't know what you think about," he said gruffly, his eyes flitting all over the restaurant. "That's why I asked."

"I've never seen a man go red that fast." She picked up

her tea and took another drink, because it was so dang hot in here. She needed a fan or an ice cream cone—or both. Or maybe she should get control of her thoughts. She tried to shrug, but her shoulders were a bit bony for the action. "I was just thinking you have great hair, and I wondered what it would feel like if I got to run my fingers through it."

His eyes hooked into hers, and the fireworks show started all over again. "Really?" he asked, clearly dumbfounded.

"Yes." She removed her arms from the table and sat on her hands. "And then I was thinking about how handsome you are. You know, with that sexy beard over that strong jaw, and how everything just lines up all perfectly. You're like a movie star." Her face grew hotter with every word she spoke, and she told herself to stop talking. Immediately.

The redness in Todd's face ebbed away, and his normal coloring returned. "Thank you, Laura."

She did the shrugging again, and something had really crawled into her stomach that had loosened her tongue, because she said, "Hans wasn't like you at all. He was blond, and quite a bit shorter, and if I'd suggested we go hiking to a waterfall, he'd have said he'd find out if we could rent scooters or horses instead."

Todd blinked a couple of times, and then sat back in the booth. "I thought you said his sister had dark hair."

"Half-sister," Laura said. "She did. She came from a different father." She picked up her drink and chugged it now. She suddenly wondered if they'd put alcohol in it, and that was why her tongue had gone so loose. She pulled the straw out of her mouth a bit harshly, and tea spurted everywhere.

"Oh, gosh," she said, quickly reaching for her napkin. She hadn't unrolled her silverware yet, but she did so and mopped up the splatter. "Sorry, now I'm all nervous."

Todd offered her a warm smile. "Why are you nervous? I thought we were doin' great. I'm the one who turned into a beet."

Laura couldn't believe she'd even said how nervous she was out loud. "I think they maybe spiked my drink." She pushed the half-gone glass toward him. "Taste it."

He did, taking his straw from his cola and putting into her tea. "There's only tea in that," he said.

Laura took the glass back and told herself not to take another drink until she'd had something to eat. Perhaps the caffeine had addled her brain.

"So Big Bill has missed you," he said, switching the topic to something safer: Horses. "Oh, and look what King Louis has been doin'." He tapped and swiped on his phone, then slid it toward her. She watched a video of the naughty horse getting up in his stall and stealing hay, giggling at the look on his face at the end.

"No wonder he's overweight," she said, grinning as she looked up from his phone.

"Sammy Boy moved him and put Winchester in there, but they have some sort of horse grapevine, and Winnie's been doing it too. So now we have to stop at the hardware store so Adam can build a wall between the stall and the hay." He shook his head as she handed his phone back.

"If it's not one thing, it's another," she said.

Their eyes met again, and Todd flipped his phone over. "Exactly." He reached for her hand before she could pull it back and he covered both of hers with both of his. "Let's make another date right now." He swallowed, his only sign of nerves now that his flushed face had completely disappeared. "You want to?"

"Yes," she said without hesitating.

"Something outside," he said. "If it's not raining."

"We can play a game inside if it is," she said.

"Tomorrow?" Todd asked, and that adorable flush came creeping back up his neck. It didn't move as fast, and it never did get all the way to his cheeks. "I mean, let me look at my schedule when we get back to the ranch."

Laura watched him cool off, and she couldn't stop smiling. He wanted to see her again, and soon, and what woman would be upset about that? She didn't want him to think she didn't want to see him again, and soon, so she lifted her fingers and slipped them through his. "Tomorrow sounds awesome," she said. "You should see how much food is in my trunk. My mama can feed us lunch or dinner. You pick."

Todd looked at her again, the moment between them light yet heavy. Filled with meaning but casual. Comfortable but a bit tense too. "I'd pick dinner," he said, immediately clearing his throat. "Then we won't have to go back to work afterward."

Laura pulled her hands back as the apple bacon jam arrived, as did the bacon-wrapped chestnuts. Everything looked brown and thick and delicious, and her stomach growled at her. "Meals should be out in a few minutes," the waiter said before walking away.

Laura looked a Todd, who picked up the spoon for the jam. Instead of taking some for himself, he dished some onto a small plate, tonged on a biscuit, and handed it to her. "Just try not to moan too loud," he said with that trademark grin of his. It didn't come out often, but when it did, it made Laura feel like choirs of angels were singing.

"Thanks," she said. He served her two chestnuts too before taking anything for himself. She split her biscuit and buttered it, then leaned over to smell the jam. She got apples, obviously, and salt, and cinnamon, and her mouth positively poured with saliva.

She slathered on plenty, because why not? Why go in with a small bite? A tiny taste? Nope, not her.

She took a big bite of the biscuit too, her eyes locked onto Todd's. The tart, salty, savory-sweet jam mixed with the flaky biscuit, and the creamy butter, and Laura couldn't help it.

She moaned loudly.

Todd burst out laughing, and then he did the same thing. She grinned at him as she chewed and swallowed. "This is seriously the best jam I've ever had." She pointed one finger at Todd. "But I will deny it until the day I die if you tell my mama it beats her raspberry rhubarb jam."

"No, ma'am," he said. "I wouldn't dream of tellin' her." He grinned at her, and she fell a little bit in love with Todd Stewart over apple bacon jam, easy conversation, and the implication that they'd be together long enough to gather chestnuts next fall and for her to introduce him to her mama at some point in the future.

Laura wanted all of that, and as she ate, talked, and laughed with Todd, she never once felt the need to apologize to Hans—or herself. She deserved happiness, and if she could find it again with a movie-star handsome cowboy who knew all the best places to eat in town and who could rescue her when she got flat tires, then that was what she wanted.

———

"THURSDAY," SHE REPEATED A COUPLE OF HOURS LATER. "Okay." She picked up the pen and started filling out the form. "Anytime Thursday?" Todd had dropped her off to deal with the paperwork for her tire while he ran to the hardware store. She'd be done before him, but he'd parked across the street, and she could walk over and meet him there.

She hadn't experienced a better lunch than she'd just had with him. Not in years, and not with Hans. Not with anyone. She smiled as she filled out her name and phone number, because while their first date hadn't been stellar, this one had been.

So far.

"Here you go." She passed back the card and Rafael took it.

"Thanks," he said. "We'll call you, but yes, anytime Thursday should be fine. My guys will get to it tomorrow at some point. Sorry it's not today; we have all of the Gilbert machines in right now."

Laura waved her hand as if shooing away a bothersome fly. "It's fine. I know how busy you can be." Hidden Hollow had one tire shop for the surrounding farms and communities too. If she needed a car to get to work every day, she might be more frustrated.

She left the tire shop and looked across the street. Todd's truck sat in the parking lot at the hardware store, and she imagined it transforming into a big, gallant steed. Then he'd don his cowboy hat crown, saddle up, and ride in to save her, no matter what peril she faced.

It was a nice thought, one that made her smile, and heaven knew that Laura needed more reasons to smile. If one of them could be a handsome cowboy, why not?

Why not indeed? she thought, and she went to meet that handsome man across the street.

CHAPTER
EIGHT

Todd stood back and watched as Adam did a great contortionist act with his body to get the drill up where he needed it. Outside the wind blew in the darkness, but Todd didn't feel it in his soul the way he sometimes did.

His date with Laura that day couldn't have gone better, and they already had two more on the calendar. Dinner tomorrow, at her place, though she did warn him she might want to relocate to his if Josie was acting up. He still needed to get the story behind that, but he hadn't asked because they'd just arrived at her cabin, and she'd wanted to get inside and check on her cats.

He'd helped her carry in the gifts, the food, and the boxes of memorabilia her mama had sent home with her. He'd laughed at a couple of old photographs and promised to see her the following day. They'd text, of course, because Laura had been gone for a few days and would be going around to various animals to check up on them. He'd get a full report on the livestock she made it to, some of which would be these silly horses in the close stable.

The sound of the drill made it feel like the screw was piercing his brain, and Todd closed his eyes against it. He'd been gone for a large portion of today, but he felt like he'd put in a full day's work in only a few hours since returning.

"There," Adam declared, sitting upright again. He handed the drill down to Sammy Boy, who bent to put it on the ground. "That should keep them out." He threw Winchester a dirty look in the stall, but Todd turned and looked at King Louis a few down. It was really his fault for nabbing the extra hay and demonstrating how to do it to all the other horses.

"I hate it," he said, looking back at the jimmy-rigged barrier. "It makes the whole stable feel smaller."

"Yeah, well, it'll save us money," Adam said as he jumped down from the platform that held their hay. His feet slapped the concrete and dislodged the drill, knocking it over. Neither he nor Sammy Boy made to retrieve it, and Todd certainly wasn't going to. "Okay, I have a woman to call back," he said.

"You do?" Todd asked, pure shock moving through him. Not the electric kind that he got when Laura touched him, but utter surprise and awe. "Who?"

"Can you get this cleaned up?" Adam asked Sammy Boy.

"Yeah." The other cowboy was fixated on his phone though. "I'll get it done, boss."

"Thanks." Adam hitched his toolbelt higher on his waist, threw Todd a look, and the two of them started to leave the stable. Outside, the wind dang near stole Todd's hat right off his head, and he pressed one palm to it to keep it on.

"Who do you need to call?"

"Just Holly," he said.

"You made it sound like a woman," Todd said with a scoff.

"Holly's a woman." He grinned at Todd. "She won't like hearing you don't think so."

"You know what I mean." Todd looked up into the darkening sky. He loved this time of night, when the sun was down, but it wasn't dark yet. Only the brightest of stars could be seen, and he liked that they peeped out of the grayness to welcome the night. "What does Holly want?"

"Oh, she's got someone at the lodge tonight she wanted me to rescue her from." Adam sighed. "I don't know. She has a lot of people she needs help with."

"She does?"

"Especially when families come and bring their single sons," he said. "I've been over there every night since Christmas, making up some story about her ex-con boyfriend." He rolled his eyes even as he chuckled. "That makes them back off a little bit."

"I had no idea."

"That's because you have your head so far up in the

clouds with Laura." Adam threw Todd a look made of ninja stars.

Todd winced. "I do not."

"Oh, brother, you do." He chuckled and slung his arm around Todd's shoulders. "I don't care, but you do."

"You don't care?" Todd usually left the harder, more pressing questions and conversations to Blake, but the oldest of the Stewart siblings hadn't been around as much lately. "When are you going to get on the dating horse again?"

Adam laughed, the sound too loud for such a still evening. "I'm not," he said, removing his arm. "Ever."

"Wow, ever?" he challenged. He wasn't sure who'd entered his body that day. He'd heard Adam say things like that before, and he'd never questioned him. "Over Marcy? I didn't think she held that much power over you."

"She holds no power over me," Adam bit out. "None. Not even a little bit."

Todd didn't want to risk his life tonight, so he simply gave Adam a look that said, *Then why won't you try again?* that he knew his brother wouldn't answer. He didn't need to give advice. Blake would've said, *Sometimes it takes more than one try. Just look at me and Gina.*

But Todd wasn't Blake, and bright light spilled from the windows along the front of the lodge. Todd had parked back at the stable, and he slowed. Adam didn't. Conversation over.

"See you tomorrow," he called, to which Adam grunted. That was behavior Todd was used to, and he didn't worry about it as he headed back to his truck and then back to his cabin. Kyle's truck sat in the driveway, but no lights shone from these windows.

His brother sat at the desk in the dining room, bent over something in front of him, his laptop open and brightly shining into the dark house.

"You didn't turn on any lights?" Todd asked as he entered. He reached to flip on the lamps in the living room, and Kyle turned toward him, his eyes looking bloodshot and dilated. "You look like a zombie. It's quittin' time."

He bent down to pat Azure, whose whole body wagged in front of him. He held a bright blue bone in his mouth, which Todd knew he wouldn't be able to take away. "Did Blake drop you off here, bud? Huh?" Azure pushed his way between Todd's legs, and he scrubbed his fingers down the dog's spine.

"I can't call it a night yet. I have a call with Rock of Ages in twenty minutes," Kyle said.

"So take a break until then." Todd eyed his brother. "Seriously, stop working on the computer in the dark."

"I didn't even realize it had gotten dark," Kyle said.

"That's not a good sign either." Todd paused to take off his cowboy boots, and instant relief flowed down to his feet. He sighed as he shed his jacket, hung it on a hook, and then rounded the couch to sit. "Anything for dinner?" Azure jumped up beside him, and Todd leaned his arm on the canine's back. He could definitely fall asleep right there, as he hadn't slept well the night before. Too much excitement over seeing Laura today, almost like it had been Christmas Eve all over again.

"I was going to go over to the lodge after my call," Kyle said. "I can bring something back."

"Sure." Todd yawned. "I'll take a cat nap."

"It's almost six." Kyle came into the living room.

"Your point is?"

"You sleep now, you'll be up all night."

Todd yawned again. "Okay." He let his eyes drift closed, and all he could think about was Laura. She'd called him a movie star that day, and he could admit it was nice to hear. He didn't want their relationship to be one-sided, and he didn't want to guess at what resided in her head.

His phone chimed, and he pulled himself back from the edge of unconsciousness. Kyle wasn't in the living room anymore, and he'd flooded the dining room and kitchen with light too. He sat back at the desk, talking, and Todd realized he'd fallen asleep for a few minutes. Probably twenty or more, as Kyle's call had obviously started.

He tugged his phone out of his back pocket, which earned him a semi-glare from Azure as he dislodged the dog, and looked at it. Laura had texted a picture, and he hurried to open it.

She smiled at him, and he couldn't help smiling back. She held the black and white kitten she'd been particularly worried about, their cheeks pressed together. *He's doing great*, she'd messaged. *They all are, so that's good.*

Yes, it is, he sent back. She'd nursed some kittens back to health after their mother had abandoned them, claiming the ranch could use good mousers. She wasn't wrong, and while Todd sometimes didn't know if the cats on the ranch were theirs or not, he wasn't going to argue with them chasing off vermin.

You out in the barn? he asked.

Yep, she sent back. *Just checking on a few things tonight.*

You had today off.

I know.

Todd waited for more of an explanation, but Laura didn't send it. He suspected she wasn't home for two reasons: She really did have a drive to make sure her cats were okay, and Josie was at the cabin. He wanted her to be comfortable, and if a housing reassignment needed to be made, then he could make it.

How are things with you and Josie? He thumbed out the message but didn't send it. She'd said very little about her cabinmate—just the one slip the one time. Still, it nagged at Todd, and he quickly sent the message before he lost his nerve.

Fine, Laura sent back.

I can make a housing reassignment, he said.

No, she said. *It's not necessary.*

He wished they could have this conversation in person, but he also wanted to take her at her word. *All right,* he said. *You'll let me know if it becomes necessary, right?*

Of course, she said, but Todd wasn't so sure that was true. He didn't want to call her on it tonight, and the conversation ended. He leaned his head back against the couch, took a deep breath, and let his eyes drift closed again.

He dreamt of Laura this time, and it was no surprise to him that her housing reassignment put her with him. He had no idea where Kyle would live, and in his dreams, that didn't matter. All that mattered was the fact that he and Laura were together, and Todd was less than pleased when Kyle woke him sometime later, though his brother had brought food.

————

Todd lifted his coffee to his lips a couple of days later, the steam tickling up into his nose. The horses walking around the ring in front of him mostly fell into line, but of course, Gemma tossed her head. She kicked up her back legs. She tossed some more, showing her teeth to Todd as she went by.

She had to keep going, because the other horses in the ring did, and she had no choice. He grinned at her, then took another drink of his coffee as Lady went by behind her. She was steady and strong, head forward, ignoring the antics of the horse in front of her. Gemma had more of a free spirit, and Todd couldn't wait to see how well she did with the cows.

He wandered away from the walking ring and over to the wash shed, where he knew Sierra and Adam would be. They were there, talking about something with serious faces. Todd avoided them, because he didn't want anything very serious right now.

Blake and Jesse were the ones in the stall with Verity, one of their bigger horses. He pulled the carriage for concerts, along with Oak, and as Todd approached, both Blake and Jesse jumped back.

"What's with him?" Todd asked, noting the pink hue in the water. He lifted his eyes to his oldest brother.

"He's injured," Blake said. "Don't worry about it. We already called Laura."

Todd raised his eyebrows. "You did?" No one thought he should know one of their top show horses had an injury? Of course, Adam and Jesse dealt with that kind of stuff on the commercial side of the ranch. Adam handled the horses to make sure they knew what they needed to do for carriage rides, horseback riding, all of it. Jesse, inside his quick mind, devised activities and uses for the horses for the guests who came to stay at the lodge.

They worked together a lot, and anything with animals required Todd's knowledge, and Laura's expertise as well.

Another pair of boots arrived, and he turned to find Laura coming toward them. His heartbeat pounced against his ribs, and he dang near dropped his cup of coffee. It was his fourth or fifth for the day, and if he didn't stop after this one, he'd be in real danger of not being able to sleep tonight.

He emitted a half-yell, half-cry as the hot liquid splashed the back of his hand, but no one looked at him. Thankfully.

Not even Laura, which stung slightly in the back of Todd's throat.

"He's bleeding," she said, stepping right up to the huge horse. Verity had to be four times as big as Laura, but she touched his flank and ran her hand along his side as if they were old pals. "Where?"

"We don't know," Jesse said. "He won't let us see."

Todd moved to his right so he could see into the wash stall better. Laura brought a calm energy with her that he craved inside his own life too. She spoke to Verity quietly, and the horse moved his enormous head as if to nuzzle her.

She didn't let him do that, but kept a few inches between them. He could easily kick her and kill her, and Todd's heart did another erratic pulse. Verity was a good horse. Well-trained and usually not flighty. He'd been working at Longhorn for a decade, and Todd swallowed at the thought of him being in pain.

Laura crouched, putting herself at Verity's left foot. She examined it, shook her head, and ran her hands up his leg to his chest. She ducked under him and repeated the motion on the right side.

He shook his head against the restraints in the wash stall, and Blake and Jesse backed up again as Verity stomped his back leg. Adam and Sierra finished whatever they'd been talking about and approached too.

"How is he?" Adam asked.

"She's checking for the injury," Todd said. He indicated the horse with his coffee cup. "How long have you known he's been hurt?"

"Ten minutes, maybe." Adam sighed and ran his hand along his face. "We called Laura, and I was just about to call you when Sierra came up and said we have a problem in the bull pen."

Todd switched his attention to her. "We have a problem in the bull pen?" Was anyone going to tell him anything that day?

"It's minor," Sierra said. "I need Laura too, but we decided she should come here first."

"It's up here," Laura called. "I need my bag."

Adam stooped to get it for her, moving completely behind the horse. Jesse yelped, and Todd could see everything in slow-motion. Someone yelled—maybe him, he wasn't sure.

Verity lifted his left hind leg, the limb moving—oh—so —slowly.

Todd abandoned his coffee, his mind only on one thing —moving Adam out of the way. He dove toward his brother and the veterinary bag, and bodies collided.

His head hit the cement. Hard. His shoulder too, and he groaned as he rolled. Above him, a myriad of voices yelled.

He knew he couldn't stay there, halfway under Verity, but the moment the horse stomped his shod hoof on Todd's ankle, he also couldn't move.

He yelled, and the next thing he knew, someone had grabbed his pantleg and pulled. He slid out from underneath Verity, feeling more pain than he ever had before.

He tried to stop himself from moving, because that hurt his ankle and foot. Bad. Without knowing what he did to do it, he managed to get his body to go still. Or maybe whoever had pulled him had simply stopped. Or maybe he'd passed out.

The next thing he remembered was looking up into a bright light, new movement underneath him that felt foreign and strange. He was in a car. He was laying down in a car.

"Todd," Blake said, and he tried to turn his head toward the sound. "You can't move your head," he said. "Don't worry. You're in the ambulance, and we're almost to the hospital." His brother's warm hand landed on Todd's, and while he didn't have anything down his throat, he also couldn't figure out how to speak.

CHAPTER
NINE

Laura finished up with Looking For Gold, the bull that Sierra had been concerned about. She'd called only ten seconds after Adam had about Verity, and Laura sighed as she ran her hand through her hair and stepped back.

Today had been one busy day.

Three creatures injured at Longhorn today, and one of them was Todd. She'd been watching her phone like a hawk, as Blake kept sending ranch-wide updates about him.

He's awake now. Doing okay. Can't remember what happened.

They're taking him for an x-ray to see if he needs surgery on his ankle. It's definitely broken, but we don't know how bad.

Laura had pressed her eyes closed at that one. A broken ankle. Todd would be miserable, as he *hated* being inconvenienced or incapable of doing what he wanted to do. She didn't know everything about him, but she knew that much.

They'd gone to town yesterday so she could pick up her car, and he'd said, "Sometimes I just like to do things myself. Then I know it's done, and it's done right."

With a broken ankle, he'd have to do a lot more delegating.

"All right," Sierra said, and Laura put on the best face she could. She was worried about Todd, of course. Even worse was the idea of having to go to the hospital to see him. She should. Of course she should. They were together. Dating. Weren't they?

She wasn't sure she'd call him her boyfriend yet, but he had kissed her a couple of times. He liked her. She liked him.

Everything ran around in her head, but she managed to give Sierra a run-down of what Looks For Gold needed. "He just scraped up his legs in that wire," she said. "They're all dressed now, and I'll check them in the morning." She smiled at the other woman. "If we can keep him dry and resting for a few days, he should be fine."

"If it would stop raining, it would be easier to keep him dry," Sierra said just as another clap of thunder filled the Texas sky. It hadn't rained yet that day, but the storms seemed to come at night and stay until morning.

Laura liked listening the rainfall against the roof, but it did make for very messy working conditions on a ranch. Especially one with big, open pastures for their pregnant cattle and plenty of dirt paddocks for their horses.

"Are you going to see Todd?" she asked Sierra, who shook her head.

"No, Blake is still in town, and he said Todd doesn't want us all to come in."

"He did?" Laura hadn't looked at her phone in the past half-hour since she'd stepped into the stall with Looks For Gold. He'd been nothing but a two-ton gentleman about her cleaning and dressing his wounds, thank goodness.

The last thing she needed was a repeat of Verity's stomping episode. Why in the world had Todd dove under the horse?

Adam had said it was to save him, and he'd looked so guilty. Laura felt it bubbling down in her gut too, because she'd asked for her bag. She'd also dropped that bag right behind the horse—one of the only blind spots on an equine.

Adam and Jesse had pulled Todd out from underneath Verity before he could stomp again—which he'd done. Everyone had congregated around Todd then, because he'd passed out cold.

Nothing she did had awakened him, and Kyle had texted in to say Todd hadn't been sleeping well for several nights. Perhaps combined with the injury and pain, his body was just like—*nope. Not waking up right now.*

Blake had called the ambulance, and he'd gone with Todd to the hospital.

Laura had stayed in the wash stall to clean up Todd's blood, then Verity's leg. Adam and Jesse stayed with her, all of them talking about how it was their fault Todd had been injured. Laura hated the pinch of guilt in her stomach, then her chest, but it would not go away.

"I think I might drive in and see him," she said to Sierra, lifting her eyebrows. "Do you think I should?"

"Yeah," Sierra said, her voice just as tired as Laura felt. "You probably should.

"I don't want him to be upset."

"It's you." Sierra smiled at her. "You're the only one Todd *won't* be upset to see."

Laura watched her for a moment. "Does he talk about me?"

"Not even a little bit," Sierra assured her. "It's just…" She sighed and pulled her ponytail tight. "I know my brother, and he's a little smitten by you. Let's say he is irritated that you came. He'll never show it to you. He's on his best behavior with you, because he wants you to like him."

Laura didn't know how to respond. She finally decided to go with something playful. "What I've gotten… *That's* his best behavior?"

Sierra laughed with her, and they walked back toward the main barn together. Sierra detoured into the office, saying, "I'd text before you go, just to be sure he's available. Blake hasn't updated about the surgery."

"Good idea," Laura said. She continued through the barn and outside, looking to the back of the lodge. Her stomach growled, and she could easily go inside and get dinner before she drove to the hospital. That would give her time to get caught up on Blake's texts and then find out if Todd could even have visitors tonight.

Inside, Holly stood with a family, all of them laughing.

How she could interact with people so easily blew Laura's mind. She went on her way to get her food, and she sat at a table by herself, out of the way. She should've known that wouldn't stand, because everyone at the Texas Longhorn Ranch was so nice.

The guests, the cowboys and cowgirls who worked there, and the family who owned it.

She'd taken two bites of her baked beans before Gina sat down. "Hey, Laura," she said.

"Oh, hey," she said as if she'd been meaning to call Gina all day long. "I didn't know you stayed this late."

"Blake's gone with Todd." She stirred her salad dressing into her lettuce and veggies. "And my parents are visiting my sister. So I stayed to help with dinner and get a head-start on the desserts for tomorrow's lunch."

"Ah, I see."

Across from her, another woman took a seat, a great big sigh hissing from her mouth as she did. "Hey, guys," Starla Masters said. Laura knew her, of course. She ran the kitchen for breakfast and lunch. She wouldn't say she and Starla were friends or anything. Gina and Starla, yes.

Laura and... No, she wasn't truly friends with anyone here on the ranch. She knew them. They knew her.

You can belong here. The thought entered her mind, unbidden. Todd had said some version of it months ago, on their first date. At the time, Laura wasn't sure she'd wanted to belong on this ranch.

Now, she suddenly felt like she did.

"Hey," she said. She leaned forward. "Do you guys know Josie Meadows? My cabinmate?"

Gina started to shake her head no, but Starla nodded. "Yeah, I know her. She's been here a while now."

"She doesn't seem to..." Laura stopped herself from completing the sentence. This wasn't about Josie. This was about her. "I wonder if I did or said something wrong when I moved in or something. We don't hardly talk."

"That's just Josie," Starla said. "She has her little clique."

"Oh, is she the one with Mick, and they only hang out with Jumpy Susannah?" Gina took a big bite of her burger. "I know them."

Laura looked between her and Starla. "She does hang out with a couple of people here at the ranch."

"That's her," Starla said, looking at Gina. She switched her gaze to Laura. "It's not you. It's her. She's a little stand-offish. She has her friends, and she doesn't really know how to make room for more."

"Okay." Laura scooped up another bite of beans, but she didn't take it yet. "I have to live with her, though. It's a little awkward sometimes."

"She loves to talk about two things." Starla leaned in like she might start giving out national secrets. "Faith Ostetler, and barrel racing. You ask her about those, and you won't be able to get her to shut up." She laughed, and Gina joined in too.

Laura knew what barrel racing was, obviously. She smiled as she looked between Gina and Starla. "Who's Faith Ostetler?"

"She's a huge country musician," Gina said. "Look 'er up. You'll see."

"I will. Thanks."

Gina made a strangled noise then, and both Laura and Starla looked at her. "What?" Laura asked.

Gina's face relaxed, and her smile turned into something coy or maybe knowing. "Look who just walked in." She nodded toward the door, and Laura only had to look. Starla had to turn around, and she did.

She gave a quiet yelp and spun back around. "Gina," she whispered, her voice almost a whine. "Why does he have to go home and shower before coming to get dinner?"

Jesse stood just inside the door of the lodge, and he chatted with Baby John. He was clearly looking for Starla, though, but Laura had sat almost in the corner.

"Because he wants to look good for you," Gina mock whispered back. "When are you going to tell Nash he's being an idiot, and you'll date who you want to date?"

Starla gave her a death glare, then hunched her shoulders. "Maybe he won't see me over here."

"He already has," Laura said as Jesse spotted them. Her own heartbeat kicked out a couple of extra beats. These Stewart men weren't kidding around with the jeans, the belt buckles, the boots, or the cowboy hats. Jesse was a handsome man, and she could admit that, even if Laura didn't feel a spark for him.

Starla obviously did.

"I need more baked beans," Laura said suddenly.

"I'm out of salad," Gina added.

"Don't you dare," Starla hissed at both of them, but Laura and Gina got to their feet and left her at the table with her plate of food, alone. Only for the five seconds it took Jesse to cross the room and sit with her, and then Laura bent her head toward Gina's as they giggled together.

She didn't know all the dynamics between Jesse and Starla and Nash, but she could practically see shooting stars and showers of sparks coming from Jesse and Starla.

"Oh, thank heavens," Gina said, and Laura pulled her gaze from the pair at the corner table. "Blake says Todd doesn't need surgery." She tucked her phone in her back pocket. "Are you going to go see him tonight?"

"Yes," Laura said, encouraged when Gina nodded her approval. "Just as soon as I'm done eating."

———

LAURA DIDN'T LOOK LEFT OR RIGHT AS SHE WALKED. SHE clutched the stuffed llama in her hands, her goal singular. *Get to the end of the hall.*

Turn right.

Todd's room should be in the next corridor, and then she'd slip inside and everything would be fine. Strangely enough, she didn't feel overwhelmed or burdened by being at the hospital. She didn't like the smell of it, as everything gave her the impression of stale plastic that had been sitting in the sun for far too long.

Everyone was kind and friendly. Even when she'd had to get out of the way for a man bringing in his hurt son, she hadn't felt too many tremors. If anything, Laura felt like she was...coming home.

Odd, and she didn't know what to do with the feelings.

She turned right, and sure enough, Todd's room sat only three down, on the left. He'd gotten a room with a window, and how Laura knew before she even went inside, she wasn't sure. She just did.

She'd just reached for the huge handle that she'd have to pull with all of her weight when the door opened. Blake backed out, causing Laura to take quick steps backward too. She fumbled the llama but managed to hold onto it, and she heard Blake say, "They'll be here in about twenty minutes. I'll be right back."

He turned as the door started to fall closed behind him and walked away, muttering, "*I'm* the one who needs a break, Todd." He didn't see Laura at all, as she'd scrambled off to the side to his right, and he'd turned and gone left.

It was probably just as well, as he hadn't sounded super happy about what had gone on inside the room. That only made her stomach swoop, but she'd already committed. She'd stopped by the store for this "get well" llama and the bag of Starburst in her other hand. She couldn't just leave with them.

She heaved open the door, and Todd glared in her direction, clearly expecting her to be Blake. His expression changed the instant he saw it wasn't his brother, and softness cascaded over his features. "Laura," he said.

Lifting the llama, she said, "Hey. Do you know how far of a walk it is from the parking lot to this room?" She giggled as she hurried toward him. He reached up with both arms open, and she gladly fell into his embrace. "I got a hike tonight already, and you weren't even there."

"I'm sorry," he said into her hair, but she wasn't sure why he was apologizing.

She pulled back, and he released her. "You don't have anything to be sorry for." She beamed at him, glad all the sparks in the world were shooting through her bloodstream at the sight of him—and he hadn't been home to shower and clean up yet. "Everyone spent the afternoon in the wash shed talking about who's fault it was that you broke your ankle."

A frown marred his handsome face. "It's my fault."

"Mm, Adam thinks it's his," Laura said, shoving the Starburst-carrying llama into his hands. "Jesse's sure it's his, and I know it's mine."

Todd looked up from the llama. "Yours? How could it possibly be yours?"

"What vet worth her salt drops her medical bag behind a horse?" Laura's smile faded as she shook her head. "It was a stupid thing to do. I was just so concerned about Verity."

"We all were."

Laura turned and pulled over the nearby chair. Blake must've been sitting in it a few minutes ago. She crossed her legs and leaned her elbows on her knees. "Who dives under a horse to save their brother?"

"He was going to get kicked."

"You *did* get kicked," Laura said. She reached out and brushed a long lock of his hair off his forehead. "No surgery, though. That's good."

"I didn't get kicked," he said darkly. "I got stomped on."

"Verity is a stomper," she said. Their eyes met, and she added, "He's fine. I found the wound, and it only needed three stitches." She wasn't sure why talking about the horse's injury felt right, only that it did. "He'll be okay in a few days. Adam's going to spoil him rotten with apples and carrots."

"Of course," Todd said dryly. "While I'm stuck eating hospital food."

Laura smiled at him and let her hand drop to his shoulder. He didn't seem to mind it there, and she sure did like the human connection. "I checked on Looks For Gold. He got tangled in some barbed wire on the edge of the field. We're not sure how it got there, but Sierra's got some cowboys on it. He's scratched up—the bull—but I got him medicated and dressed too."

"Thank you." Todd ripped open the Starburst. "These are going to save my life tonight."

Laura gave him another smile, thrilled when he returned it. "I can help you when you go back to the ranch. Bring you your slippers and stuff." She grinned wider as he shook his head. "I know you being waited on hand and foot is something you're really looking forward to."

"My mama is going to be the death of me," Todd said. "She's texted forty-seven times about maybe putting in a ramp for a little while at my cabin to coming over every morning to help me shower." He blew out his breath and popped an unwrapped pink Starburst into his mouth.

"Help you shower," Laura teased. "Wow, that's a visual I'm not sure I want."

They laughed together, but Todd sobered quickly. "I'd rather have your help," he said. "Not with the shower." He spoke the last part quickly. "Food. Entertainment. Whatever."

She'd love to help him, and she did think of herself as a good nurse. "I have some experience with taking care of a man," she said, somewhat playfully.

Todd didn't grin or chuckle, though. "Yeah," he said. "I bet you do."

Silence fell between them, and she didn't like it. "It's okay," she said. "I thought coming here would be hard, and it wasn't." Surprising, at least a little bit. "I don't like how it smells here, but I actually feel comfortable in a hospital. There's always someone who cares about you and takes care of you."

"That's true," Todd murmured. He stopped unwrapping Starburst and took her hand in his instead. "Thanks for coming tonight. You're the best person I've seen in hours." He smiled and lifted her hand to his lips.

This new silence between them felt like heaven, and Laura leaned into the side of his bed to be as close to him as she could get. "Have you ever sat with someone in the hospital?" she whispered.

"Not really," he said. "My daddy had a hernia a few years ago, and we took turns coming to visit him. That's all."

"It's not bad," she said. "There's always someone to check on you." She closed her eyes and listened for the machines. "I got used to the sound of the machines, and oddly enough, they comfort me." She opened her eyes. "Yours aren't the same as Hans's."

"No?"

She looked at the things around him. He had an IV in his other arm, but he wasn't connected to a heart monitor. That was the missing element. "There's no beeping," she said. She settled back into position. "Sometimes, after a really bad night or an aggressive treatment, I'd climb into bed with him just to keep him warm. The machines would lull me to sleep. I have an app on my phone now that makes similar noises."

"Like hospital machines?" he asked quietly.

"Like the ocean," she said. "After a while, they're the same swell and release." She sighed, pure contentment flowing through her.

After another bout of quiet, where neither of them spoke, he said, "Maybe I should pretend to be cold. Then you could climb into bed with me."

Laura lifted her head, shocked at his statement. She met his eyes and found twinkling stars in his. "You." She swatted at his chest, and he flinched slightly. "You're a devil."

He laughed and grabbed her hand as she tried to hit him again. "I just like you, Laura. I like being close to you." He knew how to make things serious again, that was for sure.

Laura searched his face, trying to find an ounce of dishonesty. She couldn't. "I like you too, Todd."

"I know you miss him," he said, but before he could continue, the door opened to a cacophony of voices.

Four adults entered, and Laura quickly slipped her hand away from Todd's, stood, and faded back toward the window.

His mother and father spoke to a doctor while a nurse flitted around and took vitals. Todd said nothing, and when Blake returned, he wore such a look of gratitude that Laura knew Todd hadn't been a picnic that afternoon.

They talked about the permanent cast, which would go on tomorrow, and what pain meds he was on. No one seemed to have seen her yet, and his mother moved the chair she'd been in and sat down. "I'll stay with him tonight," she said like that was that.

"Mama," Todd finally said. "No."

No one seemed to hear him either as his father said, "The boy is thirty-six years old. He doesn't need us staying over. He's okay." He spun toward Todd. "Tell your mother you're okay, and she doesn't need to stay overnight here with you. Without a bed. With a bulging disk in her back." He glared at his wife, who didn't move a muscle.

"No one's staying overnight," Todd said. He glared at his father and his mother. "You guys are acting like no one's ever been hurt before. It's a broken ankle. Adam's done it twice, and Nash dang near lopped off several fingers once. I'm fine."

He threw a daggered look at Blake. "I thought you told them they didn't need to come."

"I told everyone." Blake held up both hands as if in surrender. "Literally the whole ranch. No one else is here."

"Mama," Todd said. Pure exhaustion lived in his voice. "Please go home."

"You are my son," she started.

"My girlfriend's here," he blurted out. "She'll keep me company until I fall asleep, and then I'll just be sleeping."

A new kind of silence blanketed the room. All eyes came to her, one by one as they all sought her out. She lifted one hand in a wave, her face feeling like fire. She could only imagine how red it was. She wasn't sure if that was because everyone was staring at her or because Todd had called her his girlfriend.

That was only heightened when his mother said, "Your girlfriend?" and then swung her shocked gaze back to Todd. "I didn't think you two were seeing each other anymore."

"They are," Blake said at the same time Todd said, "Well, we are."

Laura swallowed, her throat so dry. She wished the doctor and nurse weren't witnessing all of this, but she knew they'd probably seen and heard worse. Make that *definitely* seen and heard worse.

"I can stay," she said.

His mother huffed, jumped to her feet, and headed for the door.

"Mama," Todd called after her.

"Shannon," his father said. He went after her, and said, "Love you, Toddy. Mama does too. I'm sure Laura will keep us updated." He left, and most of the bluster and blowing storms did too.

Blake exhaled and clapped his hands together. "All

right, now that Laura's here, I'm gonna go." He gave her a grateful smile, and she could see the pinched lines around his eyes. He stepped over to Todd and hugged him, not bothering to make his voice quiet as he said, "You be nicer to her than you were to me today, ya'hear?"

Todd said nothing, and Blake walked out too.

The nurse asked if his bed was where he wanted it, and he all but shooed her out of the room. Laura's nerves felt like she'd pinned them to a line to dry, and they whipped in the storm outside. She tucked her hands in her jeans pockets and went back to the chair she'd been in a few minutes ago.

She didn't sit, though. She looked at Todd and asked, "Girlfriend? I'm your girlfriend now?"

CHAPTER
TEN

Todd's confusion erased the pounding tension in his head. "I—what?"

"You called me your girlfriend." Laura didn't look happy about that either. He honestly couldn't keep up with the conversations tonight. His foot hurt. His leg hurt. His pride had taken a huge beating—especially with Mama coming in here and treating him like he was six years old.

"I...don't know," he said, trying to be nicer to her than he'd been to Blake. The afternoon and evening hadn't been fun for either of them, and he'd have to apologize for snapping at his brother a few times.

Blake would've done the same to him had the situation been reversed, and Todd wasn't worried about making up with Blake.

Another look at Laura, and he was worried she'd bolt. Then he'd really have to spend the night alone. Irritation that he was desperate to keep her close fired through him. Annoyance that she was challenging him on this now joined in.

"You don't want to be?" he asked. "I guess I thought we were past that."

"Past what?" She finally sank into the chair, but she didn't cuddle in close to him like she had earlier.

"Worrying about the label," he said. "Like, literally five minutes ago, I told you I liked you, and that was after I said I wanted you to climb into bed with me. If a girlfriend wouldn't do that, I don't know what to tell you." He heard the gruffness of his voice, but he couldn't soften it. The nurse had put something in his IV that made everything blurred and soft, and he didn't have true control over his body and mouth right now.

Better not to speak, he told himself.

Still, he said, "If you don't want the label, fine. If you don't want to be my girlfriend, fine." He laid his head back, neither of those things fine. His eyelids felt so heavy, and he let them close. "Fine," he said again.

"Todd," Laura said.

He jerked his eyes open again, and Laura stood beside his bed. Wasn't she sitting a moment ago?

"I'm sorry," she said. "I… Things still feel sort of new between us, that's all."

"Okay," he said. "You did say you'd take care of me." He tried to take the glaring down to a reasonable level, but he wasn't sure he succeeded. "I'm getting some mixed signals from you. Doesn't feel fair."

Laura nodded as she sat. "I did say I'd take care of

you," she admitted. She did scoot close and take his hand in hers. "I guess a girlfriend *would* hold her boyfriend's hand."

"She would."

"She'd tease him about how long his hair has gotten." She smiled up at him.

Things inside his chest started to fit back together right. "Yeah."

He watched her, wondering once again what sat in her head. He wasn't going to ask that again, though. She seemed to come to some conclusion, and she rose halfway up in her seat and brushed her lips against his cheek. Fire and electricity arced through his face and ran the length of his body, but he managed to stay very still.

They sighed together, and Todd squeezed her hand. "Will you cut my hair when I get home?"

"What makes you think I know how to cut hair?"

"Instinct," he murmured.

A few seconds passed, and then she said, "I'll cut it for you."

He smiled to himself, his eyelids drifting down again. "Will you check on Azure?"

"I'm sure Blake will take him home with him," she said.

"Yeah, but will you check on him? He'll miss me."

"Yes, Todd," she said. "I'll check on Azure for you."

"Will you text my mama? I don't want her to think I was lyin' to her about that."

"I'll text her."

Todd usually wanted pure darkness before he could fall

asleep, but the lights in the room burned brightly. Still, his breathing evened, and Laura gently removed her hand from his. Her footsteps moved away from him, and the light got dimmer. Then she returned, and instead of taking his hand in hers again, she carefully squeezed into the bed with him on his uninjured left side.

He lifted his arm so she could snuggle into his side, and once she'd settled, he didn't think he'd ever be able to sleep again without her there.

"Okay?" she whispered.

"Mm." Todd's next breath smelled like the peaches in her hair, and the very faint scent of the rain she'd probably "hiked" through to come visit him.

This afternoon, he'd wished he was anywhere but here. Right now, though, Todd couldn't think of anywhere else he'd rather be than here, holding Laura against his side, and hearing and feeling her breathe in and out with him.

His last thought before he fell asleep was that he better figure out how to be the man she needed, because he never wanted to lose her. *Never, ever…*

————

TODD DIDN'T MOVE WHEN SOMEONE RANG THE DOORBELL AT his cabin the following evening. Without surgery, he hadn't had to stay in the hospital for very long. He'd gotten his cast first thing that morning, and Adam had shown up to drive him home.

"Come in," he called needlessly, because the door was already swinging open.

KISSING HER COWBOY BOSS   113

Mama entered, and relief flooded Todd. "Mama." He tried to get to his feet, but she made several clucking noises at him.

"Don't get up," she said. "I'm just bringing some food for tonight. Starla and Gina both volunteered to bring you dinner tomorrow, and Kyle said he'd drive you over to the New Year's Eve party if you want to attend."

Todd couldn't imagine staying up until midnight when he was at full health. Last night, he'd fallen asleep by eight-thirty, and while that time sat about three hours in the future right now, he could easily go to bed. "Thanks, Mama," he said. "Listen, I'm real sorry about last night. It was not a good day for me."

"Tsk, tsk," she said, bustling around the kitchen. "You don't need to apologize. I understand." She hadn't closed the door all the way, and the wind grabbed it and threw it into the wall. "Oh, dear." She hurried to close it, and for good measure, she twisted the lock.

"Don't lock it, Mama," he said. "Kyle will be here in a minute." Laura too, as she was bringing dinner that night. Some of her mother's leftovers from Christmas. He quickly pulled out his phone to warn her of Hurricane Shannon, and she replied that she'd wait a few minutes to come over.

She named all the things she'd brought over and asked him what he wanted. "Uh, the meatballs," he said. "I'm not really hungry, Mama. Just a little bit."

His mother didn't understand the concept of *a little bit*, and she brought him a full plate of steaming hot food. Normally, he'd be grateful for it, and he did his best to act like he was. "Thank you," he said, praying Kyle would walk in.

Azure barked, and a few seconds later, in came Kyle. *Praise the heavens*, Todd thought.

"Oh, good," Kyle said. "Dinner's here."

"This is for Todd," Mama said in a pointed voice.

"He can eat it, Mama."

"There's enough here for the whole ranch," Kyle said, and Todd stopped twisting his neck to watch them. They were both adults, and he didn't need to referee. He did take a bite of the meatballs, and he sagged further into the couch with the spicy marinara and deep, rich flavor of the meat.

Kyle and Mama squabbled for a few minutes, and then she said, "I told Holly I'd help with a sewing class tonight." She sat on the edge of the couch, jostling Todd. "You're okay?"

"I'm fine." Todd put a smile on his face for her and handed back the plate. "Thanks for the food, Mama."

She took the plate, her expression going from satisfied to aghast. "You barely ate."

"Laura's coming over," Kyle called from the kitchen, outing Todd.

Mama met his eye, challenge in hers. "Mama," Todd said. "This is not a competition between you and her."

"Of course not." She got to her feet, and Todd blew his breath out of his lungs. All the way out, focusing on the pause at the bottom of the breath.

"Why are you givin' him a hard time about Laura?" Kyle asked, and Todd once again stayed out of it. "You

KISSING HER COWBOY BOSS   115

bugged Blake to death about *getting* a girlfriend, and now you're annoyed Todd has one. I don't get it."

"Nothing to get," Mama said airily.

"You take good care of us, Mama," Kyle said anyway. "Whether he has Laura coming over or not shouldn't matter."

"It doesn't matter."

"Seems like it does."

"Enough," Todd said. "Mama, can you get me my pills? I'm supposed to take them with food." He didn't want to take them right now, but maybe it would make her feel appreciated and necessary. They made him light-headed and not all there, but if she'd just put them close, he could take them when Laura left.

She came into the living room with them, and Todd took the bottle from her as Kyle said, "Mama, I need you to listen to this band I just found. You're going to the lodge?"

"Yes."

"Perfect, I'll go with you." He met Todd's eyes for a long second, and in that breath of time, Todd channeled every ounce of gratitude he had toward his brother. Not only was he leaving, he was taking Mama with him and making her feel useful.

Azure jumped up onto the couch, breaking the moment between the brothers and jostling Todd's leg. "Hey, bud." He braced himself. "Be careful, okay?"

"You're okay here?" Kyle asked, leaning over the couch with a huge meatball sub in one hand. He was going to drip red sauce everywhere, but it wouldn't bother Todd as much as it would Kyle.

"Yeah, I'm fine." If he had to say "I'm fine," one more time today, he felt certain he'd lose his mind.

"Azure, get down." Kyle pointed to the floor. "Down."

The dog did what he said, albeit reluctantly, and the moment Kyle and Mama left the house, Azure jumped back onto the couch. He gave Todd a look like it was his fault he'd gotten in trouble, circled, and flopped on the other end of the couch.

Todd chuckled. "You're not in trouble, buddy." The dog still wouldn't look at him, and Todd flipped channels until someone knocked on his door again.

A light knock. Feminine. Not too intrusive, but loud enough to be heard.

Laura.

"Come on in," he called to her, and she opened the door.

Everything about her made him light up, and he pushed himself to the edge of the couch to get up. She protested, but he ignored her. He wanted to hold her and lean on her, and he couldn't do that from his horrific nest on the couch.

He grabbed his crutches, though he had a walking boot, and hobbled over to her. "Hey. How're things out on the ranch?"

"Just fine," she drawled at him, and her "fine" sounded so much better than his. She put her bowls and bags on the counter. "Your mama brought food." She swept the countertop and looked at him. "You ate already."

"Two meatballs," he said. "It was nothing."

She leaned one hip into the counter. "This isn't going to

be as good as that. Or the apple bacon jam." Laura twisted and started unpacking the food. "But my mama makes these amazing cheddar biscuits, and I learned that if I melt some butter and add chopped garlic, then I can brush the tops and make them spectacular."

"Wow," Todd said, blown away by her enthusiasm tonight. He liked this high-energy version of her, because it still felt authentic. "I thought you said you couldn't cook."

"No, I said I wasn't a *good* cook. Anyone can melt butter." She tossed him a smile and pulled out the largest container yet. "My mama sent the barbecue." She gave him a flirty smile, her eyes sliding down to his bootless feet. "You look good on your feet."

Todd ducked his head, because none of his usual defenses were in place. No hat. No boots. No ability to walk away. "Thank you, ma'am."

She giggled and went around the island to start heating up the food. He sat on a barstool and watched her for a moment.

"Sierra has everything under control," she said as she put a dish of butter in the microwave. "Knife?"

"Block by the stove." He nodded to it, and she whipped out the biggest one.

She chopped up garlic as she told him all about Verity and Looks For Gold, as well as the couple of births she'd seen that day. "In short, things are just great."

"You're basically telling me I'm not needed," he said, quirking an eyebrow at her. He was teasing, but deep down, a pin stuck in his stomach.

"Only because everyone's pulling out everything they

have," she said. "You do it effortlessly, but we're all doing our very best not to let you down." She set a plate of brisket in front of him, then a plastic bottle of barbecue sauce. "My daddy makes that, and it'll knock your socks off."

She brushed the tops of the cheddar biscuits with her garlic butter and then lifted the lid on just enough cole slaw for the two of them. "Dinner is served."

His mouth watered, and not only because of the food. "Laura, this is amazing."

She came around the counter and sat beside him. "I'll thank my mama for you." She grinned at him, her smile slipping. "Do you want to say grace?"

"Yes, please." He reached for her hand, kissed the inside of her wrist, and bowed his head. They sat that way for a few seconds, and in these pockets of stillness and silence, Todd found his center. He allowed himself to feel exactly what he did, and he could feel his feet slipping down a muddy slope. He was going to fall for this woman soon, fast, and hard.

He cleared his throat. "Lord," he said, but his voice was still froggy and craggly. "Thank you for the good people in my life who take care of me. Thank you for Laura's mama and this food. Thank you for this woman who brought it to me." He paused, because he didn't know what else to say.

His attraction to Laura had started the moment he'd laid eyes on her. She'd been here at the Texas Longhorn Lodge for months, but their relationship was still fairly new. He heard her say that exact thing last night.

"Bless us with thy spirit here tonight, and bless

everyone on the ranch who has to pick up the things I can't do. Amen." He cleared his throat and opened his eyes. Laura took a peek at him from her position of a ducked head. Her smile started out slowly, and Todd wanted to lean over and kiss it.

He wouldn't. He didn't, and she giggled as he started to chuckle. "All right," he said, reaching for the bottle of barbecue sauce. "Let's see what skills your daddy has."

Todd didn't really care what the barbecue sauce tasted like. He just wanted to go on an adventure with Laura and try everything she loved. New spices. New tastes. New conversations. Everything with her was new and exciting, and Todd hadn't realized how much of that had been missing from his life before her.

CHAPTER
ELEVEN

J esse Stewart entered the lodge late. On purpose, of course. He didn't need to be there right when the party started. He wasn't Holly or Blake, nor Mama or Daddy. They all had customer service roles to play that were bigger than his.

He dealt with unhappy customers with complaints, not with someone who needed an extra pillow in their room or a special meal for their gluten-free son.

He'd come in through the back door, which meant he could hear the party in the front of the lodge, but he hadn't joined it yet. He reached up and adjusted his bow tie, questioning for the twenty-fifth time if he should be wearing it or not.

Holly said yes. It was fun and traditional, and he looked happy and professional at the same time. *It makes you more approachable*, she'd told him last night when he'd modeled his clothes for her and Sierra.

Sierra had said the bow tie made him look like he was trying too hard. *How many bow ties do you own?* she'd challenged.

This would be the first he'd owned and worn, and Jesse shook the jitters out of his arms and shoulders. He already had the bow tie around his neck. He wore the black slacks. The festive, light pink shirt. He'd showered, trimmed up the edges of his beard, oiled it, and swept his hair to the side.

He'd likely put on a cowboy hat when he made it out front, and he'd hold a plastic cup of sparkling apple cider while he mingled with his siblings and the guests.

He really wanted to see Starla. She'd be there tonight, as she oversaw all the food that went out to guests in her job as the kitchen manager. He had no idea what she'd be wearing, but his imagination had run wild on him the past few days.

Starla starred in his thoughts almost all the time. Even while he slept, she lingered there. He'd enjoyed their brief relationship over the summer, and he missed her more than he'd admitted to himself. To anyone.

He knew he acted too obvious in his feelings for her, but it was almost like the need to be next to her overcame him, drove him outside his rational mind, and made him act a little desperate.

Jesse squared his shoulders. "Not tonight." Or maybe tonight. It was New Year's Eve after all, and people kissed when the clock struck midnight. His chest caved in at the very thought. He'd kissed Starla before, but it had been a long time, and he'd all but forgotten what it felt like, tasted like, did to him.

Wait. He knew what it had done to him. Her kiss had changed him, and Jesse wanted to experience that again.

Stupid Nash, ran through his head now, and his jaw twitched and turned hard. His brother, who worked with Starla in the kitchen every morning, also had a crush on the woman, and he'd not done a single thing about it.

Not before Jesse's brief try with her, and nothing since. He and Starla had been talking more and more about him. They spoke in circles, though, and it drove Jesse mad. Absolutely nuts. He wanted to have a conversation with Nash all right, but not with words.

Shouts and jabs, maybe.

He also didn't want to upset his mother, or Blake, or any of the guests. Because of that, he'd done nothing about Starla—and he was slowly going insane.

He went down the hall and through the staff break room. One more hallway, and he'd join the party in the front of the lodge. He'd spent a few hours here earlier today, moving desks and chairs to create room for the dance floor. They'd folded up all of their tables where they fed guests breakfast and dinner, stacked all those chairs, and put everything outside in the storage shed.

The lodge was full tonight, as were all of the cabins. Tomorrow and the next day, everyone would start leaving, and finally, the Texas Longhorn Ranch would enter their true slow season. Tonight's concert was Fiddle & Fella, and Jesse loved their music. They played all the instruments, from banjos to fiddles to guitars. They had two men and two women who sang, and boy, could they sing.

They'd be doing an outdoor concert in about an hour, and that would take the party almost all the way to midnight. Holly didn't just turn on the TV to watch the ball drop. Oh, no. She, Sierra, and Jesse had been working on a ball of their own for two solid weeks.

It would fall from the top of the flagpole out front, and so far, the weather had been the one thing that had cooperated with them. Thankfully.

Jesse ran his hands through his hair as he approached the end of the hallway. The music boomed out a hip beat, and flashing blue and white lights almost made it seem like the police had shown up at an out-of-control party.

He took a step out of the hallway and paused to assess the situation. Really, he was looking for Starla. She seemed to attract him like a moth to a flame, because he spotted her within the first few seconds, wearing a black, sparkly ballgown that swelled and narrowed in all the right places.

Jesse licked his lips and looked away from her. Holly laughed several feet away, one hand on the forearm of a man twice her age. She was so good with people, and Jesse pasted on his professional smile as well.

He moved in the opposite direction of Starla, congratulating himself for doing so. She'd likely be checking the food and going in and out of the kitchen all night. He'd do anything to help her, but he needed to be the good guest relations specialist he got paid to be.

"Mister Bellnap," he said as he joined Holly. "How's the party so far?"

"Jesse," Holly yelled above the music. "See? I told you he'd be here, and he's wearing the bow tie, as promised." She beamed at Jesse and indicated Mr. Bellnap's bow tie. Jesse wasn't sure if he should rip his off or keep smiling.

He kept smiling, shook Mr. Bellnap's hand, and kissed both the cheeks of Mrs. Bellnap. "Enjoying the party?"

The hip, fast song ended, and a slower ballad meant for dancing came on. "This is for all the romantics out there," the DJ said—and that was Kyle. He'd spent time in the country music industry, and that made him great at his job now that he was back at the ranch.

"Gentleman, grab a cowboy hat and find yourself a partner. It's not forever; it's just one dance." He chuckled into the mic, and before Jesse knew it, someone had shoved a cowboy hat into his hands.

"Go on," Mama said, grinning at him. He mashed the hat on his head, already looking for Starla. She came out of the kitchen carrying a tray of something that would make any man's mouth water. The woman herself did that for Jesse, and he strode in her direction before anyone else could approach her.

"Will you dance with me?" he asked as she turned toward the refreshment table. Starla looked at him and nearly dropped the tray of petit fours. He only knew the name of the small, French cakes because he'd spent so much time in the kitchen with Starla. Or texting Starla. Or talking to Starla.

"I'm putting out refreshments."

Helplessness filled Jesse. They hadn't specifically

spoken about tonight, but Jesse always seemed to show up where Starla was, and she'd not rejected him in the past.

"Last call," Kyle said into the mic. "Fellas, get your dance partner and get on the floor."

Jesse cocked his eyebrow at Starla and waited for her to look up at him after she placed the tray. "I can't be the only Stewart without a dance partner." He leaned closer. "It wouldn't look good."

Starla looked at him and cocked her hip. "Jess, I don't think you could look bad if you tried."

He grinned at her and offered his hand. "Please?"

She melted in front of him, and he admitted to himself that she was the only woman he'd beg for a dance. The only he ever had, and the only one he ever would.

She put her hand in his and said, "If I must. I don't want to make you look bad."

"You work for the lodge too," he said. "We have to participate so the guests will." They joined everyone else on the crowded dance floor, and they barely had room to sway back and forth.

Starla flashed a smile to the couple only inches from them before meeting Jesse's eyes again. "I don't think that's a problem, Jess."

"Mm." He put both hands on her waist, relishing the warmth of her body in front of his. He brought her as close as he dared in public, which was pretty dang close. Starla didn't complain, even when he lowered his head and kept it right next to hers.

"Things going okay in the kitchen?" he whispered.

"Yes," she whispered back, her breath tickling his ear. "You'd know that if you were here on time."

"I was fashionably late," he said, smiling to himself. He closed his eyes, because then he could experience Starla with every other sense, and he had enough awareness not to ram them into other people. She let him lead in the dance, and he liked that. She let him lead in almost everything, even agreeing to end things between them for Nash's sake months ago.

He swallowed, the words he wanted to say piling on top of one another. He couldn't say them. He should wait.

The song continued, and Jesse couldn't think of anything to say but what he really wanted to. The silence between them felt awkward, and he finally said, "I think we should go out again, Starla."

She pulled back, as Jesse suspected she would. Her eyes had gone wide, and the lights in the big room reflected her surprise toward him. "Jess."

"Don't say no," he said quickly, glancing around. He took a deep breath and focused on Starla again. "I'm going to talk to Nash."

"I don't think that's a good idea."

"He hasn't done anything," he said, frowning. "He hasn't asked you out. He hasn't made a single move. He's just jealous, and he doesn't want me to be happy."

"Why wouldn't he want you to be happy?" Starla exhaled and looked away from him. "I just don't want to be the center of attention again. I have to work with Nash every single day, Jess."

"I'm dying a little more without you every single day."

He sucked back on his desperation, bottling it tight, and putting more distance between them. "Okay. It's okay." He dropped his hands and stepped back. "Thank you for the dance, ma'am."

Turning away from Starla was the hardest thing he'd done yet. When he walked away, he took back that thought. Walking away from her while she let him—she *always* let him lead—was the absolute hardest thing he'd endured in his life.

———

KYLE STEWART STEPPED OFF THE SMALL PLATFORM THAT ACTED as the stand for the DJ. "It's all yours, Sammy Boy." He gave the other cowboy a smile and gladly relinquished the microphone. He didn't mind calling the songs, but he didn't really have the voice for it.

Sammy Boy did, and his low, bass voice made the speakers hum the way Kyle's chest did with the timbre of it. "All right, everyone," he said. A note of happiness filled the words too, and Kyle couldn't quite pull that off either. "It's time to get your dancin' boots on."

The first notes of the next song came on, and a cheer rose into the air after only the first three notes. Kyle recognized it too, because it was the opening refrain to a very popular line dance.

His head already ached, and all the boot-stomping and yeehaw-ing wouldn't help. He wanted to duck into the kitchen and grab something to eat and drink before he had to go outside to check on the band. He needed to make sure they had the refreshments they needed too, as he'd promised them food, desserts, and drinks for the duration of the evening.

"Kyle," someone yelled, but he waved them off. He kept going until he made it past the swinging door and into the kitchen. People worked back here too, but the music quieted slightly. The floor still vibrated with the stomping, and nothing on the planet could drown out the "Yeehaw!" on every sixteenth count. The citizens in town a good thirty-minute drive away could likely hear it.

He ignored the kitchen staff and went into the walk-in fridge. He'd stowed a case of water here, and he hefted it into his arms. He ducked out the back door instead of going through the party, and the cool night air brought more relief to him.

His muscles ached by the time he arrived at the outdoor stage, and he nodded to the men on the stage, tuning up their instruments and talking. He didn't see the two women that sang with Fiddles & Fellas, and he assumed they'd be in the tent he'd set up for their staging area. That only made him more hesitant to go inside, but he did it anyway.

He didn't see Wendy or Dacia, thankfully, though part of his heart yearned to find someone he could dance with the way he'd seen Jesse and Starla dancing. Or Blake and Gina. Even Holly and one of their cowboys, Little Nick, had seemed like they were having fun.

Kyle suspected Todd would be engaged before too much longer, and then everyone would be looking at him. Not that the Stewarts had to get married in order, but he would be next in line if they were. He'd been looking through his phone, but literally every woman he'd been out with in the past three years was a Do Not Contact Again.

They hadn't contacted him either, and everyone was happier that way.

He put the cold case of water on the table, noting all the music stands, the multiple instruments back here, and the bags. He turned to go get the trays of food Starla and Gina had prepped specifically for Fiddles & Fellas, and he ran straight into a soft body.

"Oof," he said, grabbing onto whatever he could get his fingers around. Still, with his momentum and bigger size than the woman he'd grabbed onto, the two of them fell to the ground. "I'm sorry." He spoke before he even catalogued the pain shooting through his knee and his palm. The woman lay beneath him, and she had to be in a lot more pain than him.

She hadn't made a noise yet, and he quickly pushed himself up and off of her. His elbow smarted, and he crouched down in front of her. "I'm so sorry. I was just bringing in some water."

The woman smiled, and Kyle's heart did a tap and a thump and something else he couldn't name. Almost instantly, he barked *no* at himself, because he was not getting involved with anyone in country music. He was not. Absolutely not.

She put her hand in his, and he helped her up. "Sorry," she said, her voice a bit strange. She dusted herself off and looked at him again. She had a pair of gorgeous, light brown eyes, and long, straight hair that looked like it wouldn't make a very thick ponytail. She probably hated that, but Kyle sure did like it.

"I'm Kyle Stewart," he said, finally dropping her hand. "I'm the band coordinator, and I just have to grab the food and then I'll be out of the way."

"Maddy Cruise," she said. She reached up and rubbed the back of her head.

"Are you okay?" he asked.

"Yeah," she said. "Just realizing now that I fell down."

"I knocked you down," he said. "I didn't hear you come up behind me."

"My brother says I move a little like a ninja." She walked with him toward the door of the tent, and he held it open for her to go through too. "Can I help you bring down the food?"

"Sure," he said, something tingling in his chest at having her at his side. "Are you part of the band?"

"Kind of," she said, then she added, "No, not really."

Kyle looked over to her, trying to figure out which statement was true. "So that's a clear maybe."

She smiled at him, and this time he went up the front steps of the lodge. "It's gonna be loud in there." He had no hope that the line dancing had calmed down, if the thumping beat coming from behind the door told him anything.

Maddy joined him, and Kyle told himself not to get too excited. She was obviously with the band, and therefore not a resident of Chestnut Springs. If she was with the band, he didn't want anything to do with her. So she was pretty. Kyle knew lots of pretty women.

"My brother is Will Steadman," she said. "He wanted me to come with him for this concert, because his wife is almost due with a baby. She's here too, and if I didn't come, he wouldn't have been able to do your concert."

Kyle raised his eyebrows. "Will's wife is pregnant?"

She laughed, the sound far better than any song Kyle had ever played, heard, or penned. "He gets that a lot. They've kept the news very quiet."

A pinch of tension kept him quiet. "Well, I feel like a real schmuck now," he said. He opened the door and went inside, not bothering to check if Maddy came with him. She did, and they wove through the bodies to the kitchen door.

Gina worked in the back now, and when she saw him, she asked, "Are you taking the stuff down for the band?"

"Yep."

"I'll help you."

"I brought help too," he said. "Maybe we can do it in one trip." He followed Gina into the walk-in, and they each picked up a tray. He balanced a second one on top of the cookies he already carried, and they once again went out the back door.

If Will hadn't met him several paces before the tent, he might've dropped the trays, as they grew heavier with every step. Thankfully, he got rid of the top one, and he said, "Thanks," with plenty of relief in his voice.

With all the food in the tent, Gina left, and Will said,

"Let's do a sound check." The band members left the tent, leaving Kyle alone with Maddy once more.

"So you work here?" she asked.

"Yep," he said. "My family owns this lodge. I coordinate all of the music events. The concerts. When I'm not doing that, I help on the ranch." He offered her a friendly smile. "What about you?"

"I teach kindergarten," she said. She once more reached up to adjust something behind her ear.

Kyle peered at her, then turned back to the tray of sandwiches and took off the plastic wrap. "Are you sure you're okay?"

"I'm... Something got a bit mixed up with my hearing aid, that's all." She frowned as she tilted her head now. "I just need to look at it." She met his eye. "Is there a bathroom inside with a mirror?"

"Sure," he said. "I'm sorry. I hope I didn't break anything."

"Even if you did, I have excellent health insurance." She gave him another smile. "Plus, it'll be a good story for my team."

"Getting knocked to the ground is a good story?"

"Better than my sister-in-law going into labor while her husband is on the stage." She laughed again, her voice warbling a little bit once more. He recognized it now as the voice of someone who was deaf.

He followed her out of the tent, noticing that she had hearing implants in both ears, and for some reason that only endeared her to him more. "Where do you teach kindergarten?" he asked.

"Dripping Springs," she said. "That's why Will wanted me to come. It's holiday break for me, and closeby, and then Sarah would have someone with her."

"Where is Sarah now?"

"Dancing," she said with a mischievous grin. "I'm not supposed to let her do that, but the woman has a mind of her own."

Kyle chuckled, and it almost felt natural to take Maddy's hand in his. Dripping Springs wasn't so far from Chestnut Springs, and they had an elementary school here.

"Do you have a boyfriend?" he asked.

Maddy looked at him, questions in her eyes. "What?"

He wasn't sure if she hadn't heard him or if she was shocked at his bold question. He decided to simply go for it again. "Do you have a boyfriend?"

"I thought that's what you said," she said, still a tone of awe in her voice. "I just wasn't sure. I'm missing every other word."

"I'm sorry," he said one more time.

She shook her head. "I don't have a boyfriend."

Kyle let his fingers brush hers on the next step, and then on the next one, he took her hand in his. She didn't pull away. If anything, she secured her fingers right into the spaces between his and held on tight.

CHAPTER
TWELVE

M adeline Cruise wished she could hear. It wasn't the first time she'd wished for such a thing, but the ringing in her ears right now sent irritation through her with every step. She needed to get this fixed, and she had to be able to hear tonight.

Sometimes, she didn't mind that she didn't hear everything other people did. Loud music wasn't her favorite, and she could easily pretend not to hear things she didn't want to. She tried really hard not to do that, though, because it felt petty and dishonest. She worked with kids all day long, trying to teach them how to be good people—as well as how to read and add numbers.

Kyle Stewart opened the door to the lodge—a building Maddy had admired when she'd first pulled up with Will and Sarah—and he indicated she should enter first. She released his hand to do so, and the ringing in her ears intensified with the atmosphere in here.

The Texas Longhorn Lodge certainly knew how to throw a big party, and normally Maddy would've enjoyed herself. She looked around for Sarah, her sister-in-law who was due with her first baby in only two weeks, but she didn't see her. She'd come into the lodge with Kristin, Roger's wife.

Roger sang in the band with Will, and their wives often traveled with them, especially if they had concerts over holidays like this one.

Kyle led her through the fray of people to a hall across the room. The restroom sat halfway down this hall, and she ducked inside. The first thing she did was turn off the earpiece, then she removed the one that she suspected was damaged. It didn't look cracked or anything, but the ringing had stopped in her head. Something had to be wrong with the hardware.

She could probably get by with just one earpiece tonight, but she quickly wiped down the unit in her hand and reconnected it.

A slight, tinny noise vibrated in her ear, and she'd have to go in and have her doctor look at it. It wasn't crackling and ringing anymore, and she could turn it off when she didn't need to talk to the gorgeous Kyle Stewart.

That done, she checked the left side, but she'd fallen on her right harder. She hadn't meant to sneak up on Kyle. She hadn't expected him to turn around so fast, and she'd honestly thought he'd seen her when he'd entered the tent. She hadn't spoken to him, but she could've sworn his eyes had landed right on her.

"Always thinking people see you," she murmured to

herself. She didn't want to think Kyle was just another cowboy with eyes that didn't see. She'd much rather give him the benefit of the doubt. His family owned this ranch, and they were extraordinarily busy tonight. He set up all the concerts here—including Fiddles & Fellas—and perhaps he had a lot on his mind tonight.

She looked down at her hand, her skin starting to tingle as she focused on it. She hadn't held a man's hand for a while, and something fizzed in her chest. Something that lifted up and tickled her nose, making her smile.

Looking into her own eyes again, she quickly ran her hands through her light brown, almost dirty blonde, hair, wishing it wasn't so thin. She had a lot of wishes about herself, though she tried not to. She'd learned to be grateful for what she had, and she reminded herself of her blessings now.

She straightened her sweater, washed her hands, and pressed her lips together to hopefully get them a bit pinker. That was about the best she could do, and Maddy turned to leave the restroom.

Kyle leaned against the wall at the end of the hall, looking out at the party still going strong in the front of the lodge. With the music filtering her way, Maddy couldn't hear anything tinny in her ears. Thankfully.

She approached, and Kyle turned toward her as she did. So he could hear her now. See her. Sense her. "Hey," he said. "Good?"

She watched his mouth move, because she'd been reading lips since she was a tiny girl. She nodded and hugged her arms around herself. "Yeah, I'm good."

"Did I break it?"

"You didn't break anything," she said, though her hip did hurt a tiny bit. He'd mostly caught her on the way down, but they'd both hit the ground. Kyle had lifted her right back up and then lowered her to the ground, so she hadn't hit nearly as hard as she could've.

She gave him a smile. "I have to find Sarah."

He straightened from the wall. "Okay." He looked toward the party and then down the hall, then at her. She liked the way the lights glinted in his dark eyes, and on his lighter brown hair, and off that big belt buckle. He was as cowboy as they came, and she could only imagine him with a guitar in his hand.

Talk about swoon-worthy. Maddy felt her knees going weak now, just picturing him behind a mic, in that blue-and-white plaid shirt, those jeans, and a pair of cowboy boots. She licked her lips.

"I, uh, have a few things to do for the band," he said, taking a tiny step closer to her. "Maybe... Dripping Springs isn't that far from here. Could I have your number?" He took both of her hands in both of his as he asked the question, his head down like he possessed a shy streak and it had reared up.

He was absolutely adorable, and Maddy was glad he'd asked so she didn't have to try to force it on him. "Hmm," she said, hoping he could hear the playfulness in her voice. "I barely know you."

"That's why you give me your number." His eyes flicked up and met hers. "Then we can call and text, and I can ask you to dinner, and we can get to know each other better."

That all sounded wonderful to Maddy. Better than staying late at school and then eating a bowl of cereal alone at night. "How far is it from here to Dripping Springs?"

"Forty minutes," he said. "Forty-five, tops."

"You own a car?"

"A truck," he said, his fingers around hers tightening. They were so warm and not all that rough, and Maddy wanted to know how a man like him came to have hands like his. "But yes."

Maddy slipped one hand away from his and ran it up his arm. He watched the journey of it, and she brushed her fingertips along his jaw, where a light beard grew. Their eyes met, and they could've powered the flashing lights in the room only steps away. "All right," she said.

Kyle grinned, and Maddy suddenly felt shy. She ducked her head as she laughed, and then she gave Kyle her number. A moment later, her phone vibrated and a bright light flashed at the bottom of her vision.

"Wow," Kyle said. "I didn't know phones could light up."

"They can." She pulled it from her front pocket. "Yours can, I'm sure." She tapped to open his message, and she added him to her contacts while they stood right there in the hallway.

"Maybe I'll see you during the concert," Kyle said. Someone called his name, and he turned toward the crowd.

"Yeah," Maddy said as another cowboy came toward them. He had the same strong jaw as Kyle, and if she had to guess, she'd say they were related somehow.

"There you are," the man said, glancing at her. "Holly's looking for you. She wants to know how much time until she should send everyone outside."

"Yeah," Kyle said. "I'll find her." He looked back to Maddy. "See you later, okay?"

She nodded, and then both cowboys left her standing at the end of the hallway, watching the two of them weave through the crowd. She sighed and leaned her hip against the wall where Kyle's had been, and said, "Thank you for bringing me to the Texas Longhorn Ranch tonight, Lord."

———

STARLA MASTERS HAD JUST SET THE LAST BOTTLE OF SPRINKLES on the table when the doors to the lodge opened. Noise and cheering spilled out, and she faded into the darkness beyond the well-lit hot chocolate bar. Thankfully, she didn't have to man it for the next hour.

Fiddles & Fellas would play; the crowd would be entertained by them; Nash and Luke had volunteered to man the drink stations during the concert. That included a huge barrel of water and one of sweet tea. Starla had seen them used during many an outdoor picnic here at the lodge, but the hot chocolate bar was new.

Holly often had one indoors during the holidays and cooler winter months, but this outdoor idea was brand new. She and Gina had crafted everything from the mini marshmallows to the Mason jars of sprinkles, chocolate chips, and butter mints that people could put in their drink. Cans of whipped cream stood at the ready, as did jars of hot fudge, homemade caramel sauce, and peppermint sticks.

That was what she'd go for if she wanted an overly sweet chocolate drink. A dash of marshmallow, then stir with a peppermint stick to get just a hint of mint. No cream. No extra chocolate. No sprinkles.

She did consider herself a purist when it came to food, as she liked to keep things simple. She liked pairing things together that were classic, and she didn't like muddying up flavors—like chocolate and mint—which went so well together already.

Gina came to her side, and Starla gave her a weary smile. "Help me clean up inside? Then we can go."

"You're staying at Blake's with me, right?" Gina asked.

"Yes." Starla couldn't imagine having to drive home after everything tonight. When Gina had offered the room at her fiancé's cabin just five minutes down the road, Starla hadn't hesitated to say yes.

"Great. Then yes, let's go get cleaned up and get out of here."

"You're not going to stay for the ball drop?" Starla asked. The two of them turned toward the lodge, and she caught sight of Jesse out of the corner of her eyes. She focused on Gina intentionally, because she didn't want to face him right now.

He wanted to start their relationship again. If she was being honest, so did she. She simply didn't know how to do it right now. She'd let him walk away from her earlier after he'd said he was dying a little bit more every day without her.

When things got difficult for Starla, she disappeared inside herself to think, reflect, and analyze. She knew now that she should've gone after Jesse when he'd walked away. She should've told him she wanted to go to dinner with him, hold his hand, and do some more of that forbidden kissing in the walk-in fridge.

Everything had been so much easier before last summer. She sighed, and the crowd still leaking from the lodge concealed it from Gina. They'd become fast friends once Gina had started at the lodge, and Starla was so glad to have such a close confidant nearby.

She linked her arm through Gina's and asked, "What should I do about Jesse?"

Gina choked and nearly fell down. "Jesse? What did he do?"

"Nothing." Starla sighed. They pressed their way into the lodge to find almost everyone had vacated it. Trash, tables, and tall glasses remained. Starla snagged the industrial-sized garbage can from beside the door and started putting anything paper, plastic, or aluminum that had been left behind in it.

Gina didn't say anything, as there were a few cowboys who worked for the lodge there to take down the tables. Once they got back into the kitchen and started scrubbing dishes, pots, and pans, she positioned herself right next to Gina.

"Maybe you'll want to stay for the ball drop." Her

eyebrows started high and went higher. "You know, to kiss him. Let him know you're interested again?"

"I've always been interested." Starla looked back at the pan which had held cheese fondue. What a messy thing to clean up, but she attacked it with a fresh round of cleaner and a trusty piece of steel wool.

"Right, but you guys have held each other at arm's length for a while now," Gina said. "Maybe it's time to pull him close and make sure he knows you want him there."

"Maybe." Starla didn't think for a moment that Gina hadn't seen them dancing. She was pretty wrapped up in Blake these days, but she still saw everything. She was like a mother in that regard, and Starla didn't mind it. "Did you see us dancing?" she whispered.

"Yes," Gina said. Nothing more.

"And?"

"And the man is in love with you."

Starla shook her head. "He can't be."

"He is. Or a version of it."

"Puppy love," Starla murmured.

"You good here?" Damion asked, and she waved at him to go. He did, and that left her and Gina alone in the kitchen.

Someone else came through the door as Damion left, and Gina said, "Well, I'm beat," in an overly loud voice. She stepped away, blocking Starla's view of who'd come in.

She knew already.

It had to be Jesse, as Gina wouldn't run off and leave Starla alone for anyone else. Jesse's soul also called to

Starla in a way no one else's had in a while, and his voice made her heartbeat rumble through her body as he said, "Yeah, I can do that," to Gina.

Her friend left, and Jesse came toward Starla. She wanted to throw the steel wool into the sink and push him against the wall. If she could be brave for five seconds, she could tell him she should've come after him earlier tonight. Then, she could tip up onto the very tips of her toes and match her mouth to his.

"Hey," Jesse said, and Starla lost her opportunity to push him against the wall in those few moments she'd taken to daydream about doing so.

She did put down the steel wool, her heart beating like a big bass drum. Starla turned toward Jesse, her frown seemingly stuck in place. "Jesse, I'm sorry."

"For what?" He didn't make a move to touch her, and that made electricity skim the surface of her skin. He was all Texas gentleman, dressed as such with that sparkly purple bow tie and everything.

He hadn't shed the cowboy hat he'd donned when they'd first started dancing, and if there was anything better than a man in a cowboy hat and blue jeans, it was Jesse in a cowboy hat and his dress clothes.

Her mouth positively watered.

"Come with me," she said, reaching for his hand.

"Where are we going?" He stumbled along after her, as if she had the power to drag him so fast he couldn't keep up.

"I should've come after you after the dance," she said as she went through the kitchen. "That's why I'm sorry."

"Starla," he said. "It's fine. I'm fine."

She pressed the big button to get into the walk-in fridge.

"We're going in here?" he asked. He'd kissed her for the first time in this fridge after following her inside. They'd been arguing then too.

She let go of his hand and kept moving toward the back wall of the fridge. She checked left and right to make sure no one else was in there, and then she faced him. "It's not fine. I should've come after you."

Jesse folded his arms and glared at her. If he knew that only made her blood burn hotter, he wouldn't do it. He wasn't nearly as imposing and frightening as he supposed he was. "Why? What would you have done?"

Starla didn't know, just as she didn't know what she was doing right now. She strode toward him the best she could in her heels, planted both palms against his chest, and pushed him into the closed fridge door. Yes, that was satisfying. Hot.

She didn't have to tip up as far as normal, but she managed to get her face really close to his. Really close. "I'm dying a little bit each day without you too." Then she kissed him.

Jesse only stood still for a moment, and then he took her into his arms easily and effortlessly—and kissed her back.

CHAPTER
THIRTEEN

Laura moved along the long table holding all of the tasty things she could drop into her hot chocolate mug. She picked up the two in front of her and moved down to another section. She was getting some for Todd too, as he couldn't really hop-walk and carry a mug of hot liquid. He took his coffee on the couch, at the table, or his desk these days instead of carrying it around the ranch like he usually did.

He wasn't out and about like he used to be, and everyone went to the office to check-in with him. That, or texts got sent fast and furious.

Someone at the ranch had set up their portable bleachers, and Todd had secured the corner of the front row on a set of them, and once Laura had dropped in the red gumdrops he'd requested, she picked up both mugs and headed back to the concert.

Her ears ached and her head throbbed in time with the beat the band played up on stage. She said nothing—what would be the point?—as she reached Todd and handed him the mug of hot chocolate. Real ceramic mugs and everything. She didn't even want to think about the number of times the dishwasher would have to run to get them all clean.

She squeezed into the spot between him and Blake, who sat on the front row with them. Gina hadn't come outside from the lodge yet, where she was helping Starla clean up inside. They'd serve breakfast at eight a.m. tomorrow instead of seven, and no one wanted to show up earlier than they had to.

Laura didn't usually stay up this late, but when she'd heard Holly talking about the enormous ball they'd strung over five hundred lights through, she wanted to see it. Plus, she'd been thinking about kissing Todd for a couple of days now.

A real kiss, one where she wasn't crying or on the verge of tears. One where they were both content, and happy, and thrilled to be together. A kiss that would embed itself into her memory that she could reflect on and have a smile come to her face instead of a cringe to her shoulders.

"Thanks, sweetheart," Todd said, his voice right at her ear. She turned toward him, very nearly kissing him right now. "This sure is good."

She leaned back into his chest too, and he slid his arm around her and rested his hand on her hip. "The band is good too."

"Kyle always books someone fantastic for our New Year's Eve concert." Todd took a sip of his hot chocolate and added, "Mm, that gumdrop is my favorite thing ever."

She giggled, feeling the rumble of his laugh in his chest. Someone moved in front of them, and then Blake stood to make room for Gina. There was no more room, and she ended up sitting on his lap. That actually gave Laura and Todd a bit more room, and she shifted over so he didn't have to hang off the end of the bench.

Laura watched the pair of them, as they were engaged. They put their faces close together and spoke, but she couldn't hear what they were saying. Gina draped her hands lazily around Blake's neck, and he held her around the waist. They seemed comfortable with one another and full of joy, and Laura remembered keenly what that felt like.

She felt a lot of those same things with Todd, even though they hadn't spent a lot of time dating. The woman on the stage started playing the fiddle, the notes flying out at the audience in quick clips, and Laura closed her eyes to really experience it.

Her mind moved wherever it wanted, and she landed on the night she'd laid with Todd in his hospital bed. She wondered what a fly on the wall would've seen that night. Two people who were comfortable with each other? Full of joy?

Laura had loved lying beside him while he slept. His very presence had almost been too much for her to handle, because she'd thought she'd never find someone she wanted to be with as much as she'd wanted to be with Hans.

She looked out of the corner of her eye toward Todd as he clapped his hand against his knee in time with the music. He caught her looking and leaned closer as if she'd said something and he'd missed it.

Happiness poured through her, and she tilted her head back to talk to him. What, she didn't know. She'd enjoyed this evening with him, from the slow swaying in the corner of the dance floor to the tin foil dinner he'd made for them in a tiny fire out behind the barn. That got them away from the crowd for a bit, and then they'd gone back in just in time for the line dancing.

Laura had participated while Todd watched, and he'd taken some videos of her. She looked happy and alive, and Laura hadn't seen herself like that in a while.

"This has been such a great night," she said.

Before Todd could answer, the song ended, and the crowd went wild. Anything he might've said would've been swallowed up in the swell of noise. She looked forward again and started to clap along with everyone else.

"All right," the lead singer drawled. "We've got one more song on our playlist tonight, and then we'll be counting down to midnight."

Surprise moved through Laura. Already? Her pulse picked up speed, because Blake and Gina stood up. She did too, but she wasn't sure why.

"It's a new year," the man onstage said. "Let's spend it

being good to one another." He nodded, his smile huge, and he and his bandmates launched into another song.

People who didn't have a seat in the bleachers stood, and Laura lost sight of Blake and Gina as they went toward the stage. Couples started to dance, and Todd got to his feet, one crutch under his right arm.

He didn't ask Laura if she wanted to dance. He swept her into his arms and started to move with her, and Laura smiled up at him.

"It has been a great night," he said, bringing his head closer to hers. He held it there, his mouth nowhere near touching hers. Something told her that if she wanted to kiss him, she was going to have to make the first move.

Like initiating the date to breakfast last week. Or showing up at the hospital. He'd kissed her twice, and he wasn't going to crash and burn for a third time.

She swallowed as she closed her eyes and allowed herself to become absorbed into all things Todd. His cologne. The scent of his shirt and his skin in her nose. The feel of his hand along her waist and one about halfway up her back. The steady sound of his breathing.

The song ended too fast, and they turned toward the stage as the applause and whooping filled the midnight sky. Before that chaos quieted, another voice filled the air.

Holly. "All right, everyone," she yelled. "We've got seventeen seconds until midnight!"

"So precise," Laura said, and she was talking to herself at this point. She wore a huge smile as a ball easily the size of a car burst into light. It sat at the top of the flagpole, which stood beside the stage, and Laura "wow"'ed at it along with everyone else.

"Ten…nine…eight…" Holly counted down, but by eight, the whole crowd chanted with her. Laura loved the energy of the crowd, the ball, the stars. All of it. It filled her veins and her senses and her soul, and she finished with "…three…two…one! Happy New Year!"

She didn't hesitate as poppers got popped and men whistled between their teeth. The ball had started to fall, but she didn't watch it. She turned toward Todd, lifted up onto her toes, took his face in both of her hands, and kissed him.

Both of their previous kisses had been short. So short, she could barely remember them. She suspected her emotions had something to do with that.

Tonight, she lived fully in the moment, pure adrenaline buzzing from one part of her body to the next. She moved her mouth in sync with him, and soon enough, he was kissing her—which was exactly what she wanted.

He tasted like chocolate, his mouth strong and soft at the same time. She got drunk on him instantly, and she hadn't felt that intoxicating, floating feeling with a man since her first kiss with Hans.

Todd finally broke the kiss when there was more cheering than previously, but Laura didn't look around to see who was still kissing and who wasn't. She looked directly into Todd's eyes, and they might as well have been alone for how intently he watched her.

"Okay?" she asked, distinctly remembering that he'd asked her something similar before after a kiss.

"More than okay," he croaked, and Laura smiled at him.

"Happy New Year."

"Happy New Year, sweetheart," he said, and then he bent down and kissed her again.

CHAPTER
FOURTEEN

Todd liked this version of interactive kissing between him and Laura far better than where he got to touch his lips to her mouth for a moment before she broke their connection. This felt like a *real* connection, and he could taste that Laura had put caramel into her hot chocolate, and he sure did like that flavor combination too. He liked the way her lips fit against his, the way she stroked her mouth with his, the tingle her fingers created as she ran them along the side and then the back of his neck.

He could kiss her for a long, long time and still experience something new. He remembered they weren't alone, and he suddenly felt a lot of eyes on him. He kissed her one more time, then lowered his head to break their connection. She lingered in his personal space, breathing with him, and Todd kept his eyes closed as she did.

When she moved away, he blinked himself back to his

surroundings. Plenty of people had kissed at the stroke of midnight, but Todd didn't care about any of them. Surely they didn't care about him and Laura.

He looked left, where all the weight on the side of his face sat, just as someone cleared their throat. Adam stood there, half perplexed and half disgusted. He'd been following Todd around as if Todd had leashed him when he'd broken his ankle, and Todd rolled his eyes.

"Something I can do for you, Adam?"

"I was just wondering if you needed a ride home." He nodded to Laura, who pressed into Todd's side. "Evening, ma'am."

"Ma'am?" Laura asked, and while it was dark, Todd would swear that Adam's face turned a shade of red. "We've worked together fo months, Adam. You don't need to call me ma'am." She moved away from Todd and toward Adam, who only stood three paces away. Definitely close enough to have a front-row seat to the kissing.

Todd's own embarrassment rose through him, and he pressed against it. Adam could've turned around. He didn't have to watch. Or stare.

"I'm pretty sure I'm younger than you too," she said, reaching up to pat Adam's chest. "I'm going to take Todd home." She turned and smiled at him. "Right?"

"Yes, ma'am." He kicked a smile at her.

She rolled her eyes. "You think you're funny, but you're not."

"Then why are you smilin' like that?" He forgot for a moment that he couldn't just walk over to her and take her hand in his, then tow her away from his glaring brother. He took a step, then remembered his right leg couldn't really bear weight, and stumbled. He hopped, and Adam lunged forward to grab onto him.

"Hey, whoa," he said, and Todd had heard him talk like that to the horses in the past. The weak ones. The playful ones. The annoying ones. All of them. Horses adored Adam, and Todd normally got along great with him too— just not when he was on the receiving end of the soothing statement.

Todd got his good leg underneath him while Laura bent to get the crutch he'd dropped. He wasn't supposed to put any weight on his right foot, and since he didn't want to be in a cast or a boot for longer than he needed to be, he'd been following the doctor's orders.

No weight on his foot, and that meant he had to lean on Adam and Laura, even if he didn't like it. "I'm good," he said.

Neither of them moved away from him, but Adam's grip on his shoulders lessened.

"Your crutch is here," Laura said, and Todd put his arm over it and rested his hand on the handle. He truly found his balance, and only then did his brother back up. "Forgot I couldn't walk," he admitted.

Adam fell back and looked at Laura. "I'm going ot follow you home, just in case he needs help getting inside."

"I'd appreciate that," she said.

Todd growled, and they both brought their attention back to him. "I'm standing right here."

"Barely," Laura said with a smile. "I'm so tired, and I'm sure you are too. It's okay to have a little extra help."

He had plenty of arguments for that, because if Adam followed them back to his cabin, he wouldn't be able to kiss her again. This real first kiss may have happened in public, but he didn't want to repeat that. Kyle would be busy over here for a while, as Fiddles & Fellas still tinkered with their instruments and talked to fans on the stage.

People walked toward the lodge, and a line had formed for the bus that went out to the guest cabins. Right now, Longhorn Ranch bustled with activity, but Todd knew that in an hour, everything would be still and silent.

Todd glared at Adam. "You stay for fifteen minutes and help Kyle and Blake get cleaned up out here."

Adam opened his mouth as if he'd protest, then snapped it closed. "Fine," he said.

"Find Jesse," Todd said. "He has two good legs and big muscles too."

"He went inside to help Starla a while ago," Adam said. "He's probably kissing her too." He looked toward the lodge, a dark cloud moving across his face.

"Yeah, well, you could find someone to kiss if you wanted to," Todd said, turning away from Adam. He regretted the words the moment he heard them land in his own ears. He hung his head and sighed. "Adam, I'm sorry."

"It's fine," his brother barked. "I'll help for fifteen minutes, so you better kiss her quick." He walked away, and Todd inhaled and then blew his breath out in a hiss. "That was rude of me."

Laura held up his keys. "You can talk to him tomorrow. Let's not waste our fifteen minutes." She grinned at him, then danced out of his reach. "You stay here. I'll go get your truck. It'll be faster that way."

He once again wanted to argue, but he couldn't. Laura was right; if she ran around the lodge to where he'd parked his truck and came to pick him up, they wouldn't spend most of their fifteen minutes with him hobbling through the gravel.

The feeling of helplessness and weakness moved through him, and he tamped it all the way down into his stomach. It could stay there until he knew how to deal with it. He hoped.

People continued to disperse, the band quieted, Adam folded up the tables the hot chocolate bar had rested on. He returned to the front driveway with Jesse, the two of them arguing in somewhat quiet voices. Quiet for Stewart men, at least.

Todd simply stood out of the way and listened. "...can see her tomorrow. I don't want to be up all night cleaning up tables," Adam said.

"You can't say anything to anyone," Jesse said, leaning closer to Adam. He said something else, but Todd's brothers had two good legs, and they moved faster than he could hear.

It didn't matter. Todd knew who "she" was when it came to Jesse, and Adam had been right. He'd been inside kissing Starla. Most likely.

None of my business, Todd told himself just as Nash, Holly, and Kyle came out of the tent that had been set up for the band. He carried a couple of trays that were mostly empty, a woman at his side Todd had never seen before. They talked and smiled, and Todd nodded to his brother as he went by.

"You okay?" Kyle asked, slowing. The woman did too, but Kyle kept his gaze on Todd.

"Laura's getting the truck," he said.

"Okay." He looked back over his shoulder. "I think we'll be done out here in about a half-hour."

"I wish I could help," Todd said. He always helped at big family-sponsored events like this, even if he had to be out on the ranch at dawn. Tomorrow, he didn't, and he should be the one stacking chairs and taking down the band's tent.

"We're good," Kyle said. "Adam and Jesse just got here, and Blake's already working on the tent." He smiled at Todd and lifted the half-full trays. "These are deceptively heavy. See you tomorrow."

"Yep." Todd watched the two of them go inside, and then the crunching of tires on gravel told Todd that Laura had probably done some jogging to get to the truck so fast. He adjusted his position as she brought the vehicle to a stop, then hopped over to the passenger door.

She'd already jumped down as he pulled open the door, and he called, "I can do it."

Laura came and stood at his side anyway, and she took his crutch after he'd boosted himself onto the seat. She tucked it into the back seat, then went around to get behind the wheel. Todd couldn't drive, as he'd hurt his

KISSING HER COWBOY BOSS   161

right foot. He felt completely disabled, but he said nothing as Laura made the quick trip back to his cabin.

She kept the radio low, and when she came to a stop on the dirt path in front of the cabin, they both sat there. Then she unbuckled her seatbelt and deftly climbed right over the console between them, giggling as she landed in his lap.

"Oh," he said, grunting with her added weight. He encircled her in his arms and kissed her without a second thought.

"I thought this might be easier than standing on the porch," she whispered, threading her fingers through his hair. He had no idea where his cowboy hat had gone. Right now, he didn't need it.

"Mm." He touched his lips to her throat and felt the bobbing of her pulse there. The passion between them burned hot, and Todd kissed her again. After an explosive initial touch, he slowed the kiss and turned it sweet. Laura went with him, and he liked kissing her from the heart instead of his hormones.

They ended the kiss at the same time, and Laura tucked herself against his chest. He breathed in, and she breathed out. After a moment, she asked, "What are you afraid of, Todd?"

He wasn't sure how to answer the question. "I don't know," he said, but he knew she wouldn't accept that answer. Laura probed into real things, and apparently fears were the next thing on her list.

They'd talked about favorites already, as well as hobbies, and just this morning, she'd wanted to know where he saw himself in five years. This cabin? On this ranch? Wife? Children? How many dogs?

She'd teased him about the dogs, and he'd gone along with it. He'd enjoyed it.

"I'm not real fond of heights," he said. "You?"

"I don't know," she said.

Todd lightly chuckled. "That's not true."

"Would you believe snakes?" she asked, a lilt in her voice that made him lean down and inhale the scent of her hair.

"Not even for a moment," he whispered. "I'm betting you had a couple of pet snakes your mama didn't know about."

She giggled, and that was all the confirmation he needed.

"So not snakes," he prompted.

"Not snakes." She didn't say anything right away, and Todd looked out the windshield and into the darkness.

"I'm afraid to let people down," Todd said. "Or animals."

"Mm, I can see that about you."

"I'm afraid of needles," he said. "Injections. Giving blood. That kind of thing."

She shifted and looked up at him. "You did fine in the hospital."

"They had the IV in before I woke up." He smiled at her in the moonlight, everything about her fair and soft. "I'm afraid of being alone here on this ranch forever."

She kissed him, and Todd had never felt more complete than he did then. This kiss didn't last long, and she stroked one hand through his hair and down the side of his face, her eyes watching the movement of it instead of looking into his.

"I'm afraid of wasting time," she said. "Of losing time. Of not having enough time to do what I want to do."

"What's that?" Todd asked. "What do you want to do?"

"Save a really big pig," she said, a smile tugging at the corners of her mouth. They flattened as quickly as they'd lifted. "Ride a great big Belgian horse."

"You haven't done that yet?" He chuckled.

She shook her head no in all seriousness. "I want to fall in love again. I want to get married—I've wanted to be a wife for a decade." Her chin shook, and Todd wished he could erase the heartache in her life. "I want kids."

Her eyes came to his then. "Do you want children, Todd?"

"Yes." He spoke simply and from the heart, because there was no reason not to.

She pressed her cheek to his, and he let his eyes drift closed. "Where would you live?" she asked. "Here? In this cabin? Or do you Stewarts have extra houses sitting empty somewhere, just waiting for all of you to get married and have families?"

"That's a great question," he said. "Blake has a place of his own. The rest of us share, but this is the family land out here. There's room for more houses."

Laura nodded, and the glare of another pair of headlights came up behind them. "Adam's here. I'm going to let him get you inside, okay? I'm ready to drop, and I don't think I could catch you if you fell."

"Thank you for saying 'if'," Todd said.

Laura giggled and twisted to move off his lap. She went right back over the console again as Adam came to a stop beside Todd, and he opened the passenger door to get out. He let his brother help him inside, knowing Kyle would serve him coffee in the morning if Mama didn't beat him to it.

Blake stopped by all the time. Adam had become a shadow. Mama brought more food every single day— sometimes meal after meal. Kyle naturally helped, and that made sense as they lived together. Laura and Sierra helped a lot around the barn office. Everyone on the ranch had picked up any slack Todd's injury had created.

As Adam stayed at his side with every painstaking step up to the porch, Laura backed out of the driveway and headed home. Todd sighed, and said, "I don't blame you, you know." He didn't have to say for what.

"I know," Adam said, equally as quietly as Todd had spoken.

"I didn't mean to say anything about you dating." Todd looked at his brother, a fine sweat breaking out on his forehead. He realized he'd left his cowboy hat in his truck, but reasoned that it would be there tomorrow when Laura came to pick him up.

Adam's jaw hardened, and he nodded.

Todd swallowed his question about why Adam couldn't get past his dislike of dating and relationships, because they'd both had enough for one evening. They made it to the porch, and Todd leaned against the railing while Adam moved to open the door. He switched on the lights inside and turned back to Todd. "Okay?"

"I'm just tired."

"Join the club." Adam gave him a weary smile then. "I'm sure it's worse for you, though."

"Not worse or better. Just tired."

"Things will slow down now."

"For those on the guest side," Todd said, committing to take another step. If he strung enough of them together, he'd make it to his bedroom, and then his bed. "We're in the thick of birthing season, and you've got twice as many pregnant mares as usual. No one sees that."

"They see it," Adam said. He didn't try to say how, and Todd seriously wondered if his brothers and sister on the commercial side of the ranch truly understood how much a real working ranch required.

He let Adam take his coat and help him remove his single cowboy boot. He let him guide him down the hall and into the bedroom, and he let him get out his gym shorts. "Thanks, brother." Todd hugged Adam and clapped him on the back. "Now get on home, so Jesse will stop kissing Starla and go to bed."

Adam scoffed and shook his head. "That man. I don't know what he thinks has changed."

Todd didn't either, but he was too tired to worry about it right now. He used the restroom, pulled on his gym shorts, and sank into bed. He fell asleep almost immediately, only waking when Kyle cracked his door and let Azure into the bedroom. The dog jumped up onto the bed and circled before laying down right against Todd's back.

"Hey, bud," he whispered, patting the dog. He liked the warmth against his body, and he imagined Azure to be Laura, curled into him the way she had in the hospital. He didn't fall back asleep instantly, but allowed his soft mind to think about a future with Laura Woodcross.

Not in this cabin, but one like it. She'd sleep beside him, and they'd have a family together. They'd have dogs and horses and all the big pigs she wanted.

It was a beautiful dream Todd could only pray would become a reality.

CHAPTER
FIFTEEN

Laura's feet had never hurt as badly as they did right now. Every step sent a jabbing ache up her legs, through her glutes, and into her spine. To add insult to injury, it had been drizzling for four solid days.

Four.

Mother Nature seemed to cry harder the moment she realized the Hill Country had started to dry even the littlest bit. Then she'd sniffle and wheeze for a few hours. Then another torrential downpour would come. At this point, Laura was used to breathing in a mist, and she kept walking through it to get to the barn.

Todd's ankle was getting better—and faster than anyone had thought it would. It had only been a few weeks since his injury, and he could swing himself around quite adeptly on the crutches now. He still couldn't drive, which was why Laura found herself pulling open the back door of the barn and going inside.

This barn had temperature controls, one of which was a dehumidifier and another an air conditioner and a furnace. She sighed in the blessed warmth—sans water in the air—and peeled her gloves off her hands. No sooner had she done that than her phone rang.

A mental exhaustion poured through her, and at her mama's ringtone, Laura collapsed on the bench just inside the door. "Hey, Mama," she said.

"You sound tired."

"I am tired." Laura slapped her gloves down on the bench beside her. "Just got in from this very messy pen of goats." She shook her head to herself. Mama wasn't much of an outdoor person, other than to take a walk down the quarter-mile driveway to the mailbox and back a few times each week.

Laura loved being outside, just not right now. Not in six inches of mud, and not with a goat who didn't seem to understand that barbed wire was sharp and would injure her. A barn cat wound around her ankles, and she bent to pat it. "What's goin' on?"

"I just wanted to call and tell you something," Mama said, and she had a hedge in her voice.

Laura looked up from the cat, her muscles already going tense. "Okay." She didn't need to know what was going on with Hans's family, or his half-sister. That kind of news only stirred up old feelings she'd been wrestling with and trying to pin flat. "Mama, I don't need to know anything about Hans."

"This isn't about him," Mama said.

"Then why aren't you talking?" Her mama only did this when the news was such that Laura wouldn't really appreciate it.

It's gossip, she thought just as Mama said, "Word around Hidden Hollow is that Doc Lewiston is going to retire."

Laura blinked; Mama exhaled mightily. "Boy, I've been holding that in so tight for a week now." She gave a nervous laugh that Laura did not return.

Dr. Lewiston was the only veterinarian within fifty miles of Hidden Hollow. He didn't live in town, but in the next one over, and he'd been working his practice for a handful of decades. Everyone took their animals—from cats and pet rats to horses and cattle—to Doc Lewiston.

"Wow," she said.

"That's your only reaction?"

Laura leaned her head back against the wall behind her, letting her eyes slip closed. "I don't know, Mama. What do you want me to say?"

"I thought maybe you could take over his practice."

Laura shook her head, so many thoughts now perched inside. "It doesn't work like that, Mama."

"Then how does it work?" Her voice came out a bit clipped, and Laura wished she had time to educate her mother on the intricacies of buying a huge veterinary practice like the one Dr. Lewiston had built. It would likely be millions of dollars—with an established customer base that would be guaranteed income.

The thoughts bubbled like carbonation on the surface

of soda, and Laura liked the way they tickled. She could be closer to her family. She'd have a lot of business from the get-go. She was a good vet, and she'd done one of her internships with Dr. Lewiston, before Hans had gotten sick and she'd dropped out of veterinarian school. When she'd gone back, she hadn't worked with him, but the bigger doctors in Austin.

"He probably already has someone buying him out," Laura said. She opened her eyes. "It's not me, Mama."

"I haven't heard that," Mama said.

"It's all gossip anyway," Laura said. "I'm happy here." She looked down the hallway that led past the stables and storage and to the offices on the other side of the barn. "Things are going great with Todd, and…I don't know." She sighed and closed her eyes again. "I feel settled here. I don't want to think about getting another job right now."

"It wouldn't be another job," Mama said. "It would be your own practice, baby. Yours. So close to us too."

Mama had told her she didn't need to be close. Eddie lived right next door with his family, and he ran the farm now. Guilt cut through Laura, something she'd kept at bay with her parents' promises that she didn't need to be close. Chestnut Springs *was* close to Hidden Hollow. An hour was nothing.

"Maybe you should just call him," Mama suggested, and Laura would be shocked if she hadn't already done so.

"Maybe," she said, groaning as she got back to her feet. "I have to go, Mama. I have to tell my boss what's going on with the goats."

"Oh, okay."

"Love you."

"Love you too, dear."

Laura hung up, another round of guilt sliding down her throat that she'd lied to her mother. Todd didn't need to know anything about the goats. She just wanted to talk to him for a moment, go eat dinner at the lodge, and then slip into a nice, hot bathtub and forget about today.

Her phone rang again before she'd even taken a step, and she whimpered. She wasn't even sure she could continue to put weight on her feet. Todd's name sat on the screen now, and she sank back onto the bench, tears pressing into her eyes.

She answered him with a, "Hey. I'm down at the end of the hall by the back door."

He paused. "You are? Why?"

"My mama called, and my feet hurt so bad, I couldn't take another step."

"I'll come to you." His phone scuffled and scratched, and then the call ended. She heard the creaking and rubber ends of his crutches against the cement floor before he came around the corner, and then he swung toward her with power and grace in every movement.

She smiled at him, glad her tears had gone. "Hey."

"Yeah, you're in bad shape," he said, grinning as he arrived. He groaned as he sat beside her, then he twisted to rest his crutches against the wall. Turning back to her, he kissed her, and Laura let everything tremble that needed to.

He pulled away, putting only an inch or two between them. "What did your mama say?"

"Nothing." She sniffled and reached up to wipe her face. She shook her head, glad the weakness had fled in all that single shaky moment.

"Laura."

She drew in a deep breath. "She said the vet that's been working in Hidden Hollow and the surrounding area is supposedly retiring."

Todd said nothing, which was about like saying everything. Of course he wouldn't want her to go. She didn't want to go either. She couldn't stand this silence, and she reached for his hand. He easily slipped his fingers between hers and held on tight. Yes, that was what she needed. A caring touch and warmth and an anchor to hook herself to.

Azure came down the hall, and he stopped in front of Todd. He scratched the dog before he came over to Laura. She gave him a good, hearty stroke along the side of his face, everything about him making her happy.

"Did you get to nap with your daddy this afternoon? You're so lucky."

"I didn't nap," Todd said. "And he belongs to Blake."

Laura gave him a smile, feeling much more settled. "I like it here, Todd."

"You'd tell me if you didn't." He studied her face, then nodded. "Right? I'm gonna call Jesse to take me home. He'll drop you off at my place too, and then we'll have Adam send food over from the lodge." He pulled out his phone to get that done, but Laura put her other hand over it.

"I can make it to the lodge."

"I don't think so," he said. "In fact, I'm going to have

Jesse carry you to the truck." His eyes sparkled like bright lights in a dark sky. "And you're not going to argue with me about it."

"I am not going to let him carry me."

Todd let his phone sag to his lap. "Would you let me if I could?"

Laura wanted to tell him of course not. She could walk; she was a grown woman. Her feet still radiated an ache up her calves and through her knees, and she honestly wasn't sure if she could or not.

"I wanted to take a hot bath," she said.

"Then I'll have Adam send food to your place," he said. "And I'll have Jesse carry you inside your cabin."

Laura smiled at him and shook her head. "I don't want to be alone."

"Well, I'm not getting in the hot bath with you," he teased. "Think of what my mother would say." He chuckled, and Laura did too. "Jesse and Adam will do anything I ask. So you tell me what you want from them, and I'll get it done."

"Do they still feel guilty?"

"Adam especially."

"Having food sent somewhere sounds awesome," Laura said. "It's so loud sometimes."

"Sometimes," Todd said. "My place or yours?" He was really asking if she wanted to be alone or with him, because if she chose her cabin, he wouldn't be going with her. Whenever they spent time together in the evenings, it was always at his cabin. Laura had started to warm up to

Josie a little bit, but it was really Josie who needed to do some thawing toward Laura.

Because she spent a lot of time with Todd in the evenings, she hadn't had much time to talk to her about the things she was passionate about. She'd been listening to more Faith Ostetler, but she hadn't figured out a way to work her into a breakfast conversation yet.

They didn't eat breakfast at their cabin anyway. The lodge served two meals every day, and the entire staff could eat there. Laura didn't want to spend time cooking if she didn't have to.

"I think my place," she finally said. "Would Adam really carry me inside? I could hobble to the bath."

"I'm texting him right now." He didn't seem upset that she'd chosen a nice, quiet bath over an evening with him, and Laura leaned her head against his bicep.

"Thank you," she murmured.

"I'll have him take me home too, and then get someone to bring my truck to you."

"I can just go to your place," she said.

"No." He looked up from his phone. "You need a night to yourself, and it's fine. They're coming."

"They're?"

"Jesse and Adam."

Another tremor worked its way through Laura, but Todd put his phone away and took her hand in his again. He pressed a kiss to her temple, and they simply sat together until a couple of men came around the corner. Jesse and Adam, and they both wore concern on their faces.

"You need a day off," Adam said with plenty of bite in his tone. "Todd, did you give her tomorrow off?"

"I'm fine," Laura said at the same time Todd said, "No, but she can have it if she wants."

"You had to call your brother to carry her home," Adam griped. He looked from Todd to Laura. "You're taking tomorrow off."

"My feet just hurt," she said.

"Yeah, and that means you're taking tomorrow off." He picked up Todd's crutches and handed them to Jesse. "You're in charge of Todd. I'll get Laura."

She wanted to protest, but with the three of them looking at her with those dark eyes with what could've been glares, she simply reached up and put her hands around Adam's shoulders. He lifted her easily and carried her the way a husband would tote his bride across the threshold of their new home.

Down the hall and outside they went, Todd and Jesse talking in low voices behind them. Adam put her in the passenger seat, barked something to Jesse about going inside to get her a meal, and then he got behind the wheel and started down the lane.

Laura's heartbeat fissured through her body. "Thank you, Adam," she said.

"I've seen people work the way you do." His voice softened as he spoke. "You don't take a day off here and there, and you'll be forced to." He quirked his eyebrows at her for a moment and then looked back out the windshield at the dying day. "Sickness. An injury. Something. Then you'll be down for longer than a day."

She nodded. "I'll take tomorrow off."

"I brought some of the muscle tincture I use," he said. "It's there in the glove box."

She stretched forward to open it, and an orange bottle almost fell out.

"Take it," he said. "Massage it into your feet and calves. It helps a lot."

"Thank you."

At her house, he carried her up the steps and right inside. "The bathroom?" he asked, barely glancing at Josie, who sat at the dining room table with Mick. "Howdy, guys."

"What's going on?" Josie asked, getting to her feet.

"Laura just needs to rest." Adam continued down the hall and took Laura right into the bathroom. With her seated on the closed toilet, he looked down at her. "I'm going to run back to the lodge and get your food. Take Todd home. We'll get him to work tomorrow. You rest."

"Yes, sir," she said. The last word caught in her throat. "Adam…thank you."

"Of course." He gave her a rare smile and left the bathroom. Laura sighed and pushed her hands through her hair. She tugged her phone out of her back pocket, tapped, and swiped to get to a playlist.

The first few notes of a Faith Ostetler song started to play just as Josie darkened the doorway. "Why is Adam Stewart carrying you inside?" She looked from Laura to the phone. "Is that Faith Ostetler?"

"Yes," Laura said.

Josie's whole demeanor changed, what with her shoulders going down and her mouth actually tipping up into a sort of half-smile. "I haven't heard this song."

Laura grinned at her, feeling the door between them start to swing open. Wide open. "It's brand new," she said. "A new single she put out on Tuesday, I think."

"You're kidding." Josie pulled out her phone and started working on it. "This is incredible. I love her stuff." She looked up at Laura, the joy and hope there only fading slightly. "I'm sorry you're hurt."

"I just ache," Laura said.

"Adam said he's sending someone with food."

"Yes." Laura reached back and released her hair from her ponytail. "Todd called him to carry me in here, as if I can't walk." She scoffed. "Todd would've done it, but he can't even walk himself." She gave Josie a small smile. "If I'm in here too long, just knock, and I'll get out."

"Take your time," Josie said, her smile appearing fully. "Mick and I are just going over that new paddock build."

"Oh, I want to see that when you're done," Laura said. "It sounds fascinating."

The new Faith Ostetler song blasted from Josie's phone too, and she returned her attention to it. "Mick's gonna love this." She gave Laura another smile. "Do you need anything? Pain meds? Ice pack?"

"Some pain meds would be fantastic," she said.

"I'll get them."

Laura nodded as she left, a new ray of sunshine now illuminating her life. She twisted and started the hot water in the tub. She swallowed the pills Josie brought her, and then she managed to get to her feet for long enough to close the door, get undressed, and ease herself into the hot bath.

She let her eyes drift closed as she sighed, because this was exactly what she needed—and she had Todd, her cowboy atop a shining white horse, to provide it for her.

CHAPTER
SIXTEEN

Todd could barely remember January. One day, he walked into the lodge to find it decorated in a variety of pink, purple, and white hearts. He paused, because he didn't really walk into anywhere, and took it all in.

"This is disgusting," Adam said from behind him.

"Don't stop in the blasted doorway," Blake yelled, and Todd swung himself out of the way. The people behind him could now enter, and as they did, he watched their reactions to the Cupid barf everywhere.

"This is great," Sierra said, her eyes shining. "I wonder who did this?'

"I wonder," Todd said in a deadpan. She looked at him, her eyebrows up. "Holly and Ashley is my guess." The two of them had been stuck at the hip lately, and he didn't know what that was about. He worked on the other side of the operation here at the Texas Longhorn Ranch, and he didn't have to agree with valentines plastered on every desk, table, chair, and wall. The guests probably liked it.

They'd all come to the lodge today for a family meeting. When Daddy ran the ranch, they had them every single month. Since Blake had taken over, he'd not done them as often. Usually about once a quarter, or "as needed." He'd scheduled one for today, and that meant everyone was congregating in the break room in the staff area of the lodge.

Todd and Sierra would distribute any necessary information to their team of cowboys and cowgirls, as would everyone else in the Stewart family.

"Mama made the hand pies," someone said ahead of him, and Todd tore his attention from décor to focus on something better—food. His mother made a delectable hand pie, and when he finally arrived in the break room area, he found the one round table there laden with food. Not just hand pies, but chips and guacamole, salsa, potato salad, and Starla's famous brisket bundles.

He couldn't really carry a plate with the crutches, and Blake appeared in front of him, a full array of food on the plate he held. "Go sit down," he said, nodding toward one of the long tables that edged the room.

Todd grinned at his brother and did as instructed. Blake slid the plate of food in front of him and said, "I'll be right back." He re-entered the fray, and Todd simply sat back and watched. He did love his family, even if Jesse glared at Nash while their younger brother was flirting with Ashley. Even if Adam elbowed Sierra and nodded over to Daddy and then the two of them shared a smile. He wondered what that was about, but he liked his drama-free life. He wouldn't ask, and every one of them had a different relationship with the others.

Kyle sat next to him, which wasn't surprising, and Adam next to him. Jesse beside him, and then Holly, Blake, and Sierra. Nash seemed to be the odd one out all the time, and he watched as Ashley, Gina, and Starla went down the hall. They weren't family members and didn't need to be present at this meeting. They'd brought the food for the luncheon, and that was all.

Blake didn't stand up and get the meeting started. He wasn't stupid, that was for sure. He knew they needed to get together every so often and just be friends with one another. It was something Daddy had done—and lectured them about—for years.

"How's Laura?" Kyle asked, and Todd nodded as he bit into his brisket bundle.

He chewed and swallowed, the salty meat and tangy barbecue sauce the best thing he'd eaten in a while. "Real good."

"What are you doing for Valentine's Day?"

Todd's mind blanked. "Um, I don't know." He honestly tried to make it through each day without tripping. Planning a Valentine's Day date hadn't entered his mind yet.

Kyle looked to his right, but Adam was engrossed in a conversation with Jesse and Holly. It was clear Kyle didn't want anyone to overhear what he was about to say. Todd took another bite of his brisket in an attempt to show Kyle that whatever he said would be fine. A-okay. Nothing to see here.

"I want to ask this woman out," he said. "Well, we've been out once, but it was kind of…weird."

Todd raised his eyebrows. "Weird?"

"I don't know." Kyle shook his head. "Maybe I should just forget about her." He clearly didn't want to do that, and Todd leaned closer.

"Describe weird. Like, she said she had a boyfriend weird, or like a little uncomfortable weird? Or the date was just bad?"

"No boyfriend," Kyle said. "She's made that clear a couple of times now."

"You're texting her? Calling? What?" He hadn't noticed Kyle on the phone an excessive amount in the evenings, but he'd been pretty wrapped up in his own girlfriend, napping with Azure, or hobbling around the cabin.

"Both," Kyle said. "Texting more than calling." He took an overly large bite of potato salad and looked at Todd. He didn't have to speak for the questions to pour out of him.

He liked this woman. If Todd wanted to, he could find out where they'd met and more about the date. He wasn't sure he needed to know that. Kyle liked her. They'd been out once, and he'd felt awkward about it. He wanted to try again.

"Double date on Valentine's Day?" he suggested.

Relief covered Kyle's whole face. "I'll plan the whole thing. You and Laura just have to come."

Todd nodded. "I'll check with her, but I think at our stage, a date on Valentine's Day would be implied."

"I would think so," Kyle said dryly. "The way you're kissin' her all the time."

"It's not all the time," Todd said. He wished.

Kyle grinned at him. "I know. You've been very good when I'm home, and I appreciate it."

"You don't have to stay away," Todd said. "I mostly sleep, and she does the dishes, and then lays by me." It was nice, and he liked her presence in his life. It didn't have to be complex to be good.

"I know," he said. "Both of you were asleep when I walked in the other night." He turned as someone whistled through their teeth. That wasn't Blake, but Becks.

Todd's cousin. She'd come to the ranch last year to implement their new website, all of their new software for online reservations, and make their online presence shine. She'd done an amazing job—and continued to do so—and it was clear she would be running today's meeting.

"All right, y'all," she said into a microphone. "Finish up your desserts and get ready to dive into our work this afternoon."

"Here we go," Adam muttered, but Becks silenced him with a well-placed glare. Todd had always liked her. She was level-headed and cool. She knew a lot about networks, computers, and more. She'd worked in cybersecurity on the national level, and now she lived and worked here, on the family ranch.

It was a testimony to him of how strong the pull of family was. His mind flew to Laura and the conversation they'd had in the barn a couple of weeks ago. Her mama had called about a veterinarian retiring near Hidden

Hollow. Laura had dismissed it immediately, but it had lingered in Todd's mind.

The possibility of her leaving made him frown and his mind fire question after question at himself. Could he go with her? Could she commute? Hidden Hollow wasn't that far away. Did she want to go? If so, was he a strong enough pull to keep her here? If she didn't want to go, why not?

He blinked his way back to Becks just as she said, "From now on, I'll need everyone to fill out this online form for every activity planned here at the lodge. We don't have everything on our calendars, and that means we're not painting an accurate picture for prospective guests."

"Online form?" Adam said, and he did not sound happy.

Becks speared him with another look that told him not to argue with her. "It takes about sixty seconds per activity. Now." She turned toward a blank wall, which suddenly got illuminated with a slide. "I need to know the name of the activity. Where guests should gather for it. If there's an extra cost beyond their resort fee and nightly stay, and if there's a limit on registration. Any food provided. Special gear or clothing they need to wear. All of that."

"This sounds like more than sixty seconds' worth of information," Kyle said, and Todd didn't even want to think about how long it would take him to enter his concerts. They did one every weekend all summer long, but Todd reasoned that was one event, and a lot of the details were the same.

"Then, this will sync with our calendar online," Becks

said, and the image on the wall changed. "People can register for those activities right when they book, or we'll send reminder emails leading up to their stay. That will reduce the burden of our front desk on check-in, and it'll ensure that families can do activities together instead of being disappointed there's not enough spots for the horse-back riding."

"That was one family," Adam said.

Becks acted like she hadn't even heard him. "We've been working on implementing this for about five months now, and it doesn't work unless the details are put into the form."

Blake stood, wiping his mouth. He tossed his napkin to the table. "This isn't a commentary on anyone and what they've done or haven't done. This makes the Texas Long-horn Ranch an easier, faster, better place to book a reservation. There are activities here, and people can add them to their schedule as they're reserving rooms or cabins." He surveyed everyone. "As Becks said, we've been working on it for months, so it has nothing to do with one family or this concert or a brownie tasting no one knew about last week."

"Wait," Nash said. "There was a brownie tasting last week?"

"You're the morning manager," Jesse threw down the table to him. "It was at ten-thirty in the morning. How did you not know about it?"

Todd shifted in his seat, feeling like World War Stewart was about to happen. Thankfully, Blake held up one hand, as if he alone could hold back the tide. He probably could,

as everyone in the family, Todd included, looked up to
Blake.

"That's not the point," he said. "The point is, if there is
an event going on in your department, it must be in this
form no later than two weeks before the date it will be
held. Recurring events can be inputted once, saved as a
template, and then all you have to do is change the date.
Becks?"

"Right." She cleared her throat and changed the slide
again. "So Adam has horseback riding every Thursday,
Friday, Saturday, and Sunday, right? So he puts in all the
information once." She clickety-clacked on the keyboard
and put in a bunch of gibberish information. "He clicks
this button right here that says 'save as recurring event
template.'" She did that, and then she reloaded the form.

"Right here at the top, it asks if you want to use an
event template. You click the box, and they come up." It
did. "Select it, and change the date. It's now done."

"Nice," Adam said, smiling.

"Can we put them in once and say they repeat?"
Sierra asked. "We have that farm visit every Saturday
morning."

"There's a button here that says 'recurring,'" Becks
said. "Click that, and tell it how many times and the
frequency." She demonstrated how Sierra might put in the
farm visit, and Todd could easily see how much effort had
gone into this system.

He didn't oversee any events. Not really. Sierra did
several things around the ranch for guests—like the farm
visit. Adam ran all the horse-related things, like horseback

riding and carriage rides and horse-brushing and animal-feeding demonstrations.

"If you have questions on this, please see me or Becks," Blake said. Becks sat back down and the presentation on the wall went dark.

"All right," Blake said. "Adam's going to talk for a second about the horses, and then Jesse's going to go over some of his new ideas."

Todd smiled to himself. Jesse hated the spotlight, and he'd be shocked if he said much. Instead, Holly would make the presentation and everyone would be nodding with smiles by the end of it.

"Cake?" Kyle asked as he stood.

"Definitely." If Todd had to sit through Adam talking in a stern voice about the horses, and then Holly trying to charm them all into thinking offering free ice cream every Thursday was a good idea, he needed cake.

He honestly didn't care what they did on the commercial side of the ranch. If he needed to help, he would. If he didn't, he'd merrily go about his business with the ranching operation that needed to be run.

His phone buzzed while Kyle slipped behind him to get cake, and he looked at his device. *Hope your meeting isn't terrible*, Laura said.

Not yet, he said. His thumbs flew while Adam stood and said, "Along with this new system for events, Little Nick and I have decided we need to have a system for reserving horses."

Here we go, Todd thought. He grinned at his phone and sent the text without thinking too hard about it.

Are you free for a double date with Kyle and someone I don't know on Valentine's Day?

Kyle put a plate bearing a large piece of chocolate cake on the table in front of him. His phone buzzed and he caught Laura's response—*sure am.* Suddenly, with the cake and the date, he could survive anything that happened in this family meeting.

He turned the phone toward Kyle, who nodded and then he got busy on his own phone. Adam finished talking, and Kyle slid his phone closer to Todd.

Holly stood to begin the brainstorming session, but Todd kept reading Kyle's phone. He'd been texting with a woman named Maddy Cruise—and he'd put a ship and a heart after her name in his contacts—and he'd just asked her to double with him and his brother for Valentine's Day.

She'd come back with, *Up there or down here?*

Wherever, Kyle had said. *Maybe halfway between? Maybe we can go to dinner in Fredericksburg or something.*

Oh, that's the capital of tourism, she'd said. *Canyon Lake would be better. Or Johnson City. Oh, there's a GREAT place in Marble Falls.*

I'll talk to Todd about it, he'd said. *We'll plan something awesome if you're in.*

I'm in.

Todd smiled, glad that this Maddy woman had said yes to Kyle after a "weird" date.

"I think we should all get to see what's so fascinating on that phone," Holly said, and Todd looked up at the near proximity of her voice. He barely had time to slap his hand over Kyle's phone before Holly had it. Her nails scrabbled along the back of his hand, and he swept the phone off the table and into his lap a moment later.

"No," he said.

"What's the last thing I said?" Holly challenged.

Todd blinked and looked over to the wall where Becks had done her presentation. Adam stared at him with a frown, and Jesse lifted an imaginary cup and tipped his head back to drink it.

Blake smiled and shook his head, and Sierra spelled something out in sign language.

"Something about syrups and sodas," he said, though there was nothing shining on the wall and he wasn't sure he could read Sierra's hands so quickly. Jesse had been drinking, that much was certain.

Holly looked like she'd swallowed an entire lemon orchard. "I'd appreciate it if you'd put your phone away."

"You got it, sis," Todd said, sliding the phone back to Kyle under the table. They exchanged a glance, and since Todd didn't particularly enjoy the spotlight shining so brightly on him either, he actually did pay attention for the rest of the meeting.

He was suddenly really looking forward to Valentine's Day, and once the meeting ended, he said to Kyle, "Find out about the place in Marble Falls, and I'll call and see if they have any reservations."

For Valentine's Day, they would need them.

He suspected Laura would love Marble Falls, as they had a lot of hiking trails and parks and lakes, waterfalls, and rivers there. His foot wouldn't be better to the point that they could do a whole lot, but maybe they could spend the whole day up there, and simply meet Kyle and Maddy for dinner.

New adventures. Explore a new place together. Build memories as they spent time together. Those things were important to Laura, and that meant they were becoming more and more important to Todd—because she was becoming more and more important to Todd.

CHAPTER
SEVENTEEN

L aura smelled something amazing coming from her cabin as she went up the steps to the front porch. She'd just dropped Todd off at his cabin and had decided to head home for lunch. She'd done that a few times, and she'd never encountered Josie. Or anything that smelled half so good coming from their house.

She went inside, and sure enough Josie looked up from the kitchen at the back of the room. "Hey," she said, and she actually smiled. "Is Todd off?"

"Soon." Laura closed the door behind her and returned Josie's smile. It had been a couple of weeks since Adam had carried her down the hall and into the bathroom, and they'd done a little female bonding over Faith Ostetler's new song. "You cook?"

Josie giggled and shook her head. "No, Mick gave me this from his daddy. He owns a restaurant in town, and he went over the weekend to visit them."

"Ah, got it."

"Are you hungry? There's lots." Josie stirred whatever she had in the plastic container, and Laura's stomach grumbled.

"Sure, if there's enough."

"There is." Josie turned and got out another bowl. "It's just chili, but it's fantastic."

"Spicy?" Laura could smell the heat, but she didn't mind it too much. As long as there were other flavors too, she actually liked the burn in the back of her throat and nose.

"Not too bad," Josie said. She put the bowl on the counter and opened the drawer with spoons in it. "What were you doing this morning?"

Laura flinched as if Josie had flicked water in her face. Just a tiny little startle. "Oh, I texted you." She grinned at Josie as she came around the corner and sat at the end of the bar. "Guess what we got out on the ranch last week?"

"If this is a piece of equipment, you can't have any chili." Josie didn't look like she was kidding either.

"It's not a piece of equipment."

"Must be an animal then."

Laura nodded as Josie dished up chili for herself and left the rest for Laura. She could barely contain her excitement. "You like these animals, and I told Adam you should come ride her."

Josie met Laura's eyes, hope shining in hers.

"I mean, with you bein' Texas royalty and all." Laura shrugged like she didn't care if Josie rode the barrel racing horse or not. "Plus, we want to get an idea of what she can do."

"Laura," Josie said slowly. She'd learned over the past month or so that Josie was a lot more female than she was. She cried over sappy movies, and she shrieked at good news. She wasn't close to a lot of people, and she didn't care about shoes—so she was very much like Laura in some ways. In others, she very much fit the more giggly, gossipy type of woman Laura had never been.

"It's a barrel racing horse," Laura blurted out. "Her name is Shining Star, and she is gorgeous."

As predicted, Josie squealed. She jumped to her feet too. "Let's go."

"They're doing a bath right now." Laura didn't move to get up. Instead, she reached for a fork. "We can't go right now."

"But you checked her out?"

"Yep." Laura sprinkled some shredded cheese over her chili. "She's healthy as a horse." They giggled together, and Josie sat back down.

She sighed, her face still full of wonder. "Why did Adam buy a barrel racing horse?" She too added cheese to her chili and stirred it all together while Laura considered if she should tell her or not.

She took a bite of chili first, and this was fantastic. Better than her mama's, but she'd never tell her that. "He bought her because she was retiring, and he thought maybe it would be a fun event for guests to watch."

Laura watched Josie's reaction, which had mirrored her own for the first few seconds. Confusion, then some struggling to come up with the right answer, and then a brightness of clarity. "He wants me to ride her in a demo?"

"I did mention that we had a couple of former barrel racers here." Laura lifted one shoulder in a half-shrug. "He said he'd talk to you."

Josie burst out laughing, and the next thing Laura knew, her next bite of chili went flying as Josie launched herself at her and hugged her. "Oh, okay." She laughed and hugged Josie back, if a bit awkwardly.

"I *love* horseback riding," she said. "The lessons are good, don't get me wrong." She taught a lot of lessons. She led guests on guided horseback tours as well. "But this... This'll be something new and different."

"That's Adam's hope," Laura said, though she knew the idea had come from Jesse. She hadn't even mentioned anything about Josie to Adam, but Jesse had been sitting at dinner with her, Todd, and Starla a few weeks ago.

They ate for a minute, and then Josie startled too, hers much bigger and more dramatic that Laura's had been. "Oh, someone called for you."

"They did?" Laura looked at her cellphone on the counter in front of her. It must not be someone she knew, or they'd use her cell. "Who?"

"I don't know. A doctor."

Laura looked up as Josie slid off the barstool and went around the counter to the fridge. "A doctor?" Someone for Todd? Why would they call her?

They wouldn't.

So someone for her daddy. Why hadn't Mama just called?

Josie peeled off a bright blue sticky note and gave it to Laura. She smoothed her finger along the top of it so it would stick to the counter in front of her, but Laura had already seen most of the letters.

Doc Lewiston. Josie had written a number below his name.

"He wants you to call him. Said he thought about getting your number from your parents, but he didn't want them to worry."

"Worry," Laura repeated. Her mind felt slow, like it was barely moving, and she had no idea why Doc Lewiston would need to call her in the first place. If her parents would be worried about him asking for her number?

She shook her head. "Thanks," she said. "I'll call him back this afternoon."

Josie retook her seat and said something about her former rodeo career. Laura did her best to participate and listen, because it was nice to have a cabinmate she could connect with and talk to. Her mind kept wandering to town, and the hospital there. Todd had an appointment this afternoon with his podiatrist, and he'd know if he could get out of the cast by Valentine's Day.

If it didn't linger on Todd, it flowed down the highway to Hidden Hollow and Doc Lewiston. Laura hadn't seriously entertained finding out more about his practice or if the veterinarian was really going to retire. Mama could get fanciful about things sometimes, and it had been pure gossip.

After Josie hugged her again and practically skipped out of the cabin, Laura faced her phone. The blue note stared her in the face. "Just do it," she told herself in the too-quiet house.

She didn't pick up her phone, but instead, just tapped and swiped to make a call. She tapped in the number and hit the green icon. She then tapped to put it on speaker, because she didn't think she could do much more with her body than involuntary things.

"Hello?" a woman asked. Definitely not Doc Lewiston.

Laura tried to speak, but her throat felt fused together. She cleared it and said, "Yes, hi."

"Doc is out at Sandy Hills," the woman said in a bored voice. "He won't be in until tomorrow. If you have a true emergency, I can patch you through, but I'm going to need to know all the details first."

Laura frowned as surprise went through her. Of course Doc Lewiston couldn't be available twenty-four-seven, but if she did have a true emergency, by the time she gave his receptionist all the details, it might be too late.

"Not an emergency," she said. "It's Laura Woodcross, returning Doctor Lewiston's call."

"Oh, yes, Laura." The woman's voice changed instantly. "Let me ping him and see if he can talk. Hold, please." Before Laura could protest or ask how long she'd have to hold, fluffy music filtered through the line.

She had a job to do that day too, but no one checked her hours. She didn't punch a clock. She could get out to the calving shed in five minutes or fifteen. Or thirty. No one would question her or ask her who she'd been talking to.

It felt like a lifetime, but Doc Lewiston came on with,

"Hello, Miss Woodcross," only three minutes later. "Thanks for callin' me back."

"Yeah, sure," Laura said, once again clearing her throat. "My cabinmate said you wanted me to call."

"Yes." A cow lowed on his end of the line, and he chuckled. Then he gave some directions to whoever he was with, and the wind scratched across his speaker. He was out there, doing what he did. Doing what Laura loved to do—treat and care for animals.

"I don't know if you've heard, since you don't live around here anymore, but I'm fixin' to retire."

Laura saw no point in lying about it. "My mama mentioned it," she said. "It sounded like gossip to me."

Doc Lewiston chuckled. "It's funny how sometimes gossip is true."

Laura smiled.

"Anyway, you were a fantastic intern, and I'm wondering where you are and what you're doing. I mean, I know where you are. I called the Texas Longhorn Ranch and asked about you." He chuckled again. "I'm looking for a replacement, and I have several people in mind. To be honest, this practice should be split in two or three. There's enough for three full-time vets, and I'm wondering if you might be interested in being one of them."

Laura opened her mouth to answer but found she had no words. "I—"

"Maybe you'd like to come by the building, meet with the staff, see some of the animals. You could go around with me for a day on one of the ranches. Like you did when you were interning."

Laura's mind spun. She didn't know what to say. "Yes," flew out of her mouth, and then she started to giggle in a very Josie-like way. "I need to talk to my bosses here and get some time off to come down there. Can I let you know?"

"Sure, sure," he said. "I'm not planning on going anywhere for a few months."

"Okay," Laura said. "I'll let you know."

"Sounds great." The call ended just as another cow wanted to join the conversation with her deep voice. Laura stared at her phone as it went dark.

"What just happened?" she wondered to herself. Doc Lewiston had likely worked with dozens of veterinary students over the years. Had she really left that big of an impression?

She'd always felt insignificant and overlooked in her program. Men twice her size always dismissed her—until she showed them she could handle the bulls and Belgians as easily as they could. Sometimes easier, as she connected with the animal instead of using brute strength to get it to comply.

She felt pulled back down the highway. Back to the life she'd had in Hidden Hollow once upon a time. Back to the life she'd always dreamed of. One where she didn't share a cabin with another woman, and she didn't work on someone else's ranch.

She'd be closer to her family, and closer to where Hans was buried, and closer to the life she could've had.

"The life you *should've* had?" she whispered, but the

thought grew too dangerous, and she pushed it out of her mind.

No matter what, she needed to arrange to get a few days off to go visit her family. She could tack a day onto that to spend with Doc Lewiston.

She started texting her mother, and then Todd. He told her anytime, as they were nearly out of birthing season. Up next, they'd tag calves and get ready for branding, and she'd have to be there for that.

So next weekend? she asked. That should be a lull between activities.

It's Valentine's Day next weekend.

Foolishness struck her behind the lungs. Valentine's Day. With her boyfriend. How could she be thinking of interviewing for a job an hour away, when she had a good one here? A good man who cherished her and clearly wanted her to stay here?

She didn't know how to reconcile all the pieces currently swirling around her, and she picked up her phone and pushed it into her back pocket. She had to get to the calving shed, and she'd think about Todd, Doc Lewiston, Hidden Hollow, the Texas Longhorn Lodge, and everything else later.

.

CHAPTER
EIGHTEEN

Todd rode in the passenger seat of the side-by-side, bracing himself against the bar there as Little Nick pulled his foot from the accelerator. He leapt from the machine a moment later and ran toward the calf and his momma, tagging gun in his hand.

Todd watched as the tagging took all of eleven seconds, and most of that was Little Nick running to and from the side-by-side. He wore such a look of joy and freedom on his face, and Todd's jealousy raged like a white-rapid river.

He hadn't been able to get out of the cast yet. His foot needed another week, but Todd felt certain next time he went to see the podiatrist, he'd get told it needed another week. Then another one.

It had only been seven weeks since Verity had stomped on his ankle, and Todd should be grateful he wasn't more injured. He was. He was grateful he hadn't needed surgery. He was grateful he wasn't in any pain. He was grateful he'd graduated from two crutches to one.

He simply wanted the cast off too.

Even then, the doctor had told him he'd have to wear a walking boot for a few weeks, but Todd could drive with that. At least theoretically.

Laura had been a saint, driving him to the barn and home again. They'd spent a lot of time together, and he warmed with the simple thought of her. Then Little Nick gunned the side-by-side, and Todd got thrown backward.

"Hey," he protested.

"Sorry." Little Nick threw him a smile. "Only a few more."

In this field, at least. Todd was just glad to be out of the barn on a day without rain. The sun broke through the wispy clouds overhead, and he could practically feel the vitamin D soaking into his skin.

He had a date with Laura that night. A real date, where they were going to town to a variety show. Dinner, entertainment, music, dancing. Blake had told him about it, and he'd wanted a solo date with Laura off the ranch.

Valentine's Day weekend was almost upon them too, but they were doubling with Kyle and Maddy. Todd had asked, and Laura had started stopping by his office after lunch to practice dancing with him and his crutch.

Next weekend, she was heading to Hidden Hollow to visit her parents. She hadn't invited him to come, and Todd was still considering if he should suggest it. Invite himself. He'd like to meet her parents, and she should know how serious he was about her. Suggesting such a thing would do that for sure.

Everything Laura did, she managed to do with grace, elegance, and supreme acceptance. She rarely got angry or upset anymore, and the melancholy which had plagued her last autumn and into the holidays had disappeared completely.

As Todd rode in the side-by-side—paying more attention now so he didn't get whiplashed around—and thought about Laura, he could feel himself falling in love with her. Slipping and sliding and then free-falling. There was nothing about her he didn't like, and the things that had caused some tension between them had been resolved or explained by things in her past.

No one was perfect, but he thought Laura Woodcross might be as close as someone could get.

"Is that a white calf?" Little Nick asked, and Todd blinked his way back to the reality in front of him. He too saw a flash of pure white, like the driven snow, before it disappeared behind a big black mama cow.

"Uh, I'm not sure."

Little Nick cranked the wheel, and the side-by-side creaked and groaned as it turned. Or maybe that was Todd. Either way, Little Nick spun them around in a tight circle and headed back the way they'd come.

"Did we have any reports of a white calf?" Todd asked.

"No idea," Little Nick said.

Todd felt absent from his own ranch, and he frowned. He usually knew everything that happened out here, and he should this year too. Lord knew all he did was sit in his office and text people. He should know absolutely everything.

Hearing about something and being out on the ranch were two different things, and he wished he'd been more present. He could limp around the dirt and gravel paths and be where he usually was.

Committed to that, he focused as Little Nick drove right through the herd. They didn't seem to care at all, and sure enough, the white calf came into view.

"Wait a second," Todd said at the same time Little Nick stopped pressing on the gas pedal. The side-by-side engine growl got reduced to a rumble, and the two of them simply stared at the little animal.

He certainly wasn't little, but he wasn't a great big beef cow either. He wasn't a bull.

"That's not a cow," Little Nick said. "Look at his neck."

"That's…a bison," Todd said, and he looked from the white calf to the cowboy beside him. "What—?"

"There are bison here," Little Nick said, though he wore wonder on his face too.

"It's a beefalo," Todd said, and he twisted his hips to get out of the vehicle. He hopped a couple of steps to grab his crutch, and then he started toward the beefalo.

"Boss," Little Nick jogged up beside him. "I'm gonna get in so much trouble for letting you out of the side-by-side."

"*Letting* me out?" Todd scoffed and shook his head. "With who? Sierra?"

"Your mama," Little Nick said, counting on his fingers. "Blake. Adam. Jesse. Yes, Sierra. Laura. Kyle. I promised them all you could ride along—and that was all."

Todd slowed his step while keeping one eye on the beefalo. "You promised them all?" He swung his gaze to Little Nick now. "My ankle is almost better. I'm not an invalid."

"If you step on a clod wrong, you twist it," he said. Worry rode in his eyes now. "They'll blame me. Please, go back. I'll get the beefalo and you can look at it from there."

Cows didn't normally approach the side-by-side. The noise of it annoyed them, and while they weren't the smartest animals in the world, they knew enough to get out of the way of moving things. Usually.

Standing there, he realized that Little Nick had killed the engine on the side-by-side. He could get the beefalo and bring it right up to Todd. He didn't want to be in the cast or a boot any longer than he had to. He turned around, irritation scratching its way through his veins.

"Fine," he barked.

"Thank you." Little Nick did seem relieved, and he jogged in the direction of the white calf while Todd returned to the side-by-side. A minute or two later, he led the beast toward Todd. The big, black mama cow sure didn't seem to like that he'd looped a rope around her baby's neck and was taking him away from her.

She lowed and clopped after Little Nick, pure urgency in her gait and the sound of her voice. "It's all right, Mama," Little Nick kept saying. He approached Todd with a big smile on his face. "I don't think we knew this calf had been born."

They didn't always know until they completed the tagging. Even then, sometimes they'd find one or two babies who'd been hiding in the fields somehow that they'd missed. "I don't see how we could've," Todd said, marveling at the white calf.

The Native Americans held the white buffalo up as a religious symbol, but this wasn't a buffalo. He also had no idea how the mama cow had gotten pregnant by a bison. To his knowledge, there weren't free-range bison around here. Farms of them further west, sure. Just bison wandering free? No.

Little Nick led the beefalo around to his side of the vehicle, and he reached out to pat it. He'd already tagged its ear, and he sort of expected to find the pink eyes of an albino animal. The beefalo had blue eyes.

"Leucism," he said. The beefalo was shaggier than their cattle, and his fur was definitely the color of pure snow. Todd wondered how long that would last, and if he'd start to color as he grew older. He also had no idea what to do with a beefalo. Market Day wasn't for another nine months, and he supposed he could deal with it then.

"He's tagged," Little Nick said. "You wanna take a picture of him?"

"Definitely," Todd said. He dug out his phone and snapped a picture, then sent it to everyone on the ranch, the animal's bright blue eyes obvious for all to see. "Adam will love this."

"It'll be a whole class by evening," Little Nick joked, but it would probably come true. He released the beefalo much to the mama's relief, then swung back behind the wheel, and got the engine growling again.

Before they'd made it back to the road, Todd's phone rang. Adam. "Howdy," he said.

"We can do a demo class on breeding with that beefa-lo," he said. No hello. Of course not. Adam rarely used words he didn't have to, like *hello, good-bye, thank you,* or *please.*

"Is this Adam?" Todd joked. "Or Jesse?" His call-waiting sounded, and he pulled his phone from his ear as Adam said, "Ha ha. Funny."

Jesse was calling, and that did make Todd start to laugh out loud. He put his phone back to his ear and said, "Jesse's calling. Why don't you two put your heads together for the class, and then talk to me when it concerns me?"

"Great idea," Adam said dryly. He didn't say he'd talk to Jesse though.

"What's goin' on with you two?"

"Nothing," Adam said.

"Right, because that sounds believable." Todd didn't really need to be involved in the drama. If it was anything, it would be Starla and Jesse's relationship, which had apparently stirred up a hornet's nest with Adam instead of Nash.

"He just…he's annoying me lately. That's all."

"Starla?"

Adam said nothing, but Todd could imagine the way his jaw jumped. That jaw muscle always said yes when it pulsed beneath his skin.

"I'm dating," he said. "That doesn't irritate you. Why does Jesse dating bother you?"

"Everything bothers me," Adam said. "Okay? You dating. Him dating. Blasted Blake and Gina kissing all over the lodge. It's disgusting."

Todd put his teeth together and kept his mouth closed. Adam just needed to vent, and then maybe he could let go of this anger.

"None of you get it, either," he said. "Which is fine. I know you don't know, and I just don't want anyone to go through what I did. You know what? Jesse out of anyone should know. He's been married before, and he should *know*."

Todd didn't want to tell Adam—again—that not every woman was his ex-wife. Or Jesse's ex-wife. That there were good women out there, and that Adam should maybe try again. It wouldn't do any good, and Adam wasn't in the frame of mind to listen anyway.

He continued to yell for another moment, and then he quieted.

"I'm sorry," Todd said.

"I know this is my problem," Adam said.

"You have a right to feel the way you feel," Todd said. "I'm sorry Blake and Gina are being disgusting." He could say something to their oldest brother. Blake wouldn't make Adam feel bad on purpose.

"Don't say anything to him," Adam said with a sigh. "It's not his fault."

"I don't like it when you hurt." He turned away from Little Nick as he said it, because he didn't need all the cowboys gossiping about Adam behind his back. The whine from the side-by-side should drown out his voice for the most part.

"I need a break," Adam admitted.

"Then take one. Remember when you forbade Laura from working for a couple of days?"

His brother scoffed. "I didn't forbid her. Come on."

"She needed a break too," Todd said. "If you need a break, Adam, take one."

"There's a lot going on right now with this new horse, and several new ideas Jesse and I have been working on."

"Yeah, and Jesse is bothering you. So take a step back. Go hiking. Go camping. Get outside and leave us all behind."

Adam didn't immediately respond, and the ranch buildings came into view as Little Nick turned the corner.

"Next weekend," Todd said. "Laura will be gone to visit her parents, and I'll go with you. I could use a break too."

"Yeah?" Adam's voice held hope. "You? From what? Sitting in that air-conditioned office of yours?"

"Hey," Todd said, his chest stinging. Then Adam started to laugh, and Todd smiled too.

"I'm not going to tell you you can't come," Adam said. "Plus, if you do, I bet I can get Daddy to let us take the Airstream."

Todd chuckled to himself. "Talk to him, and let me know."

"Deal." Adam hung up, and Todd once again enjoyed the sunshine on his face. He had plenty of messages to check, and he should probably call Jesse back and warn him about Adam's current state of mind. They lived together, though, so Jesse probably already knew.

Someone pushed up onto the bottom rung of the fence where they kept the horses to graze, and all the messages, calls, and moods around the Longhorn Ranch simply disappeared. Laura grinned at him as he approached, and he said, "Let me out here, Nick."

Little Nick did, and Todd crutched himself over to her. The fence separated them, but her face held light and hope. "Will you show me the beefalo?" she asked, her joy contagious. "I want to check him out."

Todd leaned toward her and kissed her, and if there was anything better than kissing Laura in the country sunshine, he didn't want to know about it. "Sure," he said throatily. "You'll have to drive us though."

She adjusted his collar, her eyes suddenly down there. "Don't you have a crop rotation meeting in a few minutes?"

"They can wait," he said. He wanted to spend time with her, and if that meant he had to push back a meeting thirty minutes, he'd do it. He told himself over and over again that it was too early to tell her he loved her, and he swallowed those words for now.

He just wanted more time with her. Time for them to have their adventures and experiences together—starting with the white beefalo.

CHAPTER
NINETEEN

Kyle looped his tie over itself and pulled the knot tight. It was pale pink for the holiday, and he hated it. He wasn't a man who wore pink. Todd had told him not to wear it if he didn't like it; he was wearing a navy blue and silver tie with a short-sleeved white shirt and a pair of navy slacks.

Kyle wasn't sure why they had to wear Sunday clothes at all, but the restaurant Maddy had suggested in Canyon Lake seemed like a place that required slacks and ties. He and Todd had committed to it, but he hated his tie. He hated these pants. The pockets didn't lay right on the front, and his nerves made him frown.

"This is stupid," he said to himself. He stepped out of the slacks and pulled the tie off. He opened the closet and got out a pair of clean jeans. Instantly, he felt more like himself. He tucked in his shirt and got a different tie from his drawer. The green and white paisley looked fine with his boots and he got down the dress hat he'd worn when he'd toured with That Little Texas Band.

He'd opened for them for a solid year, and he still hadn't been able to get his own record label. Now, he was glad he didn't have that life. Then, he'd been devastated and embarrassed to return to small-town Chestnut Springs as a country artist who couldn't hack it.

He'd lost so much in that time of his life, including the woman he'd asked to marry him. Apparently, their love was contingent on him becoming super-rich and famous, but only Maggie had known that.

He pushed his ex-girlfriend—fiancée—from his mind and seated the hat on his head. It was easily the most expensive piece of clothing he owned, and it made the whole outfit seem better than it was.

"You're wearin' jeans?" Todd asked as Kyle walked into the kitchen. "I want to wear jeans."

"Then go put on jeans," Kyle said as he opened the fridge. "I didn't feel like myself in the slacks."

"I'm going to make you look bad in these," Todd said, but Kyle knew that was just a secondary excuse for his brother to go change too.

"Hurry up. Your girlfriend is expecting us." Then they had to drive all the way to Dripping Springs, and then back to Canyon Lake. He'd been down to Dripping Springs exactly once since New Year's Eve, and the date he'd taken Maddy on hadn't been fantastic.

It sort of had. He wasn't sure, and Kyle hated that he didn't know how things stood between them. They still talked every day, either on the phone or via text, and she'd readily accepted the dinner invitation for tonight. She seemed excited about it, and Kyle told himself to get out of the fridge and face his fears.

Todd hurried as fast as his crutch would allow as he went back down the hall to his room, and he returned five minutes later in a pair of jeans, one cowboy boot on his good foot. Kyle beamed at him. "We look great."

"Anyone would be lucky to go out with us," Todd said. They laughed, and Kyle led the way outside. He was driving tonight, as Todd still couldn't. He'd chauffer him and Laura to Dripping Springs, because once Todd had Laura with him, he'd want to sit right beside her.

Kyle drove over to her cabin, which had pink lights shining on the porch, and he checked his phone while Todd went to the door and picked up his date. As the two of them got in the back, he texted Maddy that he was on the way. Laura wore a dress, but it didn't have sequins or anything too fancy. Perfect for a date with a jeans-wearing cowboy.

Fifty-five minutes later, Kyle needed to get out of the truck or risk saying something he'd regret. Todd and Laura —whom he'd always liked—were seriously nauseating. Laughing and giggling and talking in whispers.

Just *nauseating* in how much they liked each other. Kyle had never noticed it before, but being stuck with them in a vehicle for the past hour had really thrown a microscope on them. He didn't need to be looking that close, and he practically jumped from the truck before it had come to a complete stop.

Maddy lived in a cute, mint green house on a lane filled

with other equally as charming homes. It wasn't a terribly big place, but her grass had started to come in green, and she'd hung some hearts on her front door.

He knocked, as she didn't have a doorbell, and her voice met his ears from inside. "Just a second!"

She took far longer than a second to open the door, and Kyle wiped his palms down his thighs a couple of times and kept telling himself to calm down. Just calm down. He didn't like this long-distance dating, he knew that. He wanted to see Maddy's face when they talked so he could judge her reaction and hear her voice.

It was too hard to tell if she was flirting or not with only words on his phone. He'd suggested video calling, and they'd done it a few times. Kyle simply wanted more. In every way, he wanted more out of this relationship. More face-to-face time with her. More experiences together. More drives to Dripping Springs to see her, touch her, maybe even kiss her.

He held no objectives for tonight other than to make sure she was still interested in him. After that first date… He just needed to see her to know.

The door finally opened, and he looked up from where he'd been studying the tips of his cowboy boots. Why, he had no idea.

His eyes traveled the height of Maddy's body, and she wore a little black dress that brushed the tops of her knees, hugged her curves and had sleeves down to her elbows. On her petite frame, it looked like it had been sewn just for her, and it also didn't have frills or whistles that would make her stand out among the four of them.

Kyle couldn't help the exhale that came out of his mouth. He had no idea how long he'd been holding his breath, and his body had to take control of some things. "You are a sight for sore eyes," he said, his gaze finally landing on and latching onto hers.

She smiled, her lips pink and glossy and making Kyle wonder what flavor he'd get in his mouth if he tasted them. His thoughts made him hotter than he already was, and he reached for her. "Just wow. I'm the luckiest man in Texas tonight."

"Oh, you." She giggled and stepped out onto her porch. Her border collie came with her, just like last time, and she said, "No, Brewster. You're not coming. Go sit with David. Go on."

From inside, a man called, "Come on, Brew. Let mama go on her date."

Kyle's confusion filled him from scalp to sole. "Who's David?"

"My brother," she said, and Maddy looked up at him. She put one hand on his chest. "It's so good to see you."

Kyle didn't back up or turn to head to the truck. "Is it?" he whispered.

"Yes." Maddy's smile slipped. "You didn't think I'd be happy to see you?"

"I think it's been a long time," he said.

"I know." She looked down at her hand as if studying her nails. "It's my fault."

"Why's that?"

"I said I'd come up to Chestnut Springs, and I didn't."

"Why didn't you?" Kyle wasn't sure why he needed all

of these answers right now. Shouldn't he wait until after the date? What if she decided she didn't want to go out with him because of this conversation?

"I got a little scared," she said.

"The first date wasn't too amazing," he admitted. "I know that."

"It's not that." She moved over to the railing on her porch and looked out at the front yard. "I don't like the long-distance dating. I did it once, and it…ended badly. So I got a little too far inside my head."

Kyle joined her, easily sliding his hand along her waist. "I don't like it either."

She looked up at him. "I don't know how to fix it, other than to not see you."

"I wasn't sure you wanted to see me," he said.

"I do."

"Then maybe we both just need to make a better commitment to do that."

The same brightness he'd seen in her eyes on New Year's Eve filled her face now. "I will if you will."

"I'm in," he said, something big and wide filling his soul. It was his slow time on the ranch right now, and Dripping Springs was less than an hour from the lodge. "What about a picnic tomorrow? My ranch? Your backyard?"

She giggled and ducked her head, her pretty blonde hair falling like a curtain between them. She'd added a wave to it, and based on what she'd said via text, he expected it to be back to stick-straight by the time he dropped her off tonight.

"Your ranch," she said. "And I'll bring the food." Her eyes sparkled when she looked at him again. That hand came back to his chest, her touch light and feminine and sending sparks straight to all his hormones. "I'm sorry I canceled last time."

"Let's just pretend like tonight's our first date," he said, taking her hand in his. He lifted it to his lips and kissed the back of it. "All right? Last time was just a bit stilted, that's all."

"I was nervous."

He led her down the steps, asking, "Why?"

"I looked you up, Mister Stewart. You're a famous musician."

Kyle sent laughter straight up into the sky, and that meant this date was already ten times better than the last one. "I am not."

"You toured with That Little Texas Band for a year," she said. "You're talented, and handsome, and I was nervous. Anyone would be nervous."

He looked at her as she came down the last step and joined him at his side. "I was nervous too."

"Of me?"

He swallowed and thought of what she'd said about her previous long-distance dating experience. "I had a pretty bad break-up a few years ago, and this is my first try back on the horse."

Maddy's eyes widened. "Really?"

"I don't mean you're a horse, I just mean...I haven't dated in a while." A good long while. Years. She said nothing, and Kyle took her to the passenger side, helped her into the truck, and then got behind the wheel.

"Everyone," he said. "This is Maddy Cruise." He smiled at her. "Maddy, this is one of my older brothers, Todd, and his girlfriend, Laura."

"You came to the New Year's Eve concert," Laura said. "I recognize you."

"My brother is the lead singer in Fiddles and Fellas," she said, tucking her hair behind her ear. Kyle glimpsed her hearing aids there, and they made him smile.

"Do you play anything?" Todd asked, and Kyle met his eye in the rear view mirror. So much was said, and while he appreciated his brother checking up on him, Kyle had done his own homework.

"I'm pretty sure I'm tone-deaf," Maddy said with a laugh. "In fact, I was born deaf, so no. I don't do anything musically."

"You were born deaf?" Kyle asked.

"Wholly in my left ear," she said as she buckled her seatbelt. "Ninety percent in my right. I've had these cochlear implants for many years." She beamed at him, and Kyle couldn't help smiling back. He was okay to take things slowly with Maddy, as long as he knew she wanted to go along for the ride. Judging by their brief conversation on her porch, and the way she'd dressed and dolled up for tonight's date, she did.

"All right," Todd said, breaking the staring spell Kyle had fallen under. "We better get goin'. You two spent forever on the porch, and our reservation is ticking closer and closer."

Laura giggled and added, "He almost blew the horn at you. You owe me that he didn't."

Kyle backed out of the driveway, once again meeting Todd's eyes. "You almost hit the horn? What kind of brother are you?"

Todd only laughed, and like music from heaven above, Maddy did too. Kyle wanted to reach over and hold her hand the way he had at the concert. With Todd and Laura in the back seat, he didn't. Of course, they were practically sitting on top of one another, but his relationship with Maddy was still new. Very new.

Possibilities stretched before him, and Kyle listened to his heart as he drove to The Vine, an Italian restaurant on the main road leading into Canyon Lake. It beat heartily, telling him how healthy it was. He could get into another relationship now, and just…see.

Yeah, he'd just see where this went, one step at a time.

CHAPTER
TWENTY

Starla Masters went into her office just inside the back door of the lodge and pushed the door closed behind her. She twisted the lock and pulled the cord on the blinds to make it so no one could see inside. The morning breakfast rush had finished, and now her cooks were cleaning up from that, assembling the to-go lunches, and prepping for dinner.

She'd be gone by then, and the night kitchen manager would handle everything for tonight's dinner service. She sighed as she sank into her desk chair and turned to her right so she could see outside.

The shade from the barn cast a shadow over her window, but the natural light still boosted her mood. So many thoughts ran through her mind. They felt like a jumble of necklaces which had all been tangled into tiny, tight metal knots she couldn't undo.

She'd been plucking at them for weeks, and just when

she thought she'd found a way to get everything to unravel, it would simply pull tighter.

Her professional life only added to the knot, and that was something she'd not anticipated. It had been her personal life that had kept her awake for the past several months, but with the introduction of a single email, Starla's whole world had started to shift.

I'm opening a new restaurant in Austin, and I want you to be the head chef.

She could still see the email subject line in her head. It seemed burned into the backs of her eyes. She'd stared at it for quite a long time before she'd even opened it, at which point Mason Colledge had gone on to explain more details of the job.

Starla would be a fool not to consider it. Consider it, she had. All day yesterday and the day before that. Now today too.

She needed to respond, and she took a seat in front of her computer at the Longhorn Lodge, feeling a bit of guilt tug through her. Using her work computer to talk about another job almost felt like cheating.

Ignoring her work email account, Starla logged into her personal one. The email was still there, so it wasn't a prank. Mason was a good-natured guy, and they'd gone to culinary school together for a couple of years. She thought of Gina and how she'd take the news.

Blake would not be happy, as he'd really struggled to find a qualified pastry chef to work here, and if she left, he'd need to find a brand new kitchen manager.

"Don't feel bad," she whispered to herself. People

moved and changed jobs all the time. She'd been at the Texas Longhorn Ranch for just over three years now, and she didn't really feel an itch to leave.

She'd simply be a fool if she didn't at least find out more about the job. That was all.

Mason had said she could email back or call, and Starla preferred the direct approach. That had been one of the most maddening things about the past few months with her and Nash. Or her and Jesse. The three of them.

Jesse Stewart's handsome face filled her mind, and Starla let her eyes drift closed. He sure did seem to like her, and she'd be lying if she said she didn't like him. He made her feel warm with a single look, but there had always been something between them, holding them back.

She thought for a while it was him. Then Nash. Then her. Since they'd gotten back together over New Year's Eve, Starla had pushed away the thoughts that all wasn't well with them. She wasn't sure why she felt like that in the first place.

After dialing Mason's number, she leaned back in her office chair and sighed. "Please let this go well," she prayed under her breath. She wasn't even sure what "this" was, but she knew she wanted to do the right thing at the right time.

Jesse had broken up with her last summer, citing that the time wasn't right. To her, it still didn't quite feel right.

"Mason Colledge," Mason said, his voice crisp and that of a tenor.

Her eyes popped open. A smile crossed her face. "Mason," she said. "It's Starla Masters."

A pause came through the line. Then he started to laugh. "Miss Starla," he drawled. "You know how to drive a man insane."

They laughed together, after which she said, "I was thinking about the email."

"I've never known you to take your time with decision-making."

"I'm a decade older now," she quipped back. "With a good job I happen to like."

"I see." He paused again, and she could just imagine him with his thinking face on. "I suppose I'll have to make this my most enticing pitch yet."

"Before you do," Starla said. "You should know I haven't spent any time in a commercial kitchen in about four years now."

"Another surprise," he said, his smile evident in his tone. "Where you at?"

"The Texas Longhorn Ranch." She noted the pride in her voice. "I'm the kitchen manager. I design the menu, do all the ordering, some of the cooking is all. I do more admin stuff than chef stuff."

"How many chefs are you over there?"

"Six," she said. "Good people too."

"Poaching ability?"

Starla shook her head, her mouth set. "I'm not taking anyone from here," she said. "They'll already be in a right state without me."

"So you're seriously considering the job." Mason didn't phrase it as a question.

"I called you, didn't I?" Starla crossed her legs and looked out the window. She couldn't see anything but the broad side of the barn across the gravel lot, but she still smiled.

"I can go over everything on the phone," he said. "A lot was spelled out in the email. But the best thing for you to do would be to come to Austin and see what Fried Green Tomatoes is. Or could be, with you."

She chuckled, because Mason was good. Good at making her feel necessary to his restaurant's success. Good at knowing who he was talking to. She reminded herself of those things, but she heard herself saying, "When's a good time?"

———

TURNED OUT, "A GOOD TIME" FOR STARLA TO GET UP TO Austin to tour Fried Green Tomatoes and meet with Mason was the very next day. She'd spent the afternoon arranging to be gone, and she'd made the eighty-five minute drive to Austin as dusk fell last night.

She'd enjoyed some amazing brisket at a great barbecue restaurant down the street from Mason's location, which of course she'd driven past a few times. Going in both directions. She'd scoped out the parking, the signage, the curb appeal, all of it.

Starla didn't go into anything blind. Not anymore.

Her chest and stomach vibrated as she pulled into the lot the next morning, the sunshine casting a new light on everything. Mason met her before she'd even gotten out of her car, laughing and running at her with both arms spread wide.

"Mason," she said.

"Starla," came among his chuckles. "Look at you." He grabbed right onto her and held her tightly. She couldn't help smiling at such a warm reception. "Thank you so much for coming." He stepped back, and she grinned up at him. He stood just over six feet tall, with blond hair and a scruffy beard he really shouldn't be encouraging. She wasn't his mother or his girlfriend, so she said nothing about that.

His dull blue eyes shone with merriment she felt dancing through her soul. She hadn't felt like this since Gina had shown up in the kitchen about nine months ago. That had been so right. She was an amazing pastry chef, and she and Blake were perfect for each other. She'd been a great sounding board for Starla, who previous to her arrival, didn't have anyone in the kitchen she could really confide in.

Sadness hit her hard, but she swallowed against it. If this was right, she'd do it. "Show me everything," she said, and Mason indicated she should lead the way inside.

———

THAT EVENING, SHE DRAGGED HERSELF UP THE STEPS TO Jesse's cabin. She wasn't sure if the long drive had slowed her down, or if the weight tied to her heart made her feet feel like anchors. She'd texted him when she'd left Austin,

KISSING HER COWBOY BOSS

but she'd been too much of a chicken to check her phone since then.

He'd texted back, and she tugged her phone out of her pocket to check his messages.

You went to Austin? I love the city.

She wasn't sure if he was saying he would've liked to have come with her or not. She frowned, because this wasn't going to be an easy conversation as it was. Her heart leapt into the back of her throat, and she looked up only a moment before she stepped right into the closed door.

Her foot thumped against the wood, and she flinched mightily as she tried to stop her forward progress. She managed to do so, but not before she hit the door with her phone as her hands instinctively came up to protect her face.

She blinked as she came to a stop. She backed up and knocked at the same time Jesse called, "Come in, Star!"

Starla took a deep breath, reached for the knob, and entered her boyfriend's cabin. He stood in the kitchen, a piping bag in his hand. He wasn't going to make this any easier on her. It was suddenly so hard that she stopped just inside the door and watched him squeeze the perfect dollop of frosting on top of a chocolate cupcake.

"Mama baked today," he said.

"Good news." Starla swallowed her nerves. "I was trying to decide if I should ask you if you'd been in the kitchen this afternoon."

He flashed her a smile that made her pulse quicken. "Why'd you go to Austin?"

Starla turned and closed the door behind her. "Jesse," she said as she faced him again. She didn't know how to get the words out. She couldn't do it. Perhaps she could just pack up in the middle of the night and move. She wouldn't show up for work, and when someone finally noticed, they'd go to her house and find it empty.

She dismissed the idea as ridiculous. She didn't run from her problems. Not anymore. She didn't ghost people who counted on her. Not again.

"Jesse," she tried again, and he looked up from the last perfectly frosted cupcake. She must've worn some agony on her face, because he sobered and put down the piping bag.

"Bad news? Is it your mom?"

Her mind seized onto her mother as a reason she had to go to Austin. That felt cheap and dishonest, because it was both. She shook her head. "Jesse," she said for a third time. "I got another job offer in Austin. This really great Southern restaurant an old friend from culinary school is opening in a couple of months."

With the words finally moving across her vocal cords and out of her mouth, Starla didn't feel so blocked. She reached for Jesse's hands and took both of his in both of hers.

"I'm going to take the job, Jess. I'm moving to Austin at the end of March."

CHAPTER
TWENTY-ONE

L aura drove through the gate announcing the property line of the Texas Longhorn Ranch, the news of Starla leaving still ringing in her ears. Nash, the morning manager at the lodge, had stood up during breakfast only a half-hour ago and made the announcement.

Starla had tears in her eyes, but not a single one had slid down her face. She'd stood with Gina, Ashley, and the rest of the kitchen chefs and staff, and she'd smiled and hugged everyone who'd come up to wish her well.

She wasn't leaving for six or seven more weeks, but Laura had seen the stress on Blake's face as he and a few of his siblings—Jesse, Todd, and Holly to be precise—had gone down the hall toward the offices in the back of the lodge.

Starla ran everything food-related at the ranch. Losing

her was a great big blow, and Laura's hands tightened on the steering wheel. Todd had acted like he'd needed a vet pretty desperately last year when he'd hired her too, and she didn't want to leave the ranch—or him—high and dry.

Her own eyes filled with tears, but Laura kept her foot pressed on the gas. She had to make her own decisions. She had to live her own life. If there was anything she'd learned from what she'd endured with Hans, it was that.

He'd promised her forever, but no one could promise that. Not even her.

Her chest ached, and her stomach swooped. She kept driving, though. She had to know what was out there in Hidden Hollow for her. She'd once thought her whole life would be contained in the small town where she'd grown up. She'd wanted that more than anything. When she'd lost it, she had felt like she'd lost part of her identity.

Therefore, she had to find out if this veterinary clinic was a viable option for her.

The drive passed quickly, and Laura went right past the turn she normally took to get to her parents' farm and house. She'd sleep there tonight, visit with them tomorrow, help Eddie with a couple of things around the farm, and then drive back to Chestnut Springs on Sunday night.

In all, she'd only be gone from the ranch for three days. She wasn't sure why it felt so much longer than that. The weather had started to warm, and Laura turned her face into the sun as she flipped on her blinker to make a turn. Just down the road and around a little jog, she'd come to the veterinary office. Doc Lewiston owned a lot of land out here, and he'd set up his practice here, a bit away from town, so people could board their dogs and their horses while they were out of town, but also so he had room to observe the ill animals brought to him.

He'd sent her a map of the property, as it didn't all come with the veterinary practice. He lived in town with his wife, their kids all grown and gone now, but he wanted to keep some of the land out here though he didn't use it for anything.

She waited for the truck coming toward her to go by, then she turned and continued on her way. The veterinary office came into view the moment she rounded the corner, and Laura took a deep breath, focusing on the way it felt entering her nose, her throat, and her lungs.

She hadn't dared pray for any guidance or help yet. She honestly didn't know if this was an opportunity for her or not, and she wouldn't until after today.

The parking lot held four or five trucks, and her little sedan stuck out among the bigger vehicles. She pulled up beside a big blue truck and got out, squared her shoulders, and headed for the door.

Only one step inside, the bell still ringing in the air, a man said, "There she is." Their eyes met, and relief sagged through Laura at the sight of Doc Lewiston. He was a little grayer, and a little slower coming around the counter to embrace her. But he was still a comforting sight, what with his smile, his big, round eyes, and his calm demeanor. "How was the drive?" he asked.

"Just fine." She stepped away from him and ran her

hands down the front of her jeans. "Doesn't look too busy today." Three dogs came around the counter too, the trio clearly belonging to Doc Lewiston. That, or they were his favorites and got to roam the clinic.

"Closed to booked appointments today," he said. "We only do boarding on Fridays, so we can get caught up on appointments, handle surgeries, emergencies, and paperwork."

She nodded, because Laura had no idea what it took to run a veterinary office the size of this one.

"Doc." Another man pushed through a swinging door that led further into the building. He spied Laura and looked from her to Doc Lewiston. "Sorry, but if you've got a minute, I need you to come look at this llama."

Laura's curiosity soared, and she stood still while Doc Lewiston turned. "Come on, Doctor Woodcross," he said. "Let's go see what awaits." He threw her a kind smile from over his shoulder, and thrilled, she hurried to follow him.

"This is Whitney Carpenter. Doctor Whit, we call him. He's one of the managing partners moving forward." Doc Lewiston stopped in front of him. "Whit, this is Laura Woodcross, the third vet I'm hoping to bring on to work with you and Cory."

"Oh, splendid," he said, and he clearly wasn't from Texas. He did possess a nice smile and a genuine air about him, and he stuck out his hand for her to shake. "It's wonderful to meet you."

"You too," Laura said. She meant it, and she followed the other two vets into the back room. Dog and cat kennels took up the first room, with various doors leading off to her right into individual rooms where she knew Doc Lewiston did his appointments. She'd interned here with him for four months, and she'd assisted on surgeries, helped clients at the front desk, handled some of that paperwork he'd spoken of, and anything else required of her.

Today, though, they went through the room and out the back door. She entered a fenced-off path, with individual "rooms" for the animals going through gates on the right and left-hand side. The llama in question stood in the middle of the first paddock on the right, another vet out there with him.

He looked over his shoulder at the sound of their arrival, and then went back to bending over as he peered at the llama's shoulder. Laura could only guess what was happening with it—injury? Insects in the wool or skin?— and she entered the paddock last.

After making sure the gate was securely latched behind her, she followed the others toward the llama. His wool was probably white up against his skin, but as grown out as it was, it held gray and yellow qualities instead. He could use a good bath, and he didn't seem excited to have three more adults coming his way.

Doc Lewiston and Doc Whit kept going, but Laura slowed her steps. "I can't tell what it is," Cory said.

"Cory," Doc Lewiston said. "This is Laura Woodcross. She's the potential third vet for the Hidden Hollow practice."

The man's face lit up, and he stepped away from the llama. "Of course. Nice to meet you." He pumped her hand with both of his, and Laura couldn't help returning his smile. He exuded charm and happiness, and while he carried a few extra pounds, he had a lot of dark hair and a quick smile. He wore glasses and gray around his temples, as well as a gold wedding band on his left ring fingers.

Laura liked him—she liked Whit too—and she went around to the other side of the llama. "Does he have a name?"

"This here is Lois," Doc Lewiston said. The llama spat, and Laura grinned at her. She reached out and put her hand on Lois's left side while Doc Lewiston and the other vets took a peek at her right.

"It almost looks like a nail," Cory said. "I just can't make sense of it."

"Gerald said it was a splinter," Whit said.

"I got the splinter out," Cory said. "This is far more than that." He looked at Doc Lewiston, who also bent down to get a closer look. The tension between the four of them and the llama increased. Laura could practically hear the questions over whether this llama had been abused or not. There was a difference between an animal rubbing up against a barn or a feeding trough and getting a splinter or having a human drive a nail into her shoulder.

"I think..." Doc Lewiston reached out and touched Lois, who did not appreciate that. She made a warning cry, which sounded halfway like a horse neighing, old man laughter, and then some hums on the end. She danced away from Doc Lewiston, and Laura's heart went out to the creature.

She settled several feet away, no weight on her right

front leg, and started moaning. That was really a warning, and Laura put herself between the llama and the other vets. "Lois," she said in a calming voice. She arced away from the llama, going left so she could see the shoulder. It was bloody and a bit ragged, so no wonder she hadn't been happy to be touched there.

Laura approached slowly, everyone else silent. She wasn't sure what came over her in moments like this. She simply knew calm, and she was able to approach Lois. "Let me look, okay? I won't touch it."

She pulled out her phone and turned on the flashlight though the sun shone down from overhead. The produced light, however, gave off a different quality and it highlighted different things.

"Oh, it's a nail, my friend," she said, probably loud enough for the other vets to hear. "The light is shining on it." She looked up at the llama. "How did this happen?" She stroked her hand down the llama's neck, feeling it tremble beneath her touch.

She turned back to the other vets. "I think it needs stitches. The cut is jagged from where it went in."

"It's a nail, though?" Whit asked.

"Yeah," Laura turned back to the wound. "From the angle of it…" Pieces clicked together in her head. "You know what? It was attached to the splinter Cory already took out." Her mind filled with light, and she faced them again. "It doesn't look like abuse to me. It looks like this little lady llama here was rubbing up against something, and a piece of wood broke off, went into her shoulder, nail and all."

"I've got the other foreign object here," Cory said, and Laura rejoined them to look at it.

Doc Lewiston pointed to the hole where a nail clearly would've gone. "I think Laura is right." He smiled at her. "Do you want to do the stitches?"

"Yes, sir," she said, because it would help Lois feel better. She stayed with the llama while the others went to prepare the utensils and medical kit, and once they had Lois sedated, Whit and Cory lowered her to the ground on her left side so Laura could work on the right.

They didn't speak much while she got the nail out, then sewed together everything that needed to be sewn together. Once she applied the last piece of adhesive to the bandage, then handed the roll back to Whit, she breathed out and looked around at them.

"You're a great vet," Cory said with a smile. "Are you going to come on here?"

Laura exchanged a glance with Doc Lewiston. "I don't know."

"I'm giving her the tour today," Doc said quickly. "Then we'll go over some numbers. Then she'll have to decide."

"I think you'd be great here too," Whit said, also grinning at her.

"So it's the two of you so far?" she asked.

"Yep," Whit said while Cory nodded.

"Did you two know each other before this?"

They looked at one another. "No," Whit said. "I have a practice in Michigan. Or I did. I'm moving down here."

"From Michigan? Wow." She wanted to ask more about that, but it didn't feel like the right time.

Whit kept smiling, so he obviously wasn't too keen to share the story anyway.

"I've been working as Doc's back-up vet for a couple of years now," Cory said. "I've been part-time at The Windmill for a long time, been seeing my own clients on the side, and then this."

"He's going to be here full-time once I retire," Doc said. "You all will."

"It's that busy?" Laura asked, peeling off her gloves and tossing them in the trashcan Cory had brought out. Whit stayed with Lois, and Cory started cleaning up from the procedure.

"Oh, yes," Doc Lewiston said with a chortle. "With three of you, you wouldn't have to close to appointments, and you could do ranch and farm visits every day of the week instead of here and there, as I'm able."

He gestured her back inside. "I know you're a good vet, Laura. Now they know it too." He smiled warmly at her. "So let's talk some numbers, and then we'll go see the horses."

Her heart lifted at that promise, because she loved horses, and Doc Lewiston had several she personally adored.

———

THAT EVENING, LAURA SAT IN THE CAR TO THINK. HER MAMA probably knew she'd arrived, but she hadn't come out onto the porch yet. Laura had been running since she'd opened the door at Doc's, so she hadn't had a moment to really think about what she should do. What she wanted to do. What was the right thing to do.

The curtains in the window fluttered, and Laura unbuckled her seatbelt to get out of the car. Perhaps if she talked it all out with her parents, then she'd have an answer for herself.

She also wanted to call Todd and let him know that she'd arrived safely. She'd said she'd check in with him, and every other time she'd come to visit her parents, she couldn't wait to talk to him. He'd already called her once, right about lunchtime, but she'd been knee-deep in felines at the time and hadn't been able to answer.

Besides, she wanted to get her own mind straight before she called Todd, so she collected her bag from the back seat and went inside the farmhouse. Her mother came around the corner only a few seconds later, and Laura dropped her backpack over the top of the couch and flew into her mother's arms.

"Oh, my baby," she said, smoothing down her hair. "It went that bad at Doc's?"

"No." Laura held tightly to her emotions. "It went great."

Mama stepped back, searching Laura's face for answers. Her eyes stung, but she did not cry. "That's good, right?"

"I don't know, Mama," Laura said. "I'm dating Todd, who lives an hour away. I love the job there too."

She'd love being a vet at Doc's as well. Cory and Whit

were both great, and she could easily see herself working with them. "It's expensive," she said. "I'd have to get a big loan." Big enough to buy a house with—a really big house in Texas. Maybe not huge in other places, but a big, massive, riverside one in Texas.

"It's your career," Mama said.

Laura nodded. "I can probably get the loan." The salary from the clinic would ensure she could pay it back. "I just don't know if it's the right thing to do."

Daddy came hobbling around the corner, and tears did fill Laura's eyes then. "Tell me what to do, Daddy." She moved around her mom to hug him, and he held her tight, right against his chest. He'd done this when she'd fallen and scraped her knee as a six-year-old. He'd held her when she and Hans had come to tell them the news of his diagnosis. Daddy had always hugged her close and given her reassurances.

Tonight, he simply held on and didn't say anything.

"Only you can decide," Mama said. "We'd love to have you close by—"

"Becca," Daddy said. He didn't speak harshly, but Mama clammed up.

"Come have dinner." Mama brushed by both of them. "Daddy obviously just brought in the steaks."

Laura pulled away from her father and looked up at him. She wiped her face and nodded. "I do think better after a good steak." She offered him a wobbly smile, and he gave her a full-force sunny one in return.

"Let's go see what you come up with then, baby." He led the way into the kitchen, and the three of them sat down to dinner. Laura started to lay out everything, and about halfway through, she knew what she needed to do.

She held onto the jewel of information, not ready to say it out loud yet. After dinner, she'd call Todd and talk to him. He deserved to know before anyone else.

CHAPTER
TWENTY-TWO

Todd hippity-hopped and made it into the passenger seat of Kyle's truck. He sighed as he sat down and twisted to put on his seatbelt. This morning had been emotionally exhausting already, and he really hoped Dr. Hoffman had good news for him.

Kyle got behind the wheel and looked at Todd. "Ready?"

"I guess." Todd looked out his window as his brother started the truck. The day in the Texas Hill Country had started out beautiful, and not only because there were chocolate croissants on the breakfast bar. The sunrise had reminded Todd of all the good in the world, and he'd truly felt at peace.

He'd known in those few minutes of pre-dawn that even if the podiatrist told him he had to wear his boot for another couple of weeks, he'd be able to do it. All would be okay.

"Wild about Starla leaving," Kyle said. He hadn't been rushed back to Blake's office the way Todd had. He cut him a look out of the corner of his eye, clearly fishing for more information. "Did you know about it?"

"I didn't," Todd said. "Blake did. Jesse did. Starla did. That's all. I guess she just decided earlier this week."

"Nash said she went to Austin on Tuesday."

"Blake said the same thing." Todd watched the landscape roll by out his window, finding it brown and drab but beautiful. They hadn't left the ranch yet, and he hoped Kyle wouldn't want to talk about this shift in their staffing at the ranch for the entire drive.

Todd understood the level of Blake's stress to make sure the ranch and lodge ran well. It had taken him a long time to find a vet, and that had put strain on everyone who worked with the animals. It was like this layer of the atmosphere that was all stress, even when nothing was going wrong.

Blake only had seven weeks to find a new kitchen manager, make sure they were trained and ready to go, and bring them on board at the lodge. Behind the closed door of his office, where Todd had met with Blake, Holly, and Jesse for a couple of hours immediately following the announcement that morning, Todd had suggested Blake promote from within. It would be easier to move someone who already worked in the kitchen into Starla's position than to hire outside of them.

It was a good idea; everyone in the meeting had thought so. No matter what, Blake had run his hands through his hair at least a dozen times, and that was his brother's tell of stress. He'd had a hard time finding a pastry chef, and he didn't think it would be easy to fill a vacant kitchen position either.

"Did Jesse say anything?" Kyle asked.

"Not much," Todd said. "He and Blake have known since Tuesday night. They met with Nash the next day. Announced it to all of us this morning."

"I meant about him and Starla."

Todd shook his head. "Nothing." He looked over to Kyle. "Austin is further thatn Dripping Springs. About twice as far."

"Yeah." Kyle looked out his window then, pretending, Todd knew, to check for traffic on the left.

"How are things with you and Maddy?"

"Good," Kyle said, his voice only a tiny bit pinched. "She's comin' up here tonight, actually. After she's done teaching." He flashed Todd a smile. "I guess she has a cousin or something in the area, and she's going to stay with her out in Green River."

"That's not a bad drive," Todd said.

"She's comin' to breakfast at the lodge tomorrow morning." Kyle's fingers on the wheel released and then gripped again.

"Why are you nervous about that?"

Kyle took a moment to answer. "I honestly don't know." He blew out his breath, a chuckle coming with it. "She makes me nervous." He glanced at Todd again, who gave him a smile.

"The more you get to know her, the less nervous you'll be." He looked down at his phone as an alarm went off. He silenced it as he and Kyle were already on the way to the doctor. "I liked her. She seems real nice, and you two look good together."

"Todd." Kyle rolled his eyes.

"Sorry." Todd had forgotten that Kyle didn't want the way he looked with a woman to be a factor in whether they should be together or not. He cleared his throat. "Laura's gone for the weekend, so I'll find out if Mama and Daddy can stand to have me loitering on their couch. Then I won't be in your way."

"You're not going to be in my way," Kyle said. "We're takin' the ATVs out after breakfast. Then Jesse and Gina are doing a caramel tasting. You want to go to that, don't you?"

"Oh, right," Todd said. "Yeah, I want to go to that."

"I'll come get you after Maddy and I get back. It's not until eleven-thirty."

Todd nodded, grateful for his brother. "I'll grab a lunch and take a nap in the afternoon."

"I'm taking Maddy to The Salty Peanut for lunch," Kyle said. "Then, we're going over to the apple orchards for the afternoon. I guess she looked up some cider demo they're doing."

"Wow, so your day is full."

"Now you know why I'm so nervous. It's like five days in a single day."

Todd grinned at him. "That's because you won't see her again for another week. You've got to do five days' worth of stuff in one day."

Kyle didn't look happy about that, but he nodded.

"Her cousin is making dinner for us. So I'm meeting her too. It just…" He exhaled again. "It feels like a lot."

"It is a lot," Todd said. "I haven't met anyone in Laura's family."

Kyle's gaze landed on the side of his face, but Todd suddenly didn't want to look at him. "You could've gone with her this weekend."

Todd swallowed his retort. It wouldn't do any good to snap at Kyle. "She didn't invite me," he finally said.

"Maybe you should invite yourself."

"Maybe I'll figure out my own relationship and you can figure out yours." Todd gave Kyle a pointed look, and Kyle only nodded, his laughter coming quickly afterward.

Todd relaxed, and several minutes later, they arrived at the podiatrist's office. He used his crutch to get inside, and his nerves only grew as the minutes passed. He and Kyle sat shoulder-to-shoulder in the room, waiting for Dr. Hoffman to enter. He hated sitting on the exam table before he had to, and today, a nurse came in and asked him to go with him for an x-ray.

He went down the hall with the man. Held still in the machine. Did all he needed to do. It felt like the clock was moving backward, and with every second he had to live over again, Todd felt a scream gathering in his soul.

Finally, Dr. Hoffman entered, and he carried an x-ray film with him. "Howdy, Todd." He flipped on the light on the box on the wall and stuck the film to it. "Come see."

Todd got up, glad when Kyle came with him. Dr. Hoffman sure seemed smiley today, and he pointed to the bones in the image. "See anything?"

Todd leaned into his crutch and leaned closer to the lightbox. "No, sir."

"That boot can come off," Dr. Hoffman said.

Todd blinked and looked at him. "Really?"

The doctor started to chuckle. "Really. Right now. Hop up on the bed, and I'm going to look at it."

Todd did what the doctor said, and the relief he felt when the boot was released couldn't be described. He'd known today was going to be a great day. There had been something floating in the dawn sunshine he'd been able to sense.

The temporary cast got removed, and Todd stared at his foot like it didn't belong to him. Dr. Hoffman started pressing on it and asking questions. Todd answered them, and then the doctor declared he could walk without the cast, the boot, or the crutch.

"Now, if you have any pain at all, you get your weight off it," he said. "Use the crutch. Come in and see me again. We don't want to re-injure it."

"No, sir," Todd said.

Dr. Hoffman grinned at him, shook his hand, and said, "Thanks for taking good care of yourself, Todd."

He didn't know what to say to that, so he simply nodded. Outside in the truck, he couldn't contain himself. He couldn't stop smiling, and he quickly put a message on the ranch text string so everyone would know he was out of the boot and cast.

"Can I call Laura?" he asked.

"Sure," Kyle said.

He did, his pulse picking up speed with every ring of

the line. She didn't answer, which took some of the wind out of his sails. He didn't bother with a message. She'd call when she could, and he couldn't wait to hear her voice.

"Can we get lunch?" he asked, knowing Kyle would never say no to lunch. "Crisp's. My treat."

"Your treat? I'm in." They laughed together, because Kyle certainly didn't hurt for money and didn't need Todd to buy his lunch.

———

AN HOUR LATER, HE ASKED FOR A CUP OF COFFEE AS THE waiter took his empty plate. There was something unique about the roast beef sandwiches here, and he'd eaten every last bite.

"Hey, it's Eli Baker," Kyle said, nodding past Todd and toward the door.

He twisted in that direction, glad to see another rancher from out their way. "Howdy," he said, sliding out of the booth and moving to intercept Eli and the other man he was with. Todd didn't know him, but he and Eli had worked together a lot. He owned Horse Haven, a part-cattle ranch and part-horse boarding stable about five miles from the Texas Longhorn Ranch. He'd bought and sold hay from and to Eli for years.

"How are you?"

"Good, good." Eli laughed and shook Todd's hand. "This here's Abram. He's my new foreman."

"Fantastic," Todd said, reaching to shake the other man's hand too. He had hair as dark as night, but a quick smile with straight teeth. He wasn't nearly as tall as Todd, or even Eli, but he seemed stocky and strong. "I'm glad you found someone good."

"It's not easy," Eli said, his smile fading. "I heard you might have to look for another vet soon."

Todd's eyebrows practically flew off his face. "What?" Many more questions streamed through his mind, but he didn't need to blurt them all out in rapid succession right now. He glanced over to Abram.

"Abram's from down south a bit." Eli looked at the other man. "Round about Willow Creek, which is close enough to Hidden Hollow."

"Okay," Todd said, still not connecting the dots.

"Word out there is that the only veterinarian for those small towns and ranches is retiring, but he's bringing in three vets to take his place. Laura's name was mentioned."

Todd started shaking his head as the puzzle came together. "Right, she knows about it. But she's not interested in the job." At least she hadn't told him she was. New doubts bloomed in his mind and flew in circles, making him slow and confused.

"Ah, I see." Eli shook his hand again, his good-natured smile back in place. "Good news for both of us then."

"Yeah." Todd turned and watched the two men go past him and Kyle and on to another booth. He sat back down, but it was really more like his legs gave out on him.

"You okay?" Kyle asked. "What's this about a job in Hidden Hollow?"

Their coffee arrived, and Todd could only stare at it.

Even Kyle didn't start doctoring up his with cream and sugar the way he usually did.

Todd finally lifted his eyes to meet Kyle's. "I don't know what it's about. There is a vet down there retiring. Laura told me her mama had mentioned it."

Kyle did reach for his spoon then, and he stirred a heaping spoonful of sugar into his mug. "Maybe she's down there finding out more about it this weekend." He spoke in a sort of forced-casual way that made the hair on Todd's neck stand straight up.

He couldn't look away from Kyle, and they had several conversations in only a few moments. Finally, Todd said, "No." He shook his head. "No, she'd tell me if she was going to talk to another vet about another job."

Kyle said nothing, and all Todd could think about was Starla going to Austin on Tuesday…and not mentioning it to Jesse until she was already back, with a new job in-hand.

No, he told himself again. *Laura wouldn't do that to me.* She knew how hard it had been for him to hire her in the first place. She loved the ranch; she'd told him that a few times now. She'd simply gone to visit her parents in Hidden Hollow; she'd done it before.

Still, Todd had the urge to call her and find out what was going on. Right now. He needed to know *right now*. Instead, he sat on his phone the whole way home, refusing to let the doubt and anxiety get a full grip over his heart.

She didn't call that afternoon, and evening had become night before his phone rang. He lunged toward it when he saw her name, glad Kyle had stayed at the lodge for dinner a little later than usual. He could probably sense the storm inside Todd.

"Laura," he breathed out in lieu of hello. He didn't wait for her to respond before he said, "Did you meet with another vet today?" He didn't mean for it to sound like an accusation, but it definitely did.

Laura didn't answer right away, and in Todd's head, that *was* the answer. A keen sense of betrayal cut through him, and numbness spread from the top of his head down to his feet as he waited—and waited—for her to answer.

CHAPTER
TWENTY-THREE

Defenses sprang through Laura's mind. She hadn't anticipated needing them for this phone call, and her questions included how he'd found out.

It's small-town Texas, she thought, all the answer she needed.

"Laura," Todd said, and she blinked her way back to the conversation. "I just need—"

"Yes, I talked to another vet today," she said, her mouth getting ahead of her ears and brain. Her heartbeat thundered up her spine and reverberated in her eardrums. "I don't know what I'm going to do."

Todd's end of the line felt deathly silent. Still. She didn't want him to find out this way. Her chest heaved. "I was going to tell you."

"Were you?" he whispered. "When, Laura? *After* you'd decided?"

"I…don't know." She shook her head, frustration rising through her. "There's honestly nothing to decide right now. I toured the place. I did some intern work there before Hans got sick, before I dropped out of the program. Then I had to go back and redo some stuff, and it's been *years*."

She hated how wild and out of control she felt.

"I think," Todd started, and he was the opposite of her. Calm and cool. His voice didn't rush or rise in pitch or volume. "That we're far enough along in our relationship for you to consult with *me* about a career change that impacts the two of us. Not your mama and daddy."

"I—" She cut off, because she had no defense for that.

"You're not as serious about me as I am about you," he supplied.

Laura scoffed, but she wasn't sure how to argue that point either. "Todd," she ended up saying, her voice full of desperation.

"I'm falling in love with you," he said. His voice remained calm and quiet, and the word *love* rumbled through her whole body. "I know that scares you. I'm a little scared too, but I'd rather you know than have you think I don't care if you choose to move an hour away from me. I *do* care, Laura. I care a lot about that."

She pressed her eyes closed, the stinging in them so sharp. "I know."

"What did your parents say?"

She wanted to deny that she'd talked to them already. "To follow my heart and mind."

"And?"

"I don't know," she said, though she had an hour ago. An hour ago, her answer had been to talk to Todd and find out his feelings on the matter.

Todd sighed. "All right, well, I have some good news. Do you want to hear it?"

"No," she said. "I mean, yes, but I'm not done with the vet job."

"All right."

"I wanted to talk to you about it," she said. "I wanted to get your opinion on it. That's where I am."

A few seconds of silence went by, and then Todd said, "When you get home on Sunday, you can lay it out for me, okay?"

Home.

The word sounded like a gong in her ears. "Okay," she agreed. She took a long, deep breath. "Tell me your good news."

"I'm out of the boot and the cast," he said. "Off the crutches. Basically, I'm back to normal."

A smile touched Laura's face and expanded throughout her. "That's so great." She sniffled, and that brought another bout of silence. "Todd, I really was going to tell you."

"Hurry back to me, sweetheart," he said, his voice barely above a whisper. Then he said in a much louder tone, "I'll talk to you tomorrow," before the call ended.

"'Bye," Laura said, letting the hand holding her phone fall to her lap. Her phone almost fell out of her hand, but she managed to grip it so it wouldn't fall to the hard floor. She'd been fighting back tears since arriving at her

ISEDr

parents', but after that conversation with Todd, she let them track slowly down her face.

The things he'd said jumbled in her head as she changed into her pajamas, brushed her teeth, and curled up in her childhood bed.

Home.

I'm falling in love with you.

Hurry back to me.

Sweetheart.

Home, home, home.

She didn't know where home was, and she desperately needed to find it, grab on, and never let go.

———

LAURA DID HER BEST TO ENJOY HER WEEKEND WITH HER family, but Mama kept asking her questions, and Eddie wanted her to lecture Daddy about his medications. She finally told him, "I'm a doctor for animals, Ed, not for humans," and left the house. She'd spent a couple of hours with the ducks and chickens after that before returning to the farmhouse with more contriteness.

She needed some of that right now too, as she turned down the lane that went to Todd's cabin. She hadn't called him again; he didn't call her. They texted Saturday and today, and the last message from her had told him she was leaving, and he'd responded with, *I have brownies and ice cream at my house. Come by when you get here.*

So that was precisely what she was doing. Laura didn't realize she'd practically taken her foot off the gas pedal and she was barely moving until another truck came up behind her. She eased off to the shoulder of the dirt road to let Adam go by, and he saluted her from the brim of his cowboy hat as he did.

She commanded herself to get in control then, and she continued toward Todd's. His truck sat out front, as did Kyle's, as did another sedan Laura hadn't seen before. There was no room in the driveway, so Laura went past the cabin to the next turnout and flipped around. She parked across the street, off the road enough so someone could get by, and got out of the truck.

In that moment, the front door of the cabin opened, and Kyle came outside, Maddy's hand attached to his. The door closed behind her, and Kyle leaned in to kiss her.

Laura felt funny watching them, but she also couldn't look away. Maddy ran her hands up Kyle's chest and into his hair, and he held her in what seemed a firm way around the waist. Laura could see and taste the sparks between them from clear down here, and she wondered if she and Todd had that.

She couldn't stand there staring for much longer, so she crunched across the road, and thankfully, when she looked up again, Kyle and Maddy had moved to the very top of the stairs and were both looking at her.

"Howdy," Kyle called.

"Hey," she called back.

He and Maddy came down the steps as Laura approached, and he added, "He's inside. Just go on in."

"Thanks." Laura gave them both a smile, then faced the cabin with some measure of fear. Doom beat through her body, but she went up the steps and right inside the cabin. Todd looked up from the folder in his lap, saw her, closed it, and tossed it onto the table.

"Hey." He jumped to his feet, and Laura grinned as she watched him walk without crutches or a limp.

"Look at you." She giggled as he rounded the couch and came down the length of it to greet her. He swept her right into his personal space, holding her tightly against his chest, the same way her daddy did.

She took a deep, deep breath of him, and everything Laura thought scrambled one more time. There was no easy solution to the situation she found herself in, and her chest trembled as she exhaled. He released her, and they looked at one another.

"I missed you." She reached up and ran her fingers down the side of his face. That seemed to spur him into action, and he kissed her. Deeply and quickly, almost a frantic message he wanted to get out before he lost his chance.

She went with him, hoping she gave the right answer. He pulled away after several seconds, took her hands in his, and said, "Come have dessert."

He led her into the kitchen, and Laura knew that was her cue to start talking. She pulled out a barstool and sat, her breath leaking from her body. "It would be a really good career," she started. She kept her eyes on him, wanting to see his reaction.

"I'd have to buy into it," she continued when he simply flicked a glance in her direction. "Right now, Doc Lewiston is the only vet for like seven small towns and twice that many ranches. He does dog boarding, goat boarding, horse boarding, llama boarding. On Friday, I did stitches on a llama who'd gotten a big chunk of wood with a nail in it in her shoulder." With every word Laura spoke, the stronger she felt.

She smiled, but Todd was digging into an enormous bucket of vanilla ice cream and didn't see her. "There are two other vets coming on. So I'd be the third. It's not cheap, but it's practically a guaranteed income for a lot of years. These people, they don't have anyone else, and they'd trust me. I'm from there."

Todd pushed a bowl of brownie and ice cream toward her. "Is that why he asked you to do it?"

"I think partly," she said. "He said I was a good veterinary student, and I have a 'way' about me."

"I agree with that," he said. He finished dishing up ice cream for himself and reached for the lid of the bucket.

"There would be some days in the office," she said. "Some days out on ranches. Surgeries, boarding, all kinds of things. It wouldn't be the same thing, day after day." She'd told him once she didn't want her own practice. She didn't; that hadn't changed. Doc Lewiston's practice was more than an office job, where people brought in their sick dogs and cats. So much more.

She took a big bite of her brownie, the creamy vanilla ice cream already starting to melt and make a delicious sauce for it. Todd said nothing, and she looked up and met his eye.

"I can tell you want to do it," he said.

"It's expensive," she said with a shrug of one shoulder.

"Are you going to ask if I'd move there with you?"

Laura focused on her treat again. "Would you?"

"Do you want me to?"

Laura felt like he was asking questions in circles, trying to find some answer she didn't know how to give. "I don't know, Todd. I can't imagine you leaving your family ranch. You'd be the only Stewart to ever do that." She took another bite of dessert, back to watching him.

"I can't imagine leaving here," he admitted.

She anticipated a "but," but he didn't say it.

"I think you're so excited about this," he said. "I can see it on your face and hear it in your voice. You should do it."

Laura narrowed her eyes at him. "I don't understand."

Todd dipped his spoon in his brownie and ice cream, his eyes down on them. "When would you need to be back there, ready to work?"

"Cory and Whit are already there." Laura swallowed as Todd did the same.

He nodded, resignation all over his face. "All right."

"Todd," she said. "I want to hear what you think we should do."

He cocked his head. "There's so many things wrong with what you just said."

"Why?"

"You don't want to hear what I think" he said. "And there is no 'we' in this decision. You went. You asked questions. You'll get the loan. This isn't a 'we' thing." He shook his head and turned toward the sink. He couldn't have eaten all of his dessert yet, but he put his bowl in the sink and faced her again.

"I'm going to make it really easy for you." Todd folded his arms. While he didn't carry any darkness or malice in his voice, plenty of it stormed on his face. Now that she could see him, he probably looked like this on Friday night while they spoke on the phone too. "You obviously want to move back to Hidden Hollow and buy one-third of this veterinary practice. So you should do that."

"Todd."

"I don't want to see you anymore," he said, his voice even and careful and not one whit louder than usual. "I think we should be done."

Laura stared at him, sure she hadn't heard him correctly. "Todd," she tried again.

"If I wasn't here, would you even be questioning whether you should do this?"

Laura opened her mouth, then closed it and nodded. "Of course I would."

"I don't think so."

Outside, Azure whined, and he stepped around the fridge to open the back door for the dog. "Hey, bud," he said. "Sorry I forgot about you out there." The canine came trotting in, saw Laura, and beelined for her. With his whole body wagging, he jumped up and put his paws on her lap.

She giggled and gave him a good scrub behind the ears. He'd distracted her and Todd for a moment, but as soon as Azure returned to all-fours, they had to face the elephant in the room. He stood over by the small dining room table and folded his arms again. "Stay as long as you want. Eat more ice cream. I've got to get out to the well before it gets too dark."

With that, he plucked his cowboy hat from the hook beside the door, jammed it on his head, and went out the back door. Azure looked his way, then at Laura.

"You better go on," she said to him, and Azure trotted after Todd. She wanted to do the same, but the cowboy had just broken up with her. What was she supposed to do? Tell him no?

Pure exhaustion ran through her, and she scraped the remains of her treat into the trash can, washed her bowl and put it back in the cupboard, and then left the cabin.

She hadn't quit here. She didn't have a loan for the veterinary clinic in Hidden Hollow. Now, she didn't have Todd either, and Laura felt truly lost in the world for the second time in her life.

––––––––

THREE WEEKS LATER, SHE DID HER BEST TO SMILE AT EDDIE AS he brought in the last of her boxes from his truck. "Thank you," she called from her new kitchen. She'd been very, very lucky to find this basement apartment. It had its own separate entrance, something not everything around here had.

Her loan had been approved, and she was waiting for it to fund. She'd given Blake—her real boss, the man who signed her checks—her two weeks notice, and today was her move-in day.

They'd spent the morning at the Longhorn Ranch loading up what she owned, and now the afternoon unloading it in her new basement apartment. It wasn't the same as a cabin, but she didn't have a roommate. Deep down, she knew that all that meant was that she wouldn't have anyone to talk to at night.

The past few weeks at Longhorn had been terribly difficult for her. Blake had made the announcement of her leaving, not Todd. Blake had organized her going-away party, not Todd. Blake had hugged her and said they'd all miss her, not Todd.

She hadn't spoken to him again, at least not outside of what she absolutely had to in order to do her job. They texted, but only about animals and their health. Everything in her life had grown stale and cold, and as Laura unpacked the last of her dishes and filled the last of her kitchen cabinets, she sighed.

She looked around. She tried to see the goodness in the world—in her life—around her. There had to be something, and she caught sight of a picture of her and the twin lambs she'd delivered the first time she'd visited the Texas Longhorn Ranch.

They were a few months old in the picture, and they'd just been bathed so they were white, wooly, and wonderful. She smiled easily at the camera, and she could see her true self in that picture.

She picked it up and wiped her finger along the top of the frame. No dust sat there, and she moved over to the dining room table-for-two and set the picture in the middle of it.

"Food for tonight," Mama said as she entered the apartment. She carried a box that would feed Laura for far more than a single night and plunked it down on the non-permanent island in the kitchen. "It looks great, dear." She gazed around at the curtainless windows and stark white walls.

Laura wouldn't do anything to dress them up either. She didn't have great sewing skills—at least as far as curtains went—nor the time to do such things even if she did. "It's clean," she said to Mama. "Did you come alone?"

This apartment sat fifteen minutes from her parents', and that was because the speed limit on the road between here and there was only thirty-five.

"Yes." Mama reached up and patted her hair. "Your daddy isn't feeling well this afternoon." She put a falsely bright smile on her face. Laura did the same. She wasn't feeling particularly well this afternoon either, but she would never let anyone know.

"Eddie got everything in," she said, giving her brother a smile. "I'm almost unpacked already, and now I have food." She started unpacking the box Mama had brought. Anything to stay busy and stop herself from looking at one of them for too long.

"I'm going to go if you're good," Eddie said.

"I'm good." Laura moved into her brother and hugged him. "Thank you so much. You're the best brother in the world."

He chuckled and squeezed her tight. "It's good to have you back," he said. Then he stepped over to Mama and kissed her cheek. "See you later, Mama."

"'Bye, dear."

With only Mama in the house, Laura felt the need to work doubly fast. She kept unpacking the food and putting it away. Then she moved on to a box of movies in the living room. Mama said nothing, which was unusual and unsettling.

Laura wanted to ask her if she needed something, but it sounded accusatory inside her head. She kept hers down and kept working. When she finally looked up, Mama watched her from across the room.

"You broke up with Todd," she stated.

"Not technically." Laura reached for the knife and used it to cut the tape on the bottom of the box she'd just emptied. She brushed her hair back out of her face as she looked up at Mama again. "He broke up with me. Three weeks ago, actually." She shook her head, needing to focus somewhere but on Todd Stewart.

She didn't want to cry over him again. Once the numbness of the break-up had worn off, then the tears had come. She'd done the same thing with Hans when he'd gotten his cancer diagnosis. She'd been numb, shocked. For days.

Then horribly sad and depressed. Loads of crying. Then came the anger, and then finally, she'd dug in and started getting things done. This grief cycle was the same, and she wondered if that meant something deeper than she realized.

"I'm sorry, baby," Mama said, and Laura let her fold her into a hug.

"It's okay," Laura said, though it wasn't. "I'm okay." She wasn't. Not yet, anyway.

Maybe never again, she thought but didn't dare vocalize.

She'd thought she wouldn't be okay without Hans too, and she'd survived that loss.

Todd, though… Todd was still here, and she hated that they were still both on the earth and not together. She simply didn't know what to do about it, so she turned up the Faith Ostetler and kept unpacking, kept praying she'd done the right thing, and kept putting a fake smile on her face for Mama.

CHAPTER
TWENTY-FOUR

Todd wanted to rip down the fluffy pink rabbit someone had taped to the door of the lodge. Seriously, couldn't they go through a single holiday without everything dressed up with frills and extras?

Inside the lodge, it looked like an Easter egg hunt had thrown up, with colorful eggs on every available flat surface. The front of the desk beside the door, the walls, the cowboy's desks to his left. In the dining area, where they served breakfast and dinner, yellow, pink, blue, and purple 3D eggs hung from the ceiling like paper lanterns.

He eyed them all like they'd strangle him if given the chance and continued toward the hallway that led to Blake's office. His foot had continued to heal over the past few weeks since the cast had come off. The problem was, now his heart was hemorrhaging. For how many pieces it currently sat in, he should be back in a hospital bed.

Todd glared at Starla and the new kitchen manager as

he entered the staff break room, but neither of them looked at him. At least Blake had listened to him and promoted Ashley up to the kitchen manager. He'd hired another chef to take her spot, so when Starla left in two weeks, they should have a fairly smooth transition.

He'd lost Laura last week, at least as the vet on the ranch. He'd lost her a month ago as a friend and a girl-friend, and he'd never felt so alone and so lonely in his life. He still talked to his brothers and sisters every day. Lots of cowboys and cowgirls too. Somehow, none of them counted without Laura in his life.

He pushed her out of his thoughts, something he did a hundred times a day, even now. He went past Jesse and Nash's office, which they also shared with Holly, and down toward Blake's. Becks had an office here too, and he heard her typing away on her keyboard as he went by.

Blake's office opened up on his left, and he went inside to find it empty. Of course. Blake tried to be on time, but he had a lot of moving pieces to manage here at the lodge, as well as on the ranch, and he ran late much of the time. Todd couldn't really blame him. His irritation spiked, though, and he'd started to grow used to living in such an aggravated state.

Everything bothered him since he'd broken up with Laura, and he second-guessed his decision to do that for at least the hundredth time. He'd spent sleepless nights berating himself for walking out on her, leaving her sitting at his kitchen counter with a bowl of brownies and ice cream. What kind of man did that?

A child, he thought.

"Hey," Blake said. "Sorry I'm running a bit behind."

Glad for the distraction, Todd gave him a smile. "It's fine. I've maybe been here for a minute."

Blake took a seat behind his desk. "What's up?"

"The vet I want to hire wants twenty thousand more than the offer." Todd sank into a chair opposite his brother. "He's good, and I don't have anyone else."

Blake stared at him and said, "Let me talk to Mama." Their mother still did the lion's share of the accounting for the ranch, something she'd been doing for decades. "I don't think it'll be a problem, but that's significantly more."

"I told him that," Todd said. "I also told him I'd let him know before the weekend." It was Thursday, which meant Todd really only had until tomorrow to get this wrapped up. Wrapped up was what he'd like it to be. Then maybe he could move on with his Laura-less life. Somehow.

"I'll text her right now." Blake pulled out his phone to do that, and Todd leaned his head back and closed his eyes. His brother said something else, but Todd had started to drift toward unconsciousness. He'd slept last night, just not very well. Azure had been sticking with Blake and Gina the past week or so, and Todd felt abandoned on every front.

"She says she's checking," Blake said, and Todd yanked his eyes open again. Blake frowned at him. "You should go take a nap. You look terrible."

"Thank you," Todd said dryly. "I'll just ignore everything I have to do and take a nap. Great idea."'

Blake quirked an eyebrow at him. "We managed while you weren't walking."

"I am walking now, though."

Blake leaned back in his chair, and he might as well have steepled his fingers. Todd didn't want to hear an older brother lecture, so he got to his feet. "Text me what Mama says, so I know what I need to do. I have to get out to the milkshed. Little Nick said we might have termites." Just what he needed to go with his less-than-stellar month here at the Texas Longhorn Ranch.

"You better be joking," Blake said.

"I'm not." Todd stepped out into the hall and kept going. Termites would be terrible, as they were hard to kill and expensive in the process. With any luck, Little Nick would be wrong.

————

LITTLE NICK WAS NOT WRONG, AND A WEEK LATER, TODD stood idly by while the pest control company fumigated right into the walls of the milkshed. The thing would have holes it in that Todd would then have to patch up.

He glared at the milkshed like his gaze alone could light it on fire. He felt like that about everything lately, and with every passing day that brought him closer to summertime, the worse his mood grew.

Kyle's busy season was upon them, and he was either working madly on a band for their summer season, out with Maddy, or locked down in his bedroom, texting or talking to Maddy. He looked at Todd with compassion, but he never said anything about Laura, which Todd appreciated. He had her in his mind plenty without a verbal reminder from someone else.

"You should take the rest of today off," Blake said.

Todd glared at him. His brother had been trying to get him to take a day off for a solid week now. "I'm fine."

"You're not fine," Blake said.

"I took last week off after we found out about the termites," Todd said. "I'm supervising this, and then I have a couple of interviews for a new vet."

Mama had not approved the budget for the man who'd wanted more money, and Todd had gone back to interviewing for a position he didn't want to fill—but desperately needed to fill.

He reached up and pushed his hat lower over his eyes. He couldn't even see the milkshed anymore, but he didn't care. He didn't want to talk about taking time off—or Laura—and he wasn't needed to actually supervise professionals as they did their job.

They'd want to be paid, though, and Todd would take care of that. Plus, then he'd know how long they'd been here and could get any additional instructions if necessary. "Why don't you go do your job and let me do mine?" He cut Blake a glare out of the corner of his eye.

"Wow." Blake actually started to chuckle, which only made Todd's mood darken further. "I knew you liked Laura. I knew it would be hard without her here. I know it's caused work for you in hiring another vet."

He paused, and Todd tilted his head back to look at his

brother. They were so close, but Todd didn't know what else Blake might say.

He studied Todd's face, his smile growing. "I just didn't realize you were in love with her."

"I'm not," Todd said, the words like chips of wood in his mouth. He folded his arms and let his gaze fall back to the milkshed. "I broke up with her when I did so I *wouldn't* fall in love with her."

Blake said nothing, and Todd stewed silently in his mind. As usual. He'd been doing that for a while now. Everyone around the ranch had so much to do—Todd included—as the days got longer and hotter. No one wanted to listen to him complain about his problems.

The animals would always need care. Someone was always going to come in late. Or get hurt. Or need time off. He and Sierra managed their cowboys and cowgirls the best they could, and Todd remembered a meeting with Adam later that afternoon to go over a new session of horseback riding.

Holly and Nash had also sent out an email a day or two ago saying that the lodge and cabins were now fully booked through Labor Day, and they'd just opened up their final quarter of the year for bookings. The holidays had filled within a few hours, and Kyle had mentioned to Todd that morning that he needed to book a band soon.

It seemed hard to believe that another year would go by. Todd would endure more holidays alone, and he couldn't imagine another New Year's Eve without Laura at his side to kiss.

He closed his eyes and prayed for relief. *Just give me five minutes where I'm not thinking about her or what could've been with her.*

"You know," Blake said, and Todd opened his eyes. "You could call her. See how she's doing in Hidden Hollow. Maybe she's as miserable as you are."

"I'm not going to call her," Todd said. "She lived here for three weeks before she moved out. She had plenty of opportunities to talk to me." He turned toward his brother. "She didn't." He gestured toward the milkshed. "Do you need to be out here?"

Blake shifted his feet. "I got nothin' better to do."

"You have to be kidding." Todd scoffed. "You wanna go back to my office and do the interviews? I mean, if you've got nothin' to do."

Blake grinned at Todd, and with a rare smile, Todd returned it. "I guess I have some things to do."

"I guess you do."

Blake swept his hat off his head and pushed his hair back. "I just think, Todd, that there might be some value in reminding Laura of what—and who—she left behind. Maybe she just needs a reminder."

Todd simply shook his head. Laura lived in the past, he knew that. Her memories of Hans and Letty, the life they'd been meant to have, and all of her hopes and dreams sat right at the forefront of her mind. He'd never been able to compete with Hans. How could he? Laura held him on the highest of pedestals, and she hadn't walked away from their life together. It had been *taken* from her. Sadly and quickly and in a terrible, terrible way.

Maybe she's just not ready, he thought.

He stood outside the milkshed while the exterminators did their job, not even realizing when Blake walked away. He could've left a moment ago or twenty minutes ago, and Todd wouldn't have known. What he did know was that he was running late. His legs hurt from the long time standing, and he caught the attention of one exterminator and told him to come find him in the barn office when they were finished.

The only thing he could see during the interviews was that the people sitting across from him weren't Laura. He ate dinner. He showered. He played catch with Azure.

He got up the next morning and did everything over again. Day after day after day. Blake's words wouldn't leave his mind, but Todd couldn't act on them.

After another week, he stood in the kitchen of his cabin and said out loud, "So what if you're in love with her? Love isn't going to bring her back."

A tiny voice in his mind whispered at him, though. The words were so soft he couldn't quite make them out. He'd never admitted to anyone—not even himself—that he was in love with Laura. Now that he had, or at least alluded to being in love with her, it felt like he'd opened a door in his mind.

The words came into focus, and Todd heard them on a loop in his brain. His ears. His very soul.

What if love is enough this one time?

Maybe you should call her.

Perhaps love will bring her back to you.

CHAPTER
TWENTY-FIVE

Maddy pulled to a stop in front of the huge Texas Longhorn Lodge. There wasn't a free parking space in the lot, and both sides of the dirt road she'd driven in on had been lined with vehicles too. After a quick glance up toward the front door told her Kyle hadn't come out yet, and she started to gather her thin hair into a ponytail.

She'd just gotten it colored with a bit of red, and she liked how it shone in the sunshine now. She felt like she was on fire whenever she went outside, and that made her smile. She'd just wrapped her elastic around the ponytail four times when the passenger door opened.

"Excuse me, ma'am," Kyle said, his voice extra twangy. "You can't park here." He slid into the seat, his smile full of happiness.

"Howdy, boyfriend," she said. She leaned toward him, and he did the same to her, and they met in the middle for a quick kiss. She giggled and added, "I don't suppose you have a cowboy valet service here. It's been a long week."

"As a matter of fact," he said. "Switch me. You go in and get dinner, and I'll park your car. Then we'll go help with the stuffing."

Maddy wasn't going to argue with him. They switched spots, and she went up the steps to the lodge alone. She'd been here several times over the past couple of months, but a nervous flutter still moved through her torso. One step inside told her why. All of the tables looked full, either with guests, employees, or Stewarts, and Maddy wasn't any of those.

You're Kyle's guest, she told herself. All she did with that information was shuffle to the side so anyone coming in after her wouldn't bump into her. The dining room bustled with laughter, chatter, and activity. The scent of salt, browned meat, butter, and chocolate hung in the air. Her stomach growled at her for something to eat, as kindergarten lunchtime had been hours and hours ago.

"Maddy," a woman said pleasantly, and Maddy blinked away from the room at-large to the woman right in front of her. Kyle's sister, Holly.

She wore a black skirt that fell in lots of lacy layers and a white tank top with the same flowers on it in bright pops of lacy colors. She looked classy and sophisticated, her medium brown hair cascading over her shoulders in beautiful waves. Holly always wore the perfect amount of makeup, and just like tonight, she could make seemingly simple clothes into showpieces.

"Are you eating with us tonight?" Holly asked. "Where's Kyle?"

"He's parking my car," Maddy said. "Yes, I'm eating. Then we're helping with the stuffing."

Her eyes lit up even more than they'd already been. "Perfect." She pointed toward the buffet as if Maddy hadn't seen it yet. "There's Beef Wellington bites on the menu tonight. Starla's doing all of her favorites before she leaves." Her attention got drawn somewhere else, and she turned to greet a guest.

They laughed and hugged, and Maddy once again edged out of the way. She wanted to ask Holly if she'd mentioned anything to Kyle about their agreement, but the other woman moved away. She'd eat later, Maddy knew, after all the guests and everyone else had. Holly managed the lodge at night, so it was no wonder she shone like the sun, brightening everyone's day for just a little longer.

Maddy did the same thing at school, and she wondered how hard Holly crashed after work. Had to be hard, because the woman was charming and the epitome of perfection with people.

She joined the buffet line, loaded her plate with delectable things like the Beef Wellington bites, tempura veggies, and Starla's flourless chocolate cake that Maddy couldn't get enough of. She'd been to the Texas Longhorn Ranch enough for Starla to offer to make it for her for her birthday, but now that she was leaving for a restaurant job in Austin, Maddy didn't think that would happen.

She turned back to the dining room and found an empty seat at the closest table. She put on the bravest face she had and approached. "Can I sit here or are you saving it?"

"It's yours," the man closest to her said. "We're done anyway." He tipped back his coffee mug and stood. He didn't have to clear his own dishes, and a busboy swooped in to do that. The table got wiped down, and a family of four joined Maddy. She'd taken a few bites of everything, deemed it all delicious, and stood to go back for more cake when Kyle arrived.

"Good?" he asked, looking at her and then her half-eaten plate. "You're going for more cake." He grinned, and with those straight, white teeth, and his golden hair, he made every hormone in her body come to life.

"Do you want me to get you some?" she asked, eyeing the platter of them. "They look almost gone."

"They have more in the kitchen," he said. "But get me a couple."

Maddy did, loading a dessert plate with four of the flourless chocolate cakes. They could be eaten in two bites, so she didn't feel bad about eating three pieces. They weren't even close to the regular size of a piece of chocolate cake.

She sank back into her seat, Kyle having taken the one beside her. "You ate already?"

"A couple of hours ago," he said. "I've been helping Jesse and Nash set up the tables for the stuffing. Then I had a late phone call from…" He leaned back in his chair. "Guess who I talked to tonight?"

Maddy looked at him, that mischievous little boy smile on his face. "By the look in your eye, it's a band."

"Check."

She grinned at him, enjoying this game they'd played a few times now. He usually told her to guess something, and he'd send her checkmarks via text, or say it out loud when they were face-to-face. She'd only quizzed him once, and he'd gotten her middle name completely wrong.

"A group or a solo artist?" Maddy took a bite of her first piece of cake.

"You have to ask yes or no questions," he said.

"A 'band' is a really broad term," she argued back.

"Fine." He chuckled and popped his whole cake bite into his mouth. After he chewed and swallowed, he said, "It's a solo artist with a band."

"They all have bands," she said, her mind working now. A solo artist… It wouldn't be someone like Fiddles & Fellas, as they were a group of musicians. A solo artist would have instrumentalists and back-up singers, but their name was on the album cover.

"Male?"

"Check."

She'd learned that Kyle booked a lot of male artists, as they seemed more popular than the female artists. She'd asked him about that, but he said he wasn't sure why. He simply wanted to please the guests, and they seemed to enjoy male country singers better.

Maddy thought, but had kept to herself, that it was because wives booked the trips for their families to come to the Texas Longhorn Lodge. And women wanted to see good-looking, talented men on stage. She'd never say that to Kyle, though, as he seemed to have a sore spot when it came to the musicians he booked to come to the ranch.

She wasn't sure why; she'd never asked him. It felt too intimate of a question for where they stood in their relationship right now.

That'll change this summer, she thought, and her stomach clenched around the flourless chocolate cake.

"That's it?" he teased. "You're done guessing?"

"You don't give very good hints," she said.

He laughed again and said, "I've mentioned him before."

She studied his face for a moment. "This is someone you're over the moon to get."

"Check."

Maddy knew who it was then, but she took another bite of her cake and made him wait. "Liam Sebastian."

Kyle grinned. "Check." They laughed together, and Maddy congratulated him on getting the Texas-born country music sensation to come perform at the lodge.

"Is he doing a summer concert?" she asked. "Or is he your holiday headliner?"

"He's my final summer concert," Kyle said. "We're goin' out with a bang." He reached for her hand. "You'll come, right?"

Maddy swallowed her last piece of cake and squeezed his hand. She wiped her mouth with her free hand and set down her napkins. "Todd, I wanted to talk to you about this summer."

His smile slipped, and Maddy couldn't wait for it to come back. "All right."

"I don't teach in the summer," she said, though they'd talked about her schedule before. "I know you're really busy and won't be able to come visit me. I usually try to find something to do to keep busy."

"Yeah." He sighed and wiped his hand down his face. "Did you hear about that job you were hopin' to get?"

"I did," she said, keeping her eyes on their joined hands. His skin was rougher and tanner than hers, but she loved the way they looked together. She finally looked up to Todd. "It's on this great family ranch. I'm going to be doing these amazing art classes with kids."

Kyle's eyes zipped back and forth between hers. "That's great. You love art."

"I have to move," she said. "Not that far. Just an hour or so."

"Oh."

"The good news is the lodging came through."

"That is good." He started to pull his hand away, but Maddy increased her grip.

"Yeah, your sister was really great about all of it," Maddy said.

Kyle's attention zipped back to her. "What?"

"Holly finalized my housing yesterday. Jesse and Blake have my signed contract here somewhere. I'm moving here over Memorial Day weekend." She grinned at him, her own version of sunshine pouring from her. It wasn't as bright as his, but it would have to do. "Surprise."

Todd blinked, then bolted to his feet. "Surprise?" He tipped his head back and laughed, drawing all kinds of attention toward them. He dragged her to her feet too, and

Maddy's face began to burn. She didn't much like the spotlight, and she'd never had much need for it.

"Everyone," he bellowed, and the dining room started to quiet. "My girlfriend just told me she's moving here for the summer!" He held up their joined hands as if they'd just gotten married, and the room began to whoop and holler and whistle.

"Kyle," Maddy said, but a laugh tumbled from her mouth a moment later.

"You're done, right?" He nodded to her plate, and she nodded at him. He tucked her hand through his arm and headed for the hallway that led toward the quieter, more administrative part of the lodge. It was dark back there, as it was Friday night, she'd finished work, and driven the hour here before the announcement.

The moment they gained the corner, Kyle ducked around it and took Maddy's face in his. He kissed her, and Maddy had been kissed by good-looking cowboys before. By Kyle before. Nothing was as magical, and as mysterious, and as life-altering as the way he kissed her there in the dark after she'd told him she'd be living just down the road from him for June, July, and August.

CHAPTER
TWENTY-SIX

L aura smiled at the middle-aged woman who'd brought in her tabby cat. "She's going to be fine, Mrs. Murphy. You can stay with her until Lena comes to take her." She glanced one more time at the gray feline, and she vowed to lock her doors that night. The glare on that cat's face…

She sighed as she left the exam room. Days spent in the clinic definitely weren't her favorite. She craved the open air and wind, the scent of freshly turned dirt and something a little foul coming from the pigsty.

As it was, she collected the clipboard from the holder outside the room only six feet from the one she'd just exited, flipped a couple of pages, and read the notes. A husky. She took a deep breath, because she did love dogs. Just not dogs—a husky—with a gash in two paws. The back ones.

She hitched another smile to her face and twisted the

doorknob. The husky immediately vocalized his displeasure at her entrance, sounding very much like he was saying, "No, no, noooo!"

"Bridger," his owner chastised, but the husky didn't care. He pointed his snout heavenward and yowled again.

"I know," Laura said, handing the clipboard to her vet tech. Randall gave her a very well concealed look that said, *It's about time. I've been dying a slow death in here.*

She stepped over to the husky and stroked both sides of his face. "What did you get into, bud, huh?"

"He went under Mrs. Cornwall's fence," Abigail Worthington said. "I've told him not to over and over again." She glared at her husky. "He doesn't listen, do you, Bridger?" She seemed cross, but Laura wasn't convinced.

"Do you know what he cut his feet on?" She started to move around the husky, and he immediately stopped howling to glare at her. She slid her hand down his back, feeling him tremble under her touch. He was likely in a lot of pain, though his chart had said Randy had given him a painkiller in the form of a shot.

"She was re-wiring her chicken coop," Abigail said. "He was back there barking and chasing those darn chickens. I'm lucky he didn't catch one, because Lilian would've taken me to court over her precious poultry." The bitterness in her voice entered Laura's ears loud and clear. She kept her smile placid as she reached the dog's hindquarters.

His feet had been cleaned, but both of them still oozed blood. The left one had a much larger cut than the right, and Laura looked at Randy. She nodded and ran her fingertip along Bridger's thigh. "This right one looks like we can probably bandage it," she said. "The left...I'd like to see if it needs stitches."

"Oh, dear," Abigail fretted.

Randy stepped over to the door and pressed the button on the wall there to call another technician. They'd muzzle Bridger and then hold him so Laura could complete a better examination. As they waited, she chit-chatted with Abigail about her garden and how it had already started to sprout this year.

It was almost May, and the corners of Laura's mouth continued to droop as the conversation went on. Finally, Esmerelda came in, a rushed look in her eyes. "Sorry," she said. "There's a pair of ducks who just got here who are in bad shape." She stepped over to the sink and washed her hands. Everything inside Laura wanted to head outside to the ranch and farm animal area of the clinic, but Whit was out there today. Cory was on ranch visits to do some cattle exams, and on this fine Friday, Laura was stuck with the dogs, cats, ferrets, and gerbils who had appointments today.

Boredom drummed through her as she examined the dog's paws, stitched up the left one, and bandaged the other one. Lunchtime came and went. She felt like an actor in a movie that had been sped up, and she walked in short little bursts of movement. In one room, talk to someone who knew all about her, her family, and her grandparents, fix a problem, walk out of the room.

Pick up another chart. Repeat, repeat, repeat.

When she got home that evening, exhaustion pulled

through her. She hadn't been sleeping very well since leaving the Texas Longhorn Ranch, and she didn't want to acknowledge why. She knew why.

One, it was too loud in the quaint little red brick house on third south in Hidden Hollow. The upstairs neighbors played their music too loud. She had to make her own dinner. She had no cowgirl roommate to talk about country music with, and no handsome boyfriend to kiss, and nothing to look forward to the next day.

More of the same, dreadful tasks.

Tonight, she stared at the steps that led down to her entrance into the house, noticing the boxes there. Two of them today. Laura was so sick of carrying in boxes, opening them to find mundane things like laundry detergent and socks.

"I just don't think this is where I'm supposed to be." She'd never said the words out loud until that moment, and a strong sense of choking overcame her. She couldn't swallow, and she couldn't breathe. Tears sprang to her eyes, and Laura reached up to her throat as if she could get her tongue out of the way with her hands.

She couldn't, and she broke down into great sobs. She couldn't think. She couldn't understand what had happened to bring this on. The episode seemed to go on and on and yet pass in a moment. She quieted gradually, and then she sat like a lump in the driver's seat.

She didn't want to go inside her basement apartment, though she'd liked it well enough to rent it. She'd once wanted a home exactly like this, with green grass extending out from it on all sides. She once wanted children to fill the house with noise and life. She'd once wanted to live right here in Hidden Hollow. Nowhere else would do. Once, she'd have passed out if she'd been offered the job she currently had.

Once wasn't her reality. *Once* was not now.

Now, Laura didn't want any of this, but she was trapped. Trapped here, in a once-life she didn't want and didn't know how to get out of.

She put her car in reverse and backed out of her pristine driveway. Everything here sat in too-perfect angles, and she wanted to take out a few mailboxes as she went down the street just to mess things up a little bit. Make them match the chaos in her life and soul.

She didn't, of course, but she could see the postal carnage in her head. She drove out of town and along the winding Hill Country roads she loved so much. She had these in Chestnut Springs.

She made the turn to go to her parents' farm. She had a turn like this to head out to the Longhorn Ranch.

She couldn't stop thinking about Todd. She'd tried to push him out of her mind for weeks now, and he would not go. She'd gotten her last paycheck from the Longhorn Ranch, and she hadn't cashed it yet. She didn't want that chapter in her life to be over. She wasn't ready to turn the page.

As the farmhouse came into view, Laura realized she'd felt like this before. She'd felt left behind as the world continued to turn without her willing and ready to go with it.

When Hans had died, she'd been in a stale, silent, still bubble for a few weeks. She felt the same way now.

Her car came to a stop, and she thought back to how she'd gotten out of that dark, dreary place in her life.

She'd taken a step.

Then, she'd had to get ready to go to veterinary school.

Now... Now, she had nothing. She didn't have anywhere to go or anyone to see. She wondered how far she could get with the gasoline in her car and who would know she hadn't gone home if she simply went back to the highway, turned south, and drove until the car wouldn't go anymore.

"No one," she said.

Maybe Todd, pinged through her head. She'd shared her pin with him once, several months ago, so he'd know where she was as she drove back and forth from Chestnut Springs to Hidden Hollow.

She hadn't *un*shared it with him. If she disappeared, would the cops go to the Longhorn Ranch and ask about her? Would he remember she'd shared her location with him?

Another round of tears stung her eyes, but she blinked this set back. She didn't need to cry. She needed someone to help her make a plan.

Pressing on the gas, she continued to the farmhouse and parked in front of it. Instead of sitting in the driver's seat, unwilling to go inside, she got out and hurried toward the front door. "Mama," she called upon entering.

No one answered, and Laura felt as though someone had punched her in the throat. She went around the corner and into the kitchen, but Mama and Daddy weren't there. No one had made dinner. No coffee sat brewing for after the meal.

She pulled out her phone and called her mom. "Hello, dear," Mama said only a single ring later.

"Where are you guys?" she asked.

"We're having dinner over at the Newburys," Mama said, and Laura suddenly recognized her dignified Texan accent.

"Oh, right." Mama had told her about that. She'd just forgotten. Helplessness filled her. "Well, do you have maybe two minutes to talk?"

"I suppose," Mama said. "Yes, I'll be right back." Her voice came softer on the last part, and Laura could just see her pulling the phone away from her mouth. A few seconds later, she said, "Okay, I can talk," in her normal voice.

"Why do you go over there if you don't like it?" Laura asked.

"You know how Helen Newbury is," Mama said with a scoff. "If I don't come, I'm gossiped about for thinking I'm better than everyone in town. When I do come, I'll be gossiped about for saying the wrong thing."

Laura didn't see why she cared, but she had lived in a small Texas town for most of her life, so she didn't argue. "Mama, I'm miserable here."

"Oh, dear, I know you are." Mama's voice immediately took on a honeyed quality.

Laura collapsed onto a barstool. "What should I do?"

Mama didn't say anything, and Laura knew this was

longer than a two-minute conversation. "I'm not going to tell you what to do," she finally said. "I think it's a miracle you've admitted you're not happy here. Daddy and I have known it since that first Sunday you came to dinner."

"How do I just…quit? How do I just say, 'I'm sorry, but I made a mistake.' There is no undo button for life." Not to mention she'd gotten a sizable loan to buy one-third of the veterinary clinic.

There were other vets who wanted to, she thought, and a plan started to form in her mind.

"Maybe you just say that," Mama said. "Find the button, Laura, and push it."

She drew in a deep breath to contain the tears and panic once again threatening her. "I want to go back to Chestnut Springs."

"No," Mama said. "You want to go back to Todd Stewart."

Laura made a horrible sound, much like that husky she'd stitched up today as a half-laugh and half-sob tore through her throat. When she managed to tame the explosive emotion, she said, "I do, Mama. I really do."

"Then *do* it, dear," Mama said. "Everything else can be worked out later." Scuffling came through the line, and Mama said, "Oh, yes, Helen. Thank you." She might as well have been speaking to the queen of England. "I must go, dear."

"Of course you must," Laura said in a false British accent. "Thanks, Mama." She giggled her way off the line, but the laughter dried up quickly. She sat in the quiet house, listening to the clock tick behind her and the refrigerator hum in front of her.

She needed to find that undo button, and it wasn't here in Hidden Hollow. She headed back out to her car, her strides long, and the plan in her head morphing with every breath she took.

She had a phone charger in her car. Her purse. She could do anything with those two items, and she got behind the wheel, said, "Call Doc Lewiston," and pulled away from the farmhouse in a cloud of dirt and dust.

CHAPTER
TWENTY-SEVEN

Todd worked by the light of day though it was barely seven a.m. He'd been up for an hour. He'd showered, shaved, fried eggs, and made coffee. He now labored over the three final applications for the veterinarian position. He had to make a decision. Today. He had to hire one of them.

He simply didn't want to.

If he didn't hire a new vet, then Laura could come back. He hadn't said as much out loud, but Sierra had called him on it last night. It wasn't his fault that the blasted ponies couldn't get along. One had taken a bite—a legit bite—out of another one, and they didn't have anyone on the ranch who could doctor up a wound like that.

Todd and Sierra had had to load up the wounded pony —shrieking and all—and drive it thirty minutes to town to the emergency vet clinic. That wouldn't be cheap, and

Sierra had lectured him for the entire drive home about hiring someone already.

"You can't wait for Laura to come back," she'd said.

"I'm not," he'd argued.

She'd scoffed and laughed mirthlessly. "You are. You think if you don't hire someone, you can call her and offer her the job, and she'll take it. She's gone, Todd. Hire someone."

He'd wanted to drive them off the road and demand she get out of his truck. That would've proven her right, so he'd settled for giving her the worst glare he could come up with. She hadn't minded at all. In fact, she'd given his attitude right back to him.

Her words ran through his head again, because she wasn't wrong. He had held back on hiring someone; he just hadn't known why until she'd accused him of holding the position for a woman who wasn't coming back. Laura wasn't looking back. Though she'd done so with Hans, she hadn't for him.

He had to hire someone. Today.

"Hey," Kyle said, and Todd abandoned the applications on the table in front of him.

He got to his feet, glad for the distraction. "Hey. What time did you get in?"

"One?" Kyle guessed. He ran his fingers through his hair, sending it flying in multiple directions. "Two, maybe?"

"Wow." Todd chuckled as Kyle pulled down a coffee mug. "To be young again."

KISSING HER COWBOY BOSS 293

"Ha ha." Kyle poured himself a cup of coffee and drank it straight-up. Black. No cream and no sugar. "I can't wait until Maddy moves here. Then I won't feel like every second is so precious."

"Mm, yeah." Todd turned away from his brother, unsure why he thought conversing with him would make him feel better. It was always Maddy-this or Maddy-that, and while Todd wanted Kyle to be happy, he also wanted to talk about something besides his girlfriend.

He'd worried he'd been like that with Laura, but Jesse had assured him he hadn't. Kyle sometimes forgot that he'd had girlfriends before, and he dropped the word like it made him better for having a significant other.

Starla was leaving next weekend, and while she and Jesse hadn't broken up, they'd decided not to stay together after she left. He looked at Starla the way Todd would look at Laura if she were still here. In all honesty, it would be easier for Jesse once she left. Maybe.

Todd had determined to be there for his brother as much as possible. Blake had been there for him. Adam and Jesse too. Kyle was a tad clueless, but Todd knew it wasn't his fault. It was those rose-colored glasses he wore.

"You eat already?" Kyle asked.

"Yes, sir." Todd sat back down at the table and picked up the top application. "I think I'm going to hire Conrad."

"All right," Kyle said, because he didn't know who Conrad was anyway.

Todd read over the application again, though he had it memorized. "No one's applied in a couple of weeks now."

They probably assumed the job had been filled and just not removed from the board. He wasn't even sure why he wanted more people to apply. He'd had some good quality vets put in for the job.

His phone pinged at him, letting him know an email had come in. Not just any email, but one to the special email address he'd put on the job listing several weeks ago. He swapped out the application for his phone and swiped to see the communication.

He blinked, sure his insomnia had finally gotten to him. Laura Woodcross had just applied for the veterinary position at the Texas Longhorn Ranch.

"Kyle," he said just as a text popped up on his screen.

Laura's name sat there too. The part of her text he could read before he got sucked back up said, *Is the job at the ranch still*

"Kyle," Todd yelled this time. He spun toward his brother, his pulse rebounding and stabbing through his whole body.

"What?" Kyle frowned at him. "I'm right here."

"Look at this." He hurried over to his brother and shoved the phone in his face. Far too close for him to see. "Laura applied."

"What?" Kyle took the phone and held it at a reasonable distance.

"You see it, right? I'm not hallucinating?"

Kyle's eyes swept right and left as he read. "I see it." He grinned and handed the phone back to Todd. "So call her. I've been tellin' you to call her for weeks."

"It's not that easy," Todd said, now staring at Laura's full message. *Is the job at the ranch still open? If so, I'd love to interview for it. I just put in my application, which has some stellar references I think you'll enjoy.*

His fingers shook as he tapped to get over to her application. They'd joked a little bit when she'd first started at the ranch about the things people put on their applications, and he couldn't wait to see what she'd done.

A smile tugged at the corners of his mouth, and his blood felt like he'd poured in rice cereal, the kind that snapped and crackled and popped when it touched liquid. He dang near dropped his phone as he tapped to download her application, and then it bloomed in front of him.

He scanned it the way he had last year when she'd applied, and at the bottom, she had a couple of links for references.

He tapped the first one, and it was a video. Laura's face was frozen on the first frame, and Todd's chest pinched at the sight of her. He wanted to hear her voice so badly. The video finally started to play, and Laura grinned at him. "Hey, Todd," she said, and she didn't seem nervous at all. "I worked on a husky today, and I asked him if I was the best vet he'd ever seen. This was his answer."

The clip switched over to a black and white dog with bright blue husky eyes. "I'm the best vet you know, aren't I?" Laura asked off-camera, and the husky tipped his head back and wailed, "No, no, nooooo!"

Todd burst out laughing, the happiness streaming through him more than he could contain. He recognized the difference between how he felt in those few moments compared to the last few weeks without Laura, and he had to see her. He must talk to her today. Right now.

He turned toward the front door and went that way as he tapped to call her. If he got outside, perhaps he could imagine her across the street, flying her kite. They'd done that a few times since their disastrous first date, months and months ago.

Todd didn't care if they had many more bad days together. As long as they were together.

"Hello?" Laura asked as if she didn't know he was the one calling.

"Hey." He stepped out onto the porch, the air entering his lungs better and cleaner than it had ever been. "Wow, I miss hearing your voice." He chuckled as a hint of embarrassment crept through him. He ducked his head, though he had nothing to hide anymore.

"You were right," he said at the same time she said, "I was wrong." They both fell into silence, and Todd puzzled through what she'd said.

"What were you wrong about?" he asked.

"Everything," she said.

"Where are you?"

"I'll be at your place in a couple of minutes if you aren't too mad."

He instantly checked down the lane, but he didn't see her car. "Laura," he said. "I'm not mad. I was never mad."

"Liar," she said, her voice full of tears.

"I had to do something to preserve my heart," he whispered. "You took it with you, you know, and I've been dying a little bit more every single day."

She sniffled, and then that black sedan made the turn nice and slow.

"We're air conditioning the whole ranch now?" Kyle griped behind him, but Todd didn't care.

Laura was here. He said, "I see you," and went down the steps to the front sidewalk. He told himself not to jog. He reminded himself that he didn't have shoes on. She was coming to him, and he didn't need to act like a fool out here this morning.

She arrived after several long moments, and Todd lowered the phone and ended the call. Laura emerged from the car, and she looked radiant and beautiful. She wore a bright pink shirt in plaid with a pair of jeans, her cowgirl boots, and her hair clipped back on the sides.

She was stunning, and Todd could hardly believe she stood before him. "Hey," he said, suddenly as shy as the first time he'd met her. "You're here." He told himself not to say another word, and he tucked his hands in his jeans pockets.

"I'm here." She took a step toward him and then rocked back onto her heels. Then she flew toward him, spread her arms wide, and he caught her as she launched herself into his arms. He grunted and stumbled a little, but she was only half his size and he barely moved.

"I'm so sorry," she said into his neck. "I made all the wrong decisions. It was a huge mistake to leave this ranch. A huge mistake to buy into that clinic." She pulled back and looked at him, her legs wrapped right around his waist.

He looked up at her, haloed in the morning sunshine, and knew she was his angel. She made everything in his life worth living and having. He loved her, and he wanted her to stay with him forever.

She leaned down and kissed him, and the fire raging in Todd's veins got poured into the kiss.

"I missed you," she said, pulling away for only as long as it took to say the words. She kissed him again. "I'm going to sell my part of the clinic." Another kiss. "I do need another job, though." Another kiss. She pulled away, and Todd wasn't sure if he was coming or going. At this point, he didn't much care. "I'll take you over a job, though, if you've already hired someone."

Todd smiled and shook his head, holding onto her hips to keep her flush against him. "I haven't hired anyone yet."

Laura smiled down at him. "I'm sorry, Todd. Will you forgive me for forgetting that the past needs to be left in the past?"

"Yes," he said simply. "Will you forgive me for breaking up with you?"

"Yes."

He kissed her this time, and the inferno between them started again.

"Hey!" Kyle yelled from the porch. "Who got upset with me for the PDA on the porch the other night?"

Todd chuckled way down deep in his chest, but he didn't stop kissing Laura. He couldn't. She'd come back, and he loved her, and he didn't care who saw them. He eventually did pull back, his chest heaving. "I love you, Laura Woodcross."

"I love you too, Todd Stewart." Those were the best words he'd ever heard, and Todd kissed his angel one more time.

CHAPTER
TWENTY-EIGHT

Jesse took a moment at the front door of the cabin he shared with Adam. He had to get over to the lodge for Starla's going-away party; he was already late as it was.

The cabin sat in silence, the gentle rush of water from the dishwasher filling the air behind him. The lodge would be the opposite of that, and he normally didn't mind.

Tonight, he minded.

Starla would be leaving Chestnut Springs for Austin tomorrow. Her house had sold fairly easily, and he'd gone to her place last night to help her pack the last few boxes. Tomorrow, he'd round up as many of his brothers as he could and make the drive to her clapboard white house in town to help her with the bigger items. Couches, bed, dining room table, all of it.

He pulled open the front door and went out onto the porch. He'd kissed Starla here once. Maybe she'd kissed him. He wasn't sure. Everywhere he looked, he saw his relationship with Starla, and the ranch was going to be boring and quiet without her here.

"Probably better for her to be gone than here and not be with her," he muttered to himself. He'd endured a few months of that too, and he hadn't been happy, not for a single day.

He wasn't sure why the two of them couldn't figure out how to be together. No matter what he did, it felt like Father Time was against them. She had a great opportunity in Austin, and he didn't blame her for taking it. He simply wished it was a restaurant here in town so he could still see her.

Jesse had spent a lot of time in his life wishing, and he pushed against the idiotic thoughts. He was tired of wishing. Praying too. Those didn't seem to go his way either. He straightened his collar as he went down the steps, a task Starla usually did for him. He didn't wear a tie tonight, but a dark red polo with a pair of jeans. It would be a big party at the lodge, with a lot of past guests, people from town, and everyone from the ranch. He didn't need to go overboard, though. He would already have more eyes on him than he liked.

He swallowed as he swung behind the wheel of his truck. Adam had left an hour ago to help get the horses put away faster so he could get to the party too. Sometimes they drove over to the lodge together, as everything happened there, at the epicenter.

Jesse liked living in the last cabin on the family lane, because no one but him and Adam had a reason to come down this far. He always knew when a guest was lost, and anyone who arrived at his cabin meant to be there.

He glanced at his siblings' cabins as he went past them, and only a few minutes later, he arrived at the lodge. Cars and trucks clogged the lot, which meant he'd have nowhere to park there. He went past the lodge and around to the barn in the back. A small family and employee lot sat there, but it was full too. He drove between the back of the lodge and the barn where Todd and Sierra had offices, found several of his siblings' vehicles there, and he pulled into a small space between a Honda Accord he didn't recognize and the huge propane tank.

He'd come this far, and he wasted no time getting out of his truck and heading inside. Through the back door, he took another breath and tried to find the center of peace inside him. He'd found it a few times in recent years, and that core of him had allowed him to start dating again in the first place.

He wasn't sure he would again, though. He'd started to fall in love with Starla Masters, and he liked her for a lot of reasons, but one was that she was as stern as him, as well as just a little bit jaded, the same as him.

He went down the hall from the back of the lodge, which housed the administrative offices, and out into the large front of the lodge.

Just like they did during holidays and other big parties, all of the cowboy desks had been pushed against the wall on the north side of the lodge. The dining room had been cleared of the dinner tables, and smaller, taller tables had been set up. Groups of people milled around those, putting down their flutes of champagne and tiny plates of one-bites.

He only knew that term because of Starla, who'd teased him that he didn't have the same culinary knowledge she did. "A one-bite, Jess," she'd told him. "Is something you can eat in one bite. Savory, sweet, anything. They're small, so you can make a lot in a short amount of time, and they go a long way."

He'd chuckled with her, asked her what else she'd be serving at her own party, and then kissed her until she ducked away from him. They hadn't officially broken up, but she'd drive away from him tomorrow, and Jesse couldn't imagine they'd try to keep things going between them.

He could barely manage a girlfriend he saw simply by showing up to work. Starla knew that, and she'd known she'd lose him when she took the job.

His throat narrowed, but he swallowed against the emotion. If he was lucky, he could attach himself to Adam, Blake, or Todd, and pass the hours until the party died down, the guests left, and he could kiss Starla one last time.

He took a step out of the hallway, and Blake called, "Jesse, over here." He made room for Jesse at the table, and Jesse moved into the spot effortlessly.

"You made it." Blake grinned at Jesse like this was the party of the century.

Jesse looked back at him. "Yeah. Have you seen Starla?"

"Oh, she's in and out," Blake said. "She and Gina just

went back into the kitchen to solve some problem with the ricotta."

Jesse nodded and turned sideways as a waiter appeared with a tray of drinks. He took one after confirming it was tonic water and not alcohol. He'd struggled with that addiction in the past, and everything was better in his life if he didn't even take a sip.

His phone vibrated in his pocket, and he pulled it out as he took a drink of his water. Starla had texted with, *Are you coming?*

I'm here, he sent back. *You're the one hiding out in the kitchen.*

That would get her to come out, and he wasn't surprised when she squished into the narrow space between him and Adam a half-minute later. Gina did the same on his other side, really pressing into Blake.

He put his arm around his fiancée, and they'd be married very soon. Jesse wanted to do the same and bring Starla all the way into his personal space. Blake leaned down and chuckled as he kissed Gina, and Jesse would like to mimic that.

He didn't. He slipped his phone back into his pocket and lifted his drink to his lips. "Problem with the ricotta?"

"Samuel thought we didn't have more, and they were serving mozerrela with the prosciutto." Starla shook her head. "Apparently I'm the only one who knows how to find things in the walk-in fridge."

Jesse gave her a smile that felt tight on his face, which meant she could see how tense he was.

She looked over to Adam, and then across the table to

Todd. Jesse did the same, really taking in how many of them had gathered at this single table. His family—and all the people who loved Starla.

Her hand found his down at his side. She pressed in a little closer. "Do you want to go take a walk?"

"It's your party," he said, leaning closer. He almost felt flirty, but he pulled back on that. He couldn't be flirting with her at her going-away party. "Don't you have to be here to talk to people?"

"They won't miss me for ten minutes." She took his hand in hers now and squeezed. "I left something in my car. Come get it with me." She said the last couple of sentences in a loud, commanding voice everyone at the table could hear despite the music and chatter from others around them.

"All right." Jesse turned, releasing her hand as he did, and led the way toward the hallway he'd already come down. She followed him, and they went all the way outside before she said anything.

"I was afraid you weren't going to come," she said.

"Of course I'd be here." He slowed and waited for her to catch up. She wore a low heel, something Starla didn't do very often, to go with her glitzy black dress. She had womanly curves, and dark eyeshadow, and she ticked all of Jesse's boxes. Over and over, she'd checked every item on his list of what he found attractive and who he wanted in a wife.

They'd never talked about marriage, family, children, none of it. Everything in their relationship had stayed surface-level, as if both of them had somehow known they

KISSING HER COWBOY BOSS **307**

wouldn't end up together.

Not so surface, Jesse thought. If that was really true, he wouldn't be so upset she was leaving. Disappointed? Mad? Heartbroken? Jesse honestly didn't know how he felt in this moment.

Starla took his hand again, and Jesse sank into the touch this time. "I'm glad you came," she said. "I know it wasn't easy for you."

He didn't know what to say. He looked to the horizon beyond the employee lot. "Do you think we could do the long-distance thing?"

Kyle and Maddy had been, for the past several months at least. She was coming here for the summer, and Jesse wouldn't be surprised if Kyle was the next to get engaged.

For a while there, Jesse had thought it would be Todd, but Laura had left several weeks ago, and Todd had turned into Oscar the Grouch. Jesse understood that, as he'd done the same after his divorce. One of the only people who'd let him feel what he wanted to feel, and act the way he wanted to act was Todd. Adam had been nothing but sympathetic, and without the two of them, Jesse didn't think he'd be at the family ranch at all.

Now that Laura was back, Jesse had Todd back in the running for the next Stewart to get married.

"I don't know," Starla said with a sigh. "Doesn't seem like your kind of thing."

"Or yours," he said.

"No," she admitted.

Jesse paused in the evening shade of the huge oak tree beside the barn. "We can still call and text," he said. "I want to know how your first day goes. I want to be there on opening day."

"I'll tell you everything," she said. They fell into silence again, and Jesse normally didn't mind it. Today, he just wanted to go back to the party and let the noise overwhelm him. He wouldn't have to think that way.

"I wish things were different," she said. She turned into him. "Maybe the restaurant will be terrible, and I'll be back —like Laura."

Jesse gave her a smile. "Maybe." He didn't really think so—neither did she—but he didn't argue.

"You'll be okay without me." She reached up and brushed his long hair off his forehead. She wasn't asking. She stated it. A gorgeous smile touched her lips, and she lifted up onto her toes and kissed him.

White noise filled Jesse's head, and his hands knew exactly where to rest on Starla's back and hips. He brought her closer, and her hands moved around to the back of his neck and into his hair.

He could honestly kiss her forever, but she didn't let him. She pulled back after only a few seconds, and she said, "I better get back."

She stepped away, pulling her hands with her, and gave him another smile. He didn't want to stand out at the oak tree alone, so he started back toward the lodge with her, knowing he'd just been given his good-bye kiss.

———

KYLE WOKE TO THE SOUND OF HIS PHONE RINGING. HE reached to the right, where his nightstand stood. His eyes opened, but everything stayed dark. It was far too early in the morning for anyone to be calling him.

In that moment, his pulse pounced up his throat. If his phone was ringing before five a.m. the person had called at least three times. Or else it was after five a.m.

He found his phone and managed to squint at the brightness of it. He saw Maddy's name and that it was before five a.m., both of which sent his heart palpitating again.

He swiped on the call and sat up at the same time. "Mads?" he asked.

"Thank goodness." She breathed out the words. "I remembered that you told me to call three times before it would actually ring, so I did, but I had to wait through your voicemail each time."

"Sorry," he said. "What's going on?" She sounded rushed, panicked, and scared. "Are you okay?"

"I am," she said. Her voice pinched now, turning tinny when she added, "My momma fell last night. Daddy just called me to go get her and take her to the hospital a couple of hours ago. I guess they were thinking she could just go to bed and wake up fine in the morning."

Todd could imagine her shaking her head the way she did. She was the youngest of three girls, and her parents were getting up there in age.

"They just took her back for surgery, and they think it might be bad." She sniffled, and Kyle wished he was there to comfort her.

As early as it was, it took him a moment to think about his day ahead. "I'll shower and come down," he said.

"Okay," she said.

His heart swelled.

"Kyle," she said. "I'm not going to be able to come to the ranch this summer."

The words landed heavily in his ears. Kyle reached to snap on the lamp, as if that would help him see the situation clearer. "You don't think so?"

"Tammy and Kristen live out-of-state," she said. "They have year-round jobs. I don't work in the summer. I'm going to have to stay here and take care of my mom."

Of course she should. Kyle sighed, regretted it, and said, "It's fine, Maddy. We'll make it work."

"How?" The desperation in her voice pierced his heart, and he shook his head.

"I don't know," he said. He'd watched Todd let Laura pull away from him last year, and it felt like Maddy was doing the same to him now.

He told himself that wasn't a fair evaluation. She had been planning to come to the ranch for the summer so they could be closer. She'd done it all without his knowledge, as a surprise to him. She was upset she couldn't come. This wasn't her choice.

"I'll swing by Hiller's and get you that coffee you love," he said. "I'll be there in an hour."

"Okay," she said, and she ended the call.

Kyle stayed on the edge of his bed, trying to think through everything that had suddenly come barreling into his life. Blake's wedding was in a couple of days, and

Maddy likely wouldn't be able to attend that with him either. He told himself not to be upset. Plenty of his siblings would be at the wedding without a date.

Of course, now that Laura was back, Todd would have someone on his arm. Starla had left the ranch last weekend. Jesse might never date again. Adam for sure wouldn't. To his knowledge, Holly and Sierra didn't have anyone hanging on their arms in the evenings. If any of them had a date, it would be Nash, and Kyle could do what he'd always done—hang out with his family.

He'd be fine.

As he showered, texted Todd so his brother wouldn't worry, and got behind the wheel of his truck, Kyle kept thinking about how he wanted more for his life than *fine*.

He wanted spectacular. He wanted amazing. He wanted love, happiness, and crowds screaming for him as he walked on-stage with a guitar in his hand.

His dream of becoming country-music famous hadn't died. He'd only buried it for a little while.

"Maybe it's time to resurrect it," he told himself as he started south in the pre-dawn grayness spreading across Texas.

CHAPTER
TWENTY-NINE

Blake Stewart entered the appointed room, feeling like he'd left something behind in his cabin on the ranch. He'd lived there alone for so long, he wasn't sure how things would go after tonight.

Gina would live there with him once they returned from their trip to Italy. She'd always wanted to go and "taste the country," and Blake figured he could provide that for her before their real lives crept back in and took over again.

They both wanted children, and they both worked busy hours on the ranch. It was a good life, and Blake loved it.

Only two people stood in the room, and he wasn't surprised to see his mom and dad there ahead of him. "Mama," he said. "You'll have to leave when I have to get changed." He noted the three black garment bags hanging on racks in front of the mirrors.

His mother sniffled, and Blake opened his arms to fold

her into them. "It's a non-crying day," he said. "This is a good thing, Mama."

"I know," she said into his chest.

"You love Gina."

"I do." She leaned back and smiled at him. "Maybe I'll finally get some grandchildren."

Blake just smiled, because the last thing he needed to give Mama was fuel. Once she got going on all the things she lacked in her life, they could be there for hours and then it *would* become a crying day for Blake.

She stepped out of his arms, and Blake moved over to Daddy. "Morning, Pops." He hugged him tightly too. "We got everything here?"

"Some of the boys are bringing their own things," he said. "Adam won't let anyone touch his cowboy hats." He shook his head like Adam was uppity, and maybe he was. About cowboy hats, Blake could agree that Adam had… peculiar tastes, but he didn't begrudge him for them. If he wanted to carry everything over from the ranch, Blake didn't care.

"As long as I have my clothes," he said.

"You do. Mama went through them three times."

Blake thought he detected a hint of dryness in Daddy's tone, and they shared a secret smile. Blake went to inspect his tuxedo and indeed found it all present and ready for him.

Over the course of the next half-hour, all of his siblings arrived in the family room at Vines and Ivy, the elite wedding and reception center Gina had chosen for their wedding.

Blake would've been happy to walk up to the doors at the lodge to say "I do," but Gina wanted something a little fancier. She'd made their wedding cake, and not only that, but a groom's cake too. German chocolate, with the traditional coconut frosting pulled and sculpted just right to make it look like a weathered saddle.

She'd sent him pictures late last night. So late, he hadn't seen them until this morning, and he'd responded that he was worried she'd been up too late.

Gina hadn't responded yet, so perhaps she was running late this morning. He didn't worry that she wouldn't be here. They both seemed anxious to get this ceremony done so they could start the next, new chapter in their lives.

Blake's pulse skipped like a flat stone over water, and he swallowed as Todd came to his side. "Ready?" his brother asked. He'd been Blake's best friend for as long as he could remember, and Blake loved him for being at his side today.

He wore a smile and a black cowboy hat, and that was the image Blake always had in his head for Todd. "Yes," he said. "I feel like I've been waiting for a long time to get married."

"You're no spring chicken." Todd chuckled. "We better get started. A woman just came in to tell us we have to be headed out to the ballroom in forty-five minutes." He leaned closer. "And Jesse looks like he hasn't showered yet." He nodded over to where Jesse stood with Adam and Holly.

Blake followed his nod and scoffed. Jesse wore a dirty

pair of jeans, the rattiest pair of tennis shoes Blake ever did see, and a white striped shirt. Well, it had been white at one point. Now, it looked a shade of yellow Blake didn't think should ever be at a wedding.

"My word," he said under his breath when he wanted to use stronger language. He turned back to Todd. "I guess I'll be grateful he's here at all?"

Todd nodded. "Him and Adam, as this whole Starla-leaving thing has them both declaring that they'll never date again."

Blake rolled his eyes, then looked right into Todd's. "Are you glad you're not declaring that with them?" Laura had returned to the ranch a little over a week ago, and Todd had turned into a completely different version of himself.

Todd only gave him a smile before he bent down and started to unzip the garment bag in front of him. "The girls want to give you a hug."

Blake turned around to find Sierra and Holly, and they stood with Mama near the door. Blake made quick work of the distance between them, taking all three of them under his wingspan.

Holly giggled; Sierra laughed; Mama glared. "You're ruining my curls," she said, and Blake only laughed at her. He did drop his arm and take Holly into a single embrace. "I love you, Hols."

"I can't believe you're getting married." She'd dated here and there, but nothing serious. She worked every evening, and Blake knew that wasn't great for rela-tionships.

He didn't tell her it would be her soon. He didn't even know if she wanted to hear something like that.

He simply held her tightly so she'd know she could come talk to him anytime, and then he stepped over to his younger sister. "Thanks for everything, Sierra."

Her arms went around him too. "What do you mean?"

"I know you've picked up a lot of slack recently," Blake said real quiet, right into her ear. "I appreciate it. I think you're awesome."

She smiled as they parted, and Blake turned to face Mama. "You look so pretty," he told her as he hugged her properly. "Holly needs your touch with her hair."

"I do not," Holly said instantly, and Mama laughed.

He held her until she started to pull away, and he let her take his face in both of her hands, the way she had when he'd first gone to kindergarten, decades ago. "You're a good man," she said. "I love you."

"I love you too, Mama."

"I need all of the women with me," someone called, and Holly and Sierra linked their arms through Mama's and guided her toward the door. Without them, Blake had his doubts about whether or not she would've gone.

As the door closed, he turned back to the room, all eyes on him. He normally didn't mind that so much, but these were his brothers. Cousins. Uncles. Everyone important to him.

The door opened again, and the same woman said, "Mister Stewart, I need you ready to go to the altar in thirty-three minutes." She gave him a hawk-like look that told him not to take an extra second.

"Yes, ma'am," he said, tipping his cowboy hat at her. She vacated the room again, and Blake faced his family. "All right, boys. You heard her. Thirty-three minutes." He grinned around at them, giving a single cocked eyebrow to Jesse.

His brother ignored him, and Blake told himself to let Todd deal with that particular brother. It was his wedding day, and he needed to get dressed for his bride.

———

GINA BARLOW SMOOTHED HER HANDS DOWN THE FRONT OF her dress. "I think it looks fine," she said. "I'm going to be holding a bouquet right here." She mimed where the flowers would be. "No one will even see it." She knew about the tiny rip—as did everyone else in the room—but no one else would.

She nodded to her sister, and Ella reached for the shoe box. Gina held Jenna Johnson's hand to steady herself as she stepped into the heels, took another moment to find her balance, and then cocked one foot to see it with the dress in the mirror.

"Still perfect," she said, admiring the hot pink heel. It wasn't tacky-high, but added three inches to her height so she'd be closer to Blake's shoulder than his belly button.

Her nerves fired at her. She couldn't wait to see him standing at the altar, expecting her to come toward him. Go, she would, because she couldn't wait to become his wife.

She hadn't imagined herself getting married and

settling down in the same small Texas town she'd grown up in, but now that it was happening, she couldn't picture anything else for herself.

Blake said they could've gotten married on the ranch, but it was the first week of May, and the temperature outside had made her point for her. She'd gotten sweaty just loading her clothes into the back of her sedan that morning.

She'd brought the wedding cakes over last night, when the temps were cooler and there were no deadlines to meet. She wasn't rushed, or stressed, and she'd enjoyed making the seven-tier cake immensely. Seven for luck, as she'd told Blake. He'd laughed and told her the two of them didn't need luck.

She didn't really think so, and she turned away from the mirror. "Is Blake ready?"

The wedding coordinator for Vines and Ivy stood near the door, a clipboard in her hand and a speaker in her ear. She pressed a button on the wire, spoke into her headset, and then nodded to Gina.

"My daddy's outside?"

"He's ready," the redheaded woman confirmed. She looked like she could use a good meal of only desserts, and Gina wanted to fatten her up a little bit. She smiled at the woman as she approached and said, "You should try the wedding cake today."

"We don't eat the customer's food," she said without missing a beat.

"Or come out to the Texas Longhorn Ranch and let me feed you some banana sheet cake. You'll love it."

Her smile didn't slip. "I will, ma'am." She stepped sideways to open the door, and she gestured Gina out first. "Your daddy is right there." She indicated the left side of the doorway. After turning back to the other women in the room, who included all of her female family members, as well as Blake's, she called, "The bridal party will line up right here in the hallway. I'll lead you over to the ballroom, and we'll go right in, so we need to be ready."

Gina went out into the hall and linked her arm through her father's. "Thank you, Daddy," she said as the coordinator exited next and the other ladies started streaming out behind her. Not everyone would be in the wedding party, and the redhead let them go past her and toward the ballroom so they could take their seats.

"Of course," Daddy said, lifting her hand and kissing the back of it. "You look beautiful."

Gina felt beautiful, and she took the bouquet from Ella as her sister came out into the hall. She paused and helped Gina get all the layers of lace and fabric where they needed to be. She brushed her fingers along her hairline, then deemed her, "Ready," before joining the group.

"Men are right here at the end of the hall," the redhead yelled. She had a loud voice for such a small body, and Gina's pulse beat rapidly again.

She stayed still as the group started to move out, a man in a dark suit stepping into place beside each of the women wearing a bridesmaid gown of their choice. Gina had opinions about some things—mostly food—but what someone wore at her wedding wasn't one of them.

Ella was the first person in line, and Starla the last. She

turned around and faced Gina. Sudden tears filled her eyes, and Starla grabbed onto her shoulders and hugged her, being careful not to mash the flowers between them.

"You're amazing," she said. "I'm so happy for you." Her voice sounded like she'd inhaled helium, and she wiped her eyes as she stepped back. She was a dark goddess, with tan skin and dark hair, eyelashes, eyebrows, and eyes against the pale pink dress she'd chosen for today's wedding. She too wore a pair of bright pink heels —identical to Gina's—and she smiled through her emotion.

"You're okay to walk with Jesse?" Gina asked. She'd questioned Starla about this before, and she'd spent no less than ten minutes text-lecturing Jesse a couple of nights ago about what he could and couldn't do or say to Starla. Her taking the job in Austin had been very hard on both of them, and she'd reminded both of them that this was *her wedding*.

They'd both agreed to be on their best behavior. Because Starla was last in line, Gina watched Jesse cock his elbow for her, and she watched as Starla effortlessly slipped her hand into it. They didn't break stride, and Gina looked at her daddy. "Our turn."

"Let's go, princess." He started down the hallway, where the redhead waited at the end of the hall. How she'd already gotten to the ballroom and back baffled Gina, but the music from the room where she'd be married very soon entered her ears. Her nerves fired again, and she focused on walking without tripping on her long skirt. What a spectacle that would be.

The wedding party had been swallowed by the room by the time it came into view for Gina. She crossed the grand foyer, admiring it the same way she had the first time she and Blake had visited Vines and Ivy.

Fresh flowers sat on the front table, and the scent of oranges and lavender hung in the air. The temperature was strictly controlled, and she could breathe easily that no one would get sun stroke or sweat through their clothes.

The redhead nodded to a brunette just inside the ballroom, and the music changed on Gina's next step. She'd been told to wait at the door if the crowd was still getting to their feet when she arrived. She and Daddy did so, though the crowd now stood and seemed mostly settled.

She looked left and right, finding friends and distant family members in the back rows. All eyes in the entire room landed on her, and she reminded herself not to grip the stems of the flowers too tightly. She didn't want to look tense or scared as she walked down the aisle.

Straight ahead of her, something moved, and her eyes went that way. Blake had stepped in front of the altar from the right side, and everything inside Gina calmed instantly.

The breath whooshed out of her body at the handsome sight of his broad shoulders in that dark tuxedo. He wore a huge, black cowboy hat and big, black cowboy boots. He clasped his hands in front of him as if he could wait for hours for her to get to him.

She took the first step, and Daddy went with her. It seemed a long time, and yet only a single second, before she reached the altar too. Daddy kissed both of her cheeks before passing her to Blake, who leaned down and pressed his cheek to hers.

"Wow," he said, and as he was the more eloquent of the two of them, that said something.

The sound of moving feet and scuffling chairs filled the hall as the crowd sat, and then the pastor moved to stand on the other side of the altar.

"What a beautiful sight to see," he said. "A man and a woman who clearly love one another. Friends and family and loved ones gathered here to witness that love." He touched his chest where his heart beat. "I love seeing this sight every time I have the opportunity to perform a wedding."

"That's the extent of your speech," Blake muttered, and the pastor looked at him and laughed. They were old friends, and in fact, Cedar Mullen was a few years younger than Blake and Gina.

"I've been given my instructions," he said. "Blake and Gina will say their vows, and we'll get the ceremony started."

Gina turned toward Blake, as they'd practiced. She took both of his hands in hers and said, "Blake, I love you. I love working with you on the ranch, and I love how you put so many things and so many people first. I'm glad you didn't give up on me when I made it hard to want to be with me, and I just know we aren't going to need the seven layers of luck on our wedding cake to make it. I can't wait to be your wife."

She nodded, because she really couldn't wait, and the more she talked, the longer the wedding would go.

Blake grinned at her. "Gina said I could say whatever I wanted for my vows. I did a little Internet research, but it all felt stale and silly." A few people in the crowd chuckled, and Gina's cheeks hurt for how hard she smiled.

"I thought it best to just say something simple. I hope you'll forgive me, sweetheart, because I know you like elaborate for occasions like this."

She shook her head, her heartbeat thumping inside her chest.

"I love you. I've loved you since I was sixteen years old, and that never went away just because we weren't in the same town. The moment I saw you back here in Chestnut Springs, my heart started to hope we could be together. And here we are. I will do my best to always make sure you're happy. I love you, sweetheart."

They faced the pastor, and Cedar got the important, official questions out of the way. Gina said, "I do," as loudly as she could, but Blake still beat her as he practically bellowed, "I do," as the answer to his question.

The crowd cheered, and Blake pulled Gina toward him. Laughing, she handed her bouquet to Ella, and Blake planted a kiss squarely on her mouth.

This wasn't meant to be a passionate, tender kiss. They were both smiling, but in the few seconds of "kissing," Gina definitely felt the tender passion with which Blake loved her.

They'd done it. They were now man and wife.

Finally.

CHAPTER
THIRTY

aura swayed and step-touched along with the rest of the crowd in the arena. It was the first concert of the summer season, and Kyle had booked Josie's favorite country music star—Faith Ostetler. Laura loved her music too, and she couldn't wait for the private meeting with her tomorrow.

Kyle had arranged that for all staff and family members at the ranch, and Josie had cried real tears when she'd found out. Laura had been living with her for the past five weeks since she'd returned to the Texas Longhorn Ranch, begged for her boyfriend to forgive her, and then gotten the job she'd walked away from by mistake.

Todd slid his hand along her waist now, and she leaned into his side. He was so *good*, and Laura had always pictured herself with a good man. When she thought about her future now, it was with Todd. It was here on this ranch, with all these quirky animals and big personalities. It was the two of them driving the hour to visit her parents or having her family here to the ranch to celebrate holidays and birthday, anniversaries and maybe just to fly a kite.

She looked up at Todd and smiled, but he kept his attention on the stage ahead of them. The past five weeks had made up for the tortuous several before them, and Laura couldn't believe the marked difference between living her life in the right place at the right time and living it in the wrong place, doing the wrong thing, with the wrong people.

It was like night and day, and she was so glad the sun had come out again.

The song finished, and the crowd whooped and cheered, Laura along with them. She loved the electricity that flowed through the air at concerts like these, and this summer season opener sure seemed to have a lot of it floating in the air.

"All right, folks," Faith said into the mic, her voice carrying easily out over the rolling land. The concert arena sat across the road from the lodge, with huge cleared fields for the parking. It wasn't the same spot as they'd had for the holiday concert. This one was much bigger, with a stage Kyle set up over the course of a week that wouldn't come down until fall arrived again and the guests had to go back to their regular lives, with work and school.

"I think we have something special happening tonight." The spotlights started to flash above her, and then they swooped out over the audience. "Where's my cowboy?" She put her hand up to her eyes as if she was peering into a bright sun.

Todd eased away from Laura, and she let him go as the sound of drums filled the air. She began to clap along with them, looking over to Josie with delight. "What's going on?" she asked. "Is this a normal part of her concerts?"

"I don't know," Josie yelled. "She didn't do this last time I saw her." They both looked back up to the stage, and Laura stopped clapping as she watched Todd swing himself up onto the steps. He climbed them as the crowd went wild. Josie started jumping up and down and screaming, and she grabbed onto Laura. "He's going to ask you to marry him!" she said over and over.

Laura let herself get jostled around, because it sure seemed like Todd was going to do that. She wasn't sure why he thought that would be a good idea. They weren't two people who loved being in the spotlight, and out of everyone who worked and lived here at the ranch, they weren't the ones to get engaged in public.

She looked over to Josie and then back up to Todd. "Howdy, y'all," he drawled into the microphone. "I just wanted to take a minute here to thank you for coming." He shifted his feet and cleared his throat, and Laura's heart dropped all the way to her toes.

"My brother Kyle is usually the one up here on stage," he said next. "He hasn't missed a concert here at the Texas Longhorn Ranch for about five years now. He's around tonight—or he will be in a little bit—which is why I'm standin' here in his place."

A smile finally touched his face. "He doesn't know I'm telling you this, and if he asks how y'all found out, you're to tell them Nash told you, okay? Say it with me—Nash."

He chuckled into the mic, and the crowd started saying Nash's name though not all together.

Laura relaxed, because Todd wasn't dropping to one knee and pulling out a diamond ring. He was selling out Kyle, and she hoped he wouldn't wake up with his head shaved or his face colored with red marker. She giggled at her junior high prank thought just as Kyle said, "He's not here, because he's got a meeting with a music producer out of Nashville. He's wanted to be in country music since the day he was born, so if you're the kind to pray, send up a prayer for my brother Kyle that he'll finally get his chance."

The crowd cheered again, and Laura watched the emotion roll across Todd's face. He loved his brother so very much, and that made her heart sing.

"All right," Todd said, his voice strong again. "Let's get back to the concert, shall we?" He replaced the mic on the stand, nodded to Faith Ostetler, and started to leave the stage.

Laura started to push through the crowd to get to the side aisle so she could go meet him as he came down the stairs. It took her a bit longer than she anticipated, and she met him halfway up the aisle. His eyebrows went up as he reached for her hand. "You okay?"

"Yeah." She hugged him. "I'm kind of concert-ed out. Can we go back to your house for ice cream?" She fiddled with his collar as she asked, and when she added a flirty look through her lashes, he laughed.

"All right," he said, and he slung his arm around her as she turned around to go in the same direction as him. They had to walk quite a ways back to the lodge, and then around it to his truck. She didn't mind, because the summer night was barely starting to cool, the darkness just about to swallow the dusk.

When they finally couldn't hear any strains of music from the concert, Laura said, "Josie said you were going to propose when you went up on stage."

Todd chuckled, his voice sending vibrations through Laura's veins. "That's not really our style."

"No, it's not," she said. "Is Kyle going to be upset with you for telling everyone about his call with Nashville?"

"Probably," Todd said good-naturedly. "He needs the prayers, and he's too stubborn to ask for them himself."

"They're strangers," she said. "He might have a point."

"They're guests here," he said. "Our motto is, once you're here, you're family."

Laura did feel like that around the Stewarts, and she snuggled into Todd's side. "Like you said I could belong here if I wanted to."

"Exactly like that." He opened her door for her and helped her into his big truck. Once he was behind the wheel, he glanced over to her. "You do belong here, Laura."

"Yes," she said, smiling back at him. "I do."

He cleared his throat and shifted into gear. "How do you feel about saying that while wearing a white dress, with me at the altar with you?" He gave a little cough, a sign of his nerves.

"I do?" she asked, teasing him. "I feel great about

saying that to you." She held out her left hand. "I don't have a ring though, so I think it's gonna be a while."

Todd said nothing, and Laura didn't mind the silence. Sometimes it told her more than when he did speak. Right now, he was thinking about being her husband and having her as his wife, and Laura liked those thoughts too.

He pulled up to his cabin, and they went inside together. He started dishing up ice cream, and Laura pulled out her phone to check some of the pictures she'd taken during the concert. Todd came toward her, and she reached up to take the bowl of ice cream.

"Laura," he said, and she looked away from her phone. He stood in front of her, but he didn't carry a bowl of ice cream. Instead, the tiny little thing pinched between his fingers glinted in the lights beaming on it from the kitchen.

She sucked in a breath; Todd dropped to both knees, not just one.

He held up the ring; he smiled. "I love you," he said. "Today, and yesterday, and forever. I want you right here in this cabin. Or if not this one, then one we build together just down the road." He looked at the ring, his expression softening. When he looked at her again, his eyes shone just like the diamond.

"We can fly kites without wind, or drive to bad restaurants, or just sleep together on the couch. As long as you're mine, and I'm yours, I'll be the happiest man in Texas." He extended the ring so it was a little closer to her. Laura had looked at it, but the rest of her body felt numb.

"Will you marry me?" he asked.

Laura nodded, her voice sounding like a frog as she

said, "Yes." She cleared away the rustiness. "Yes," she said again, nice and loud. A squeal built beneath her tongue, and she couldn't believe she'd managed to find the perfect cowboy for her. Again.

"I love you," she said as Todd slid the diamond onto her finger. With it in place, she took his face in her hands and kissed him, this man she loved.

"I love you too," he whispered, and then he kissed her again.

The moment between them after they'd parted was silent and sweet, and Laura wanted to live inside it for a long time. "When do you want to get married?" she asked.

"That's up to you, sweetheart," he murmured back. "Don't you want to talk to your mama about it?"

"Yeah," she said. "I want to get married here, though, Todd." She opened her eyes and looked straight into his. "On the ranch. Not in Hidden Hollow." Her life was here now; Todd was here; she knew there was nothing in Hidden Hollow for her anymore.

"I'm sure we can do that," he said with a smile.

"Blake and Gina didn't get married here," she said.

"It was too hot outside." He smoothed her hair back. "You want an outdoor wedding."

"I want an outdoor everything." She smiled at him, glad he knew her so well. "So maybe October? Beginning of November? It cools off by then."

He gave her a kind, sexy smile. "I suppose I can wait five months to be your husband."

"Let me talk to my mama," she said. "Yes to outside,

yes to cooler weather, so we're going to be looking at those months."

"I'll talk to Holly about reserving the event barn for whatever date you give me," he said.

Laura once again marveled at this man. "I love you, Todd."

"Mm." He closed his eyes and touched his lips to hers in a chaste kiss. "I love you too," he whispered just before kissing her like he meant it.

———

Keep reading for the first couple of chapters in the next book in the series, **CLAIMING HER COWBOY KISS**, which you can preorder now.

SNEAK PEEK – CLAIMING HER COWBOY KISS CHAPTER ONE:

Madeline Cruise glanced over to her momma even as she stuffed another T-shirt into her bag. "Are you sure?" she asked.

"I'm going to be fine," her mom said. "I mean, I am fine already. The surgery was three weeks ago, and Tammy's already in town."

"For a week," Maddy said, straightening from her half-packed suitcase. "Momma." She sank onto the bed and combed her fingers through her shorter hair. It felt like she had hardly any, and she considered wearing a wig for at least the dozenth time since her sisters had come to Dripping Springs.

They'd come right after Momma's fall, but they'd only stayed for a couple of days. Tammy had returned to Colorado to arrange time off from her accounting job, and she'd returned yesterday. Kristen hadn't come back from Louisiana yet, but that was because Maddy lived ten minutes from their parents, and she'd committed to taking care of her this summer.

When Momma asked about the job at the Texas Longhorn Ranch, though, Maddy hadn't been able to conceal the truth. She'd told her that she'd had to give up the summer job teaching art lessons for any guests who wanted to take them. Mostly children, but she'd said she could do an adult painting class too. When she'd proposed couples' painting night, Holly Stewart had gone nuts with, "Yes, that's *exactly* what we need," and "Great idea, Maddy. I can't wait for you to get here."

Maddy had been excited about it too, because it meant she'd live five minutes from her boyfriend, instead of almost sixty.

Momma had not been happy she was the reason Maddy couldn't go north, couldn't do the art classes, and hadn't heard from Kyle in over a week now. They'd argued, but Momma was more stubborn than Maddy, and she said she wouldn't let Maddy into the house if she didn't go to Chestnut Springs for the summer job.

If she couldn't get in the house, she couldn't take care of her mother. Daddy had said he'd be fine, and they has neighbors and friends who could help out too. Momma was doing really well in her recovery, because she was meticulous about using the walker, applying heat and ice to her hip, taking her medications, and doing her physical therapy.

She really was a very good patient, and Maddy had called Holly only three days ago to beg for the job back. Holly, who was Kyle's sister, had immediately said yes.

The cabin they had for her hadn't been filled, and they could add or remove classes at any time. If she needed to come home for a week to help with Momma, she could.

Thus, she'd started packing, as she was set to be on the road tomorrow just after breakfast. Holly was the evening manager at the lodge on the ranch, but she'd told Maddy that Blake—the Stewart brother who ran the whole she-bang—knew she was coming and would have her paper-work ready.

Kyle did not know she was coming. With everything else that had been going on, she hadn't found the time to call him. *False*, her mind whispered at her. She'd had time. She hadn't had the courage. She didn't want him to react like everything was fine, that he hadn't stopped speaking to her for the past eleven days. If she told him she was coming, and he was all, "Oh, I'm so happy. I can't wait to see you," then she'd know that the distance between them was a real issue.

She still had a job here in Dripping Springs, teaching kindergarten. She had the next ninety-four days off, but they'd go fast, just like they did every summer. She'd be moving back here, then there'd be the same physical distance between her and Kyle there'd been for the past five months.

At the moment, their relationship wasn't strong enough to weather the distance. She knew that. Kyle did too, which was why he'd gone silent. She'd let him too. She had an operational phone. It texted and made calls. She hadn't put forth the effort either.

Her stomach writhed as she pushed off the bed to go to

her bureau to get out her socks. "I just think you have to be realistic."

"I sit in the garden and read," Momma said. "I don't need help. Daddy can get me out there. I take all of my medications. You'll be bored out of your mind if you stay here."

They'd already had all of these arguments and conversations, so Maddy picked up all the clean socks she had and put them in her bag. She had access to laundry facilities, but they weren't in her cabin. So didn't need to take everything she owned.

She looked down into her bag, not even remembering what she'd packed and what else she needed. The truth was, she didn't need anything. Chestnut Springs had stores, and if she forgot her toothbrush, she could buy another one.

Maddy wiped he hand across her forehead and looked at her mother again. "You're sure?"

"Madeline." She looked disgusted and she pushed herself to standing with the help of her walker. Maddy made no move to help her, though she itched to do so. "You're going. I'm going home."

"You can't drive."

"I've been texting Estelle."

"Estelle?" Horror moved through Maddy, and she darted in front of her mom. "Momma, if you're going to get rides from Estelle Gardner, I'm definitely not going." She stood taller than her mother, but not by much.

"What is wrong with Estelle?" Momma put one hand on her hip. "Girl, you better move."

"Momma." Maddy did not move out of the way. "Estelle is ninety if she's a day. She's legally blind. She shouldn't be driving."

"Oh, pish posh," Momma said, pushing her walker into Maddy's foot.

"Hey." She jumped back, as she wasn't wearing shoes, and she didn't want to get run over.

"Estelle had her cataracts fixed," Momma said, no remorse for running over Maddy's toes. "She can see fine." She went into the hall in her slow gait from the hip surgery after her fall a few weeks ago. "I can't ask you to drive me. You have packing to do, and laundry and dishes, and when was the last time you vacuumed?"

She continued listing chores that needed to be done around Maddy's house until the front door closed behind her, sealing her voice out. Maddy stood in the mouth of her master suite, dumbfounded.

No, she wasn't the best housekeeper. She worked a busy job, and since her mother's fall, she'd been going straight to her parents' house every night after work. The end of the school year was insane, and she hadn't done laundry for a couple of weeks. It wasn't a crime.

She didn't want to go down the hall and see the work that waited for her. She did have a lot of dishes in her sink right now, and the dishwasher was full of clean dishes she hadn't had time to put away yet.

Usually, when she was busy and stressed like this, Momma would come over and stand at the sink, doing dishes and then move to the dining room table to fold Maddy's laundry. Everything had been thrown out of their normal routine when her mother had tripped up the front steps, and then fallen down them.

"She's just pushing you away, because she doesn't want you to miss this opportunity," she told herself. She'd lived near Momma for her whole life, except for the few years she'd gone to college, and Momma could say some cruel things sometimes, just to get her way.

She turned back to her bedroom, realizing she hadn't packed any sundresses. She hurried into her closet to get them, because they'd be casual and fun for the kids and sexy and summery for Kyle.

Maddy finished packing her clean clothes, then went to start the ones in her laundry basket. With every task she finished, her excitement grew. She'd cried when she'd told Kyle she wouldn't be able to come to the ranch for the summer. If they'd kept talking, she wouldn't be so nervous to make the hour-long drive. She'd have called him the moment she'd finished yelling at her mom about going to the ranch.

She worked and worked, doing dishes and vacuuming, folding laundry, and packing, packing, packing. She was really doing this.

"You are," she said about midnight, when she finally collapsed into bed.

She was.

———

THE FOLLOWING MORNING, MADDY LEFT LATE. HONESTLY, A lot of what she did happened late. She managed to arrive at school before the children, and she told herself it didn't matter when she got to the Texas Longhorn Ranch. Holly had said to "stop by" Blake's office when she got there.

She took a few extra minutes to wait in the long line at Hiller's to get the spiced coffee she loved, along with a chocolate chip muffin top and lemon poppyseed muffin top. When she got nervous, she ate, then she'd try to burn off the calories and the nerves in the gym.

"Thank you," she said, taking her goodies from the girl in the window. She finally hit the road, and her thumbs drummed against the steering wheel. She found her rhythm about halfway to Chestnut Springs, and by the time she pulled into the parking lot at the lodge, the same excitement she'd had until her mother's fall bubbled up inside her.

She found a parking spot, pulled into it, and got out of the car. She wasn't sure where Kyle would be at this time of day, on a Saturday, but she knew tonight was the ranch's concert. Jackie Cliffton, one of the best guitar players in Texas.

Maddy liked how Kyle booked local celebrities and big legends in the country music industry. She hadn't heard anything more about his call with a top music producer in Nashville, either.

She headed for the entrance of the lodge, and she watched as the door opened and a couple of people came outside. A man and a woman, both of them laughing like a comedian was telling jokes inside. For all Maddy knew, there could be. The Texas Longhorn Ranch provided a variety of activities for all ages, and she wouldn't put anything past them.

Her feet froze when she realized the man was Kyle Stewart. Her boyfriend.

The way he put his hand on the small of the back of the woman he was with—a beautiful brunette with thick, long hair with just the right amount of wave in it—suggested he perhaps wasn't Maddy's boyfriend after all.

They came down the steps, seemingly in their own bubble of joy and happiness. She wore a pencil skirt on the cusp of June, with a blouse with little black dots all over it. She put her hand on his forearm, and if Maddy had seen them going into a restaurant, she'd have assumed they were dating.

Something horrible and hot boiled inside her. She folded her arms and cocked her hip, but that didn't do much for a tall, tough cowboy like Kyle. She wasn't exactly curvy, and her power stance really only worked on five-year-olds.

Kyle saw her, and his laughter dried up instantly. He froze too, and the two of them stood several feet apart, staring at one another.

"Hello," Maddy said, finally taking another step through the gravel. "Who's this?" She switched her gaze from Kyle to the woman at his side. She had the where-withal to remove her hand from his arm as the smile slid from her face.

"Maddy," Kyle said. He came toward her too. "What are you doing here?"

SNEAK PEEK – CLAIMING HER COWBOY KISS CHAPTER TWO:

Pure embarrassment pulled through Kyle Stewart. He had not expected to see Madeline Cruise standing in the parking lot outside the lodge. He hadn't spoken to her in several days. Over a week. Maybe longer.

Humiliation drove through him. He hadn't even had the guts to break up with her properly. He sort of thought he'd just be able to stop talking to her, and that would be that.

"What am I doing here?" she repeated, her voice like acid. "I have a job here this summer." She started walking, her arms falling back to her sides. Kyle had dated enough women to know the folded arms meant something bad.

She wore a pair of cutoffs that went halfway down her thigh and a pale yellow T-shirt covered in blue and purple hummingbirds. Her hair barely brushed the tops of her shoulders, as she'd cut it, and she didn't wear much makeup. She still made his heart pitter and pound in a strange way, and he couldn't believe he hadn't been calling and texting her.

He used to barricade himself in his bedroom just to talk to her.

"Maddy," he said as she went past him.

"I have to talk to your brother," she said, breezing by him. "Maybe I'll find you afterward." She gave him a glare out of the corner of her eye and continued toward the steps. Up she went and right through the door.

Kyle stood in the parking lot, stunned and still frozen. His mind whirred and his pulse buzzed, and he barely registered the sound of the gravely steps of Elaine Trumaine.

"Who was she?" she asked.

Kyle focused on her. "I'm sorry. We were headed over to the stage." He indicated the golf cart, and the music executive put her mega-watt smile back on her face. Kyle tossed another glance toward the lodge door, but he knew he couldn't leave Elaine out here in the heat while he went to talk to Maddy. He could send her a text, and he pulled out his phone to do that.

It was great to see you, he typed out quickly. *I'm just showing this woman from Legacy Records the stage for tonight's concert, and then I'll be back for a grab-and-go lunch. Maybe we could find somewhere and eat together.*

She didn't answer immediately, and Todd's pulse pounded up into his throat. This was bad. Very bad. His stomach clenched, and he hated how he felt like the ground was going to open beneath him.

He got behind the wheel of the golf cart and put on his professional winning smile. Truth be told, it was less flirtatious. He didn't feel as glowy inside as he had a few minutes ago. The only reason he could hold his head upright was because Elaine had only been at the lodge for thirty minutes, and he hadn't really had the chance to embarrass himself too badly.

Like asking her out, he thought as he drove the golf cart across the road, and they bounced over the cattle grate. His chest felt like someone had poked a hot branding iron through his ribs, and he gripped the steering wheel like he could get rid of his emotions that way.

"There is it," he said a moment later. "See it?"

"Wow," Elaine said. "It's much bigger than I anticipated." She threw Kyle a flirty smile, and he prayed for a solution to this situation. He'd met and worked with plenty of country music executives in his life. He couldn't get past them several years ago, so he'd used his contacts to bring the bigger talent to the ranch for their summer concert series.

In the past several weeks, however, he'd had a few doors open for him, and he'd been meeting with Jolene Gillespie from Black Hill Records. They were interested in his music, and he felt about two breaths away from signing a contract with them. That would take him away from Longhorn Ranch, and he didn't know what his family would do without him. The work he did couldn't just be handed off to someone else. Blake would have to hire someone full-time, and Kyle... Well, Kyle would have to leave Texas for a little while.

He thought of Maddy inside the lodge, signing her employment paperwork. Was he willing to leave her behind if he had a shot at a country music career? He'd struggled when she'd first told him about her mama's injury which would prevent her from coming to the ranch this summer.

He desperately wanted to know what had changed and why she'd decided to come. She was so fond of surprises, and Kyle wished this one time, she'd called or texted him. It would've saved both of them a lot of trouble.

After he brought the golf cart to a stop, he twisted the key but left it hanging in the ignition. "We have full facilities here, Miss Trumaine. Walter and Jane won't want for anything. We've got private rooms under the stage, and top-of-the-line lighting. Our ranch is booked solid for the summer, and we open our weekend concerts to the public at-large, for a nominal price too. We get lots of residents from neighboring towns coming out here."

Elaine stood from the cart. "Great parking too."

Kyle joined her near the front of the golf cart. He sometimes came to the stage in the middle of the day like this just to imagine himself up on it, a guitar in his hand, charming thousands of people who'd all come to see him.

His imagination ran overtime sometimes, and he tried to pull himself back to earth. As he'd grown up, his mama had often told him he was a dreamer—and he was. He couldn't help it, and over the years, he'd learned some coping mechanisms to get his feet back on solid ground.

Elaine walked around and took pictures, asked questions which Kyle answered without difficulty, and ended the tour with a beaming smile. He drove them back to the lodge, his pulse picking up speed with every foot they covered.

Back in the white and gold gravel, Elaine gave him a nod. "I'll be in touch, Kyle. Thank you for the entertaining morning." She gave him a smile he could only categorize as suggestive, and had he not seen Maddy an hour ago, he might have returned it in kind. He might have asked her for her number. He might have made a complete fool of himself.

Instead, he shook her hand and nodded her toward her company car. He waved like he was thrilled she'd come, and the moment the dust lifted into the air behind her tires, he breathed out a great, heaving exhale.

"Oh, boy," he said to himself. The door opened behind him, and a loud group spilled outside. They laughed and talked in noisy voices, as if they'd already had too much to drink. Kyle knew they hadn't, because the lodge didn't serve alcohol until dinnertime. Guests could bring their own, he supposed, and he stood out of the way as a group of seven or eight men came roaring down the steps.

"Cornhole?" one of them asked, and he pointed across the parking lot to the lanes where cornhole got played. At nearly noon, no one stood out in the sunshine, and Kyle wouldn't choose this time of day to play. The men didn't seem to mind at all, and they sloshed through the gravel in their cowboy boots, obviously not used to wearing them.

Kyle went up the steps and inside the lodge, breathed in the blessed air conditioning, and then looked around for Maddy. He hadn't checked for her car outside, and he moved around the check-in desk to look out the window in the administrative side of the front lodge.

The dark red sedan sat in the same spot it had been in earlier, and his heartbeat skipped dangerously over itself. If he wasn't careful, he'd have to get it checked just to make sure he didn't have an arrythmia.

He turned around, scanning for Maddy. She walked over to a table with Adam and Jesse, all three of them seemingly talking at the same time. She looked radiant and alive, and Kyle mentally kicked himself for not staying in touch with her.

She didn't text or call you either, he thought. That alone buoyed his spirits—and his courage—enough to get him to move toward her. The three of them had grabbed their lunches, and Kyle detoured to pick up one of the boxes for himself too. He usually checked the stickers to get the type of chips and salad he wanted, but today, he simply grabbed the nearest one without taking his eyes from Maddy.

Yes, he'd been flirting with Elaine, but the very idea of going out with her had dried to dust the moment he'd seen Maddy. He swallowed as he approached the table, his ears doing their job as he heard Jesse say, "…need to do it at least once during the week. Not everyone comes on the weekend."

"Couples more than families, though," Adam said.

"Right." Jesse glanced up as Kyle pulled out the chair next to him. He gave him a brief smile. "That's why I think we need to do it on Tuesday or Wednesday, as well as

Friday and Saturday." He lifted his turkey sandwich to his mouth and took a bite.

Maddy looked at Kyle, and their eyes locked. He swore the world froze except for the two of them. She sat on the other side of Adam, the furthest from him, and he could've chosen to sit directly beside her. He'd wanted to give her some breathing room.

Could she feel that spark? Did she want to be alone with him as badly as he wanted to be alone with her? How could he apologize enough and get her back into his life without coming across as desperate?"

"I think that's fine." Maddy pulled her eyes away from Kyle, and he thought it took her some effort. He hoped.

"It's four nights a week," Adam said. "You'll have to be careful not to work more than your contracted time." He gave Maddy a nod and trained his attention on Kyle. "How did the stage tour go?"

"Good." He opened his box and found a ham and cheese sandwich inside. Not his favorite. He had gotten the sour cream and cheddar chips he liked, so he pulled that bag out first. "I think she'll recommend that Double Barrel come." He opened his bag of chips and pulled out the top one. "Did you get your paperwork signed, Mads?"

"Yes," she said. "I didn't think I started until Monday, but these two were waiting for me in the hall the moment I left Blake's office." She gave Jesse and Adam a smile that said she wasn't really upset by that.

Jesse actually chuckled. "We're just so excited to have you here," he said. "It's something new and different for the guests."

"Right," Adam said, never one to add more to a conversation than necessary.

The conversation stalled there, and the words piling up in Kyle's throat prevented him from eating too much. Maddy didn't seem to have that problem, and Jesse and Adam started a conversation about saddling classes and demos.

Kyle caught Maddy's eye again and hooked his chin toward the door. Her eyebrows went up, and then she reached to close the top of her lunch box. He did the same and got to his feet. "See you later, boys," he said.

Jesse said something about eating a mint before kissing, but Kyle ignored him. He didn't think there'd be any kissing between him and Maddy right now. Soon, he hoped, but first, he had some groveling to do.

"I can help you move in," he said.

"You can?" she asked. "This afternoon?"

Kyle thought of his schedule, which included meeting the band coming in for tonight's concert at three o'clock. He'd be busy the rest of the afternoon, evening, and night. He nodded anyway. "Sure." He led her down the hall to the staff area, and by a miracle, no one sat at the single table there. "Do you want to sit here or go outside?"

"It's hot outside." She claimed a seat at the table, and this time, Kyle did sit next to her. She started to open her box, but Kyle couldn't.

"I'm really sorry, Maddy," he said. "I shouldn't have... stopped talking to you."

Her brown eyes had always captivated him, and today,

they blazed with energy and light and...displeasure. Probably that. "Why did you?"

"I don't know," he said miserably. "I mean, I kind of know why. It felt like we were on two different paths." He flipped open his box. "Diverging paths."

She nodded and pulled out a small plastic container of potato salad. "Are you upset I'm here this summer?"

"Absolutely not," he said.

She nodded again, but he didn't like how she wouldn't look at him. Like it took so much concentration to open the container and pick up a spoon.

"Are you mad at me?" he asked.

She did level her gaze at him then. "Should I be?"

Kyle swallowed, his guilt raging through him like wildfire. What did he say here? He'd apologized—she hadn't. "I don't think so." He pushed back the guilt and nerves. "I apologized. I hope you can forgive me, and maybe we can try again this summer, while you're here."

Maddy nodded, and he hated feeling like one of her naughty kindergarteners. "I suppose I could've called you too."

"Mm." He didn't want to make any big movements right now. Not when she was coming toward him like a nervous squirrel. After another handful of seconds of companionable silence, he reached over and covered her hand with his. Pure lightning arced up his arm and into his shoulder, and she had to feel that.

Her eyes came to his, indicating she did. "I just have one more question, Kyle."

"Okay." He barely got the word out of his tight throat.

"What do you think will be different come summer's end? I'll have to leave. You'll stay here." She recapped her potato salad and looked at him again. Right at him, which he loved and appreciated. "If we have a second chance this summer, what will be different when it's over to make you want to keep talking to me?"

What a great question. One he didn't know how to answer, because she was essentially asking him to read the future, and no one could do that. Not even him.

———

Coming soon.

TEXAS LONGHORN RANCH ROMANCE

Book 1: Loving Her Cowboy Best Friend: She's a city girl returning to her hometown. He's a country boy through and through. When these two former best friends (and ex-lovers) start working together, romantic sparks fly that could ignite a wildfire... Will Regina and Blake get burned or can they tame the flames into true love?

Book 2: Kissing Her Cowboy Boss: She's a veterinarian with a secret past. He's her new boss. When Todd hires Laura, it's because she's willing to live on-site and work full-time for the ranch. But when their feelings turn personal, will Laura put up walls between them to keep them apart?

Book 3: Claiming Her Cowboy Kiss: He's tried and failed in country music - and women - before. She wasn't supposed to be at the ranch that summer. When Maddy shows up unexpectedly, will she and Kyle have their second chance romance? Or will the call of the stage lure him away?

CHESTNUT RANCH ROMANCE

Book 1: A Cowboy and his Neighbor: Best friends and neighbors shouldn't share a kiss...

Book 2: A Cowboy and his Mistletoe Kiss: He wasn't supposed to kiss her. Can Travis and Millie find a way to turn their mistletoe kiss into true love?

Book 3: A Cowboy and his Christmas Crush: Can a Christmas crush and their mutual love of rescuing dogs bring them back together?

Book 4: A Cowboy and his Daughter: They were married for a few months. She lost their baby...or so he thought.

Book 5: A Cowboy and his Boss: She's his boss. He's had a crush on her for a couple of summers now. Can Toni and Griffin mix business and pleasure while making sure the teens they're in charge of stay in line?

Book 6: A Cowboy and his Fake Marriage: She needs a husband to keep her ranch...can she convince the cowboy next-door to marry her?

Book 7: A Cowboy and his Secret Kiss: He likes the pretty adventure guide next door, but she wants to keep their relationship off the grid. Can he kiss her in secret and keep his heart intact?

Book 8: A Cowboy and his Skipped Christmas: He's been in love with her forever. She's told him no more times than either of them can count. Can Theo and Sorrell find their way through past pain to a happy future together?

BLUEGRASS RANCH ROMANCE

Book 1: Winning the Cowboy Billionaire: She'll do anything to secure the funding she needs to take her perfumery to the next level...even date the boy next door.

Book 2: Roping the Cowboy Billionaire: She'll do anything to show her ex she's not still hung up on him...even date her best friend.

Book 3: Training the Cowboy Billionaire: She'll do anything to save her ranch...even marry a cowboy just so they can enter a race together.

Book 4: Parading the Cowboy Billionaire: She'll do anything to spite her mother and find her own happiness...even keep her cowboy billionaire boyfriend a secret.

Book 5: Promoting the Cowboy Billionaire: She'll do anything to keep her job...even date a client to stay on her boss's good side.

Book 6: Acquiring the Cowboy Billionaire: She'll do anything to keep her father's stud farm in the family...even marry the maddening cowboy billionaire she's never gotten along with.

Book 7: Saving the Cowboy Billionaire: She'll do anything to prove to her friends that she's over her ex...even date the cowboy she once went with in high school.

Book 8: Convincing the Cowboy Billionaire: She'll do anything to keep her dignity...even convincing the saltiest cowboy billionaire at the ranch to be her boyfriend.

ABOUT EMMY

Emmy is a Midwest mom who loves dogs, cowboys, and Texas. She's been writing for years and loves weaving stories of love, hope, and second chances. Learn more about her and her books at www.emmyeugene.com.

Printed in Great Britain
by Amazon

47286902R00209